Ashton

THE K9 FILES

Dale Mayer

ASHTON: THE K9 FILES, BOOK 32
Beverly Dale Mayer
Valley Publishing Ltd.

ISBN-13: 978-1-834088-77-8
Print Edition

Books in This Series:

Ethan, Book 1

Pierce, Book 2

Zane, Book 3

Blaze, Book 4

Lucas, Book 5

Parker, Book 6

Carter, Book 7

Weston, Book 8

Greyson, Book 9

Rowan, Book 10

Caleb, Book 11

Kurt, Book 12

Tucker, Book 13

Harley, Book 14

Kyron, Book 15

Jenner, Book 16

Rhys, Book 17

Landon, Book 18

Harper, Book 19

Kascius, Book 20

Declan, Book 21

Bauer, Book 22

Delta, Book 23

Conall, Book 24

Baron, Book 25

Walton, Book 26

Cage, Book 27

Trey, Book 28

Austin, Book 29

Mateo, Book 30

Wilden, Book 31

Ashton, Book 32

Riley, Book 33

Boxed Sets and Bundles

https://geni.us/Bundlepage

About This Book

Welcome to the all new K9 Files series reconnecting readers with the unforgettable men from SEALs of Steel in a new series of action packed, page turning romantic suspense that fans have come to expect from USA TODAY Bestselling author Dale Mayer. Pssst... you'll meet other favorite characters from SEALs of Honor and Heroes for Hire too!

At Kat's request to find out what happened to a missing K9 dog named Khan, Ashton Nelson returns to his family estate after years away, only to uncover a tangled web of family secrets and betrayal. With his grandmother Johanna's gambling addiction threatening financial ruin and his grandfather Alexander mysteriously missing, Ashton is thrust into a perilous investigation that starts with the missing dog and ends with something that could change everything.

Crystal, adopted at an early age by Ashton's aunt, becomes his ally in unraveling the mystery. Together with Khan, the retired K9 dog, they delve into the dark underbelly of family and not-so-neighborly ties, revealing hidden motivations and dangerous plots.

Amid the intrigue and danger, Ashton and Crystal's rekindled romance adds a layer of emotional depth as they navigate the treacherous waters of loyalty and greed, offering hope and a new beginning for the family estate... if anything is left.

Sign up to be notified of all Dale's releases here!
https://geni.us/DaleNews

BADGER HEARD KAT'S phone chime as she picked it up to see a text that had just come in. She read it and smiled.

Badger looked over at her. They were tucked up in bed and should have been asleep a long time ago, but something was just so special about being together at this hour when they were both still awake. "What's that smile all about?" he asked.

She held up her phone so he could see.

"Who's it from?"

"Wilden," she said, with a smile.

"And he's thanking you?" He raised one eyebrow.

"Yep, he is."

"Why?"

She chuckled and shrugged. "Not sure, but I imagine that right now he's in a place where he's ecstatic to be. I'll let him have his moment, then ask when the time is right."

"Ah." Badger gave her a smile. "I can see how that might deserve a *thank you*."

She chuckled. "It's nice to know that I've still got the magic touch."

He rolled his eyes. "Nobody quite understands how you manage it," he muttered, "but you do, and everybody is grateful. However, one of these days, you'll run out of K9 cases."

"Maybe," she acknowledged, "but that day is not today."

He shifted and looked at her.

She nodded and then planted a kiss on his lips. "Yeah, I'm not stopping anytime soon. I'm about to send Ashton out on another one."

"Really? I didn't hear about that."

"I did mention it, but you were a little bit busy," she noted, with a wry smile.

"What was I doing?"

"Oh, I don't know, trying to build more houses for other people who need them more than anything else. And by the way," she added, raising a hand to his lips, "this one's in Missouri. The dog's name is Khan, presumably after Genghis Khan, but I don't know that for sure. In fact, I don't know much about this case at all. Sounds more typical with each file these days."

He frowned. "Why Ashton then?"

She laughed. "I'm pretty sure he went to school in Missouri."

Badger thought about it, and then a smile crossed his lips. "You mean, before he went into the military?"

"Yeah. In case you didn't know, he's some financial planner. Then there was this big free-for-all with his family, and he ended up leaving."

"Do you know anything about what happened with the family? One of these times you'll get into trouble and not even know which end is up when you send these people out there."

"His grandmother is an issue, and his grandfather has gone missing. There was quite a bit of turmoil over it, at least according to the news."

"And why is that?"

"Because it's been a few days already and nobody has found him. I thought maybe Ashton should head over and see."

"Don't tell me. Is a great-granddaughter or someone involved?"

She smiled up against him and wrapped her arms around him. "Maybe."

"But, if so, they would be related."

"Not in this case. She's a cousin to Ashton, by way of adoption."

He started to chuckle. "And you already have it all figured out."

"Not quite," she admitted, "but I have a good start. Now it's just a matter of leaving it up to them and seeing if it works."

"You have such a sweet look to you, yet you are deviously conniving."

"*Nah*, I just have faith."

He turned to face her, tilted her chin, and gave her a kiss. "And I have faith *in you*."

CHAPTER 1

ASHTON NELSON PULLED up to the gas station, hopped out and started the process to fuel up his truck. He glanced around at a place he knew well but hadn't seen in at least six years, and that visit had only lasted a couple days, if that. While *eventful,* he wondered if it even counted because he had pulled out on the second night like a demon out of hell.

But then, what did he expect? The family's Missouri home came with … issues.

Some things hadn't changed, and he didn't expect them to change now either. He was here for a War Dog, and that was it. Then again, he could lie to himself as much as he wanted, yet he still knew that wasn't the whole truth.

Something was going on in his family, with his grandparents. His grandmother was, well, she was a case all to herself, and, as much as he loved her dearly, he didn't exactly like her very much lately. He couldn't handle her lies and cheating or his grandfather covering up her antics, especially when she'd touched Grandpa's client accounts for her personal gambling funds.

She didn't consider gambling an issue. Her solution was to always get more money to continue her addiction. Ashton could remember a time when she used to borrow money from everybody else in the family—and never repay them.

Those were the good ole days in retrospect. She then branched out to dipping into the household fund. Now she had graduated to stealing other people's money. He and Grandpa had called her on that, had stopped her outright thievery, forcing her to begin monthly payments to return that money where it belonged, which she did for about four years. She still owed much more to make those accounts whole.

Then a couple years ago she resumed her old tricks again.

So now Ashton was back home again. He couldn't believe it himself. It had been twelve years since he'd lived here. It had been a good six years ago that he came here, even for just those two days. He'd made that trip strictly for Crystal's benefit—and only hers.

Now he didn't even know if she would be there or not. He didn't have that contact with her any longer. Granted, he had been the one to cut ties just so he could focus on healing and rehab. Looking back at that, he had to shake his head.

So to hear from Kat what was going on with his own family was a little disconcerting.

If Crystal had reached out, he would have come, but she hadn't; and that went back to the visit six years earlier, no doubt. He groaned in frustration, finished fueling up his tank, paid, and hopped back into his truck. Without a second glance, he headed up to the corner, taking a right and traveling several miles before he took a left onto the family property.

Family property.

He almost laughed at that thought because, sure, it was family property, as long as *he* wasn't the family. That's where the challenge came in. Multiple wills had been written over the years, writing him in, writing him out.

Bottom line was, he had walked away from the family business. And, since he walked away, everybody was of the opinion that he shouldn't get anything. They didn't stop to consider the fact that he'd walked away because of things being done or not done, even when the ongoing activity was downright criminal. They all just wanted to cover it up, but he, as a financial advisor, just like his grandfather, could not and would not deal with their shady shenanigans, even if his grandmother thought it was nothing but harmless *borrowing*.

His grandfather knew better and had asked Ashton to help keep her in the clear, so Grandpa didn't have to worry about Grandma. Ashton did his best from afar over the last twelve years. However, Grandma was now in so deep that he and Grandpa knew there was no keeping her in the clear. Time to pull in the authorities.

As Ashton pulled up to the front of the huge mansion, passing several smaller dower cottages off to the side, he hopped out and looked around, frowning.

No vehicles were parked close by.

No sign of life was anywhere.

Frowning, he slowly walked up to the front door and knocked. It felt funny to knock on the door of his ancestral home, where he always thought he would live and eventually raise his family, but life hadn't been that easy, particularly in his case.

His parents had both died in a freak accident years ago during a serious flood. Being hard-headed and stubborn, his father insisted on driving across the flooded creek, and both his parents drowned when their vehicle had gone in. Since neither one had been able to get out of the vehicle—weren't swimmers even if they had—they lost their lives.

The catastrophe had left a traumatized teenage boy, still surrounded by family, but the only one who was a direct descendant of this estate. He'd gone on to complete high school and various university programs, but, in the end, he couldn't come to terms with too many of the family members living off money that wasn't theirs. They called them *loans* initially, getting away with not paying some back. Then that part of the family decided they shouldn't pay back any of it. As far as they were concerned, it was their money after all. An advance inheritance of sorts. That led to Ashton and his grandfather having one hell of a fight some six years ago.

His grandfather used to have strong morals, but his grandmother's penchant for sticky fingers and meddling in other people's accounts had messed that up too. Ashton knew his grandfather's misguided actions were done out of love for his wife, but that didn't change the fact that a lot of the townspeople were depending on his grandfather's investment firm to safeguard their own retirement funds, investing them wisely, keeping those funds safe.

If things weren't cleared up, Ashton would be forced to call the authorities about it.

That had been the crux of his visit six years ago.

Back then his grandfather had promised, absolutely promised, that they had replaced almost all the money and that his grandmother had stopped taking what wasn't hers to fuel her addiction. When Ashton demanded to see paperwork to prove it, his grandfather took offense and got angry, saying that Ashton should trust him.

"Well, trust is a hard thing when you're already a criminal." Those were the words Ashton had used, and that had been the last straw as far as his grandfather was concerned. Grandma had taken it a step further and had essentially thrown Ashton out.

When Ashton left that last time, he'd warned his grand-father that, if it wasn't fixed, Ashton would do something about it himself. "When I come back the next time, I will fix it permanently."

There had been a gray cast to his grandfather's face as he understood the threat, but Ashton was prepared to let go of only so many things in life, and his personal integrity was not one of them. Over the last six years, he'd given his grandparents enough time to fix the crooked books, and, if they hadn't bothered to do that, well, Ashton would see the entire company and, therefore, most of the family, potential-ly behind bars for the rest of their lives.

Back then his grandfather understood and, to a certain extent, agreed. Since it was primarily about the family, secondarily about his business reputation with the towns-people, Grandpa intended to do everything possible to keep them above water, which was fine by Ashton. He was okay with that, as long as it got done.

Not getting any proof of it happening? That was an en-tirely different story.

He pushed open the front door when no answer came, not surprised that it wasn't locked. They'd never locked the house as far back as he could remember. As he walked in, he called out, "Hello." Still he got no answer, but, given that no vehicles were out front, maybe that made sense too.

He walked through the living room, with the same old furnishings, the same old wallpaper. It brought both a pang of nostalgia and a wince to his face as he realized just how caught up or lost in time this place really was. As he stepped into the kitchen, he found Jenny.

She had to be almost as old as his grandmother at this

point. Jenny lived in the main house, was treated like family, but she insisted on working for her keep. As she put it, she wasn't up for charity. He wondered how she would feel if she understood the entire family was criminally involved in stealing money from the Nelson accounts as well as from Grandpa's clients—stealing money that was not theirs.

Not wanting to startle her, he called out gently, "Jenny?"

Jenny looked up, froze for a second, then a big smile spread across her face when she saw him. She got up, and, with obviously pained movements, walked toward him. He opened his arms and gently hugged her.

When he finally stepped back, he looked at her and nodded. "You look exactly the same."

She laughed, a bright pealing one. "Except for a few more creaky joints and a few more lines," she noted, with her chin up. "Other than that, I am who I am."

"And who you are is absolutely beautiful."

She smiled. "You were always such a charmer."

"It's not charm to say the truth," he told her. "You've always been a golden-hearted soul, and that has always shone through."

She stared at him, the tears forming in the corner of her eyes. She shook her head. "I think that's the nicest thing anybody has ever told me."

"I'm not surprised," he muttered. "Sometimes we forget to say the things we should, and we don't necessarily do all the things we should either."

She frowned as she eyed him intently. "Are you okay?"

"I am okay," he replied. "I mean, the last six years have been tough, but I'm doing okay."

She sighed. "I did hear something about your having a bad accident." He nodded. "And, of course, if you hadn't left, it wouldn't have happened."

"Sure, … but you remember why I left, don't you?" She gave a short nod. "Grandpa's always been a stubborn old coot," Ashton stated.

"I know. Both of them can be … passionate."

Ashton let her be with that guarded comment, since she was just trying to be considerate. She may have been like a family member, but, at the end of the day, she was an employee of the Nelson estate. Ashton announced, "And now I understand there are more problems." He watched her intently to see her reaction.

Jenny's gaze slid sideways. "I don't really know what to tell you," she began. "You should probably talk to Crystal."

"I will talk to Crystal," he confirmed, "and everybody else, … as long as anybody else is left to talk to."

CRYSTAL PATTERSON FROWNED, hearing a vehicle driving up. Vehicles never brought good news these days. She peeked out the barn door to see who it was and didn't recognize the truck at all.

Again, not necessarily good news in her book. She was a loner by nature but even more so with all the problems that had happened recently. Way too many reporters and any number of other leeches came around, looking to make sensational headlines out of Alexander Nelson's disappearance. He was the prominent figure of the estate and her grandfather.

It was heartbreaking and brutal to recognize what the world was really like when people did crap like that.

Crystal stepped out of the barn and headed toward the

house, realizing that the driver had already gone inside, and that surprised her. Not very many people were bold enough to do that, and the ones who were? Generally they didn't come back twice. Not if she had any say about it.

She walked into the front of the house and called out, "Hey."

When she heard no reply, she headed to the kitchen, finding Jenny gently held in some stranger's arms. Then Crystal caught sight of the stranger's profile and gasped. Both of them turned to her. "Ashton?"

He nodded and smiled. "Hey, Crystal."

She just blinked back tears several times, the emotions overwhelming. She didn't even know what to think—joy, fear, anger—the whole works flooded her system. She let out a very slow, exhausted breath, and she didn't even expect the words that came out of her mouth. "It's about goddamn time."

He raised one eyebrow at her. "Nice to see you too."

She glared at him and spat, "Our grandfather is missing."

"I know that … now," he replied, his tone rather calm.

She felt a pang of jealously inside. He was always the cool-headed one.

"Apparently nobody felt like telling me."

She frowned at him and then shook her head. "John said he contacted you, and you blew him off, didn't have time to come home."

"John *didn't* contact me, which you would have known if you had contacted me yourself," he pointed out. "We also know that John can't be trusted to give out information or to even do a basic follow-up, not without lying through his teeth."

She glared at him for a long moment, as his answers ticked across her brain. She realized that was quite likely exactly what had happened, versus a malicious refusal to come home, which could also have been his response. Damn.

"The fact that you didn't follow up," he stated, "also makes me question just what's been going on."

"I'm not your keeper," she replied stiffly, still off balance at his sudden appearance.

"No, you're not."

Jenny stepped away from the two of them. "I'll just go upstairs," she shared. "I could use a nap." And, with that excuse, she bolted off the main floor and headed upstairs.

Ashton turned to Crystal and smiled stiffly. "She still has the same rooms upstairs?" he asked.

"Yes, of course. … Why?"

"Well, she's physically exhausted for one and emotionally exhausted for another. Why doesn't she use the guest room downstairs?" The question was rhetorical, so he continued. "I'm not sure what the hell's going on here, but apparently people aren't keeping others in the loop," he explained coolly.

She glared at him again.

He nodded. "I get it," Ashton began. "You think I'm to blame because I haven't been here, but I can't fix what nobody was willing to tell me about."

She laughed at that. "Your version of *fix* isn't the same as everybody else's. You do realize that, right?"

"No, it isn't," he agreed, "which is also why I left. However, I had Grandpa's assurance that he was fixing things."

She stared at him for a long moment and finally asked, "Fixing what?"

He snorted, shaking his head. "If you don't know, believe me that I won't go down that pathway. What is this about Grandpa being missing?"

She swallowed and stared out the kitchen window. She wanted desperately to ask him what he meant about *fixing things,* but he wouldn't talk if he didn't want to. That much she knew. He had this locked-down sense of honor that was damn near impossible to get around sometimes.

She turned and stared at him for a long moment, before gathering her thoughts. "He's been missing for three days now. … Are you sure John didn't call and let you know?"

"John, no. Nobody at all called me and let me know," he declared. "I'm here for something completely unrelated, but, once I found out about Grandpa, of course I had to come."

She blinked at that too, wanting to question him further, but he wasn't up for that either.

"So, who saw Grandpa last and where did he go missing from?"

She frowned at Ashton, not sure if she should go there. Yet he was a family member, and he needed to know. "He went missing from the house." He blinked and she nodded. "I know. So, we don't really have a clue what's going on," she snapped.

"So, how many people are involved in the search? Does he even have his mental faculties at capacity?"

His questions came in a rapid fashion but perfectly crafted, so very typical of him. She took a deep breath. "Yes, Grandpa was doing well, which you could see for yourself if you were just here. Now the deputies are involved. They worry about his age and what they consider his possible advanced mental state."

He stared at her, raising an eyebrow. "*Possible advanced mental state?* You just said that he was all right."

"He is." She sighed. "John implied to the deputies that Grandpa might be … forgetful," she shared, with a wave of her hand. He just glared at her as she absentmindedly tucked back some hair. "Don't go getting mad at me. I'm just the messenger."

He kept quiet.

"I don't think John meant it on purpose, but he does have a tendency to say things without really thinking about them."

"*Ya* think?" he muttered. "Where's Grandma?"

Crystal hesitated. "At the moment, I think she's in town, … at the bank."

He did a double take, giving her a searching look. "And what would she be doing at the bank?"

Such a lethal note filled his tone that she flinched and stepped back. "I don't know." She looked around, wrapping her arms around herself, something he took notice of. "I don't handle any of the business."

"How long has she been there?" he asked, turning back toward the front door.

"Hey, wait, hang on a minute. What's going on?"

He didn't answer and asked again forcefully, "When exactly did Grandpa go missing?" He stood at the front door, a strained look on his face.

"If you won't give me a chance to explain," she began, "I can't tell you exactly what's going on, not that I know very much."

"Then get in my truck and tell me, so we can get going."

"Going where?" she cried out. "God, … you're scaring me."

"We're going to the bank," he repeated, his voice like steel.

She stared at him, slowly walking toward him. "Look. You've just blasted into town in your usual fashion, and now you're creating all kinds of drama."

"No, I'm not," he snapped, his tone sharp. "Yet, if I find out she's doing something she's not allowed to do, believe me that there *will* be all kinds of drama, such as you've never seen."

She blinked at that. "I feel like—"

He cut her off. "I don't care what it feels like. Either you come with me, and we'll continue the conversation on the way, or don't come with me, and we'll pick it up when I get back." And, with that, he stormed out the front door.

She raced behind him. "I'm coming with you, dammit. What the hell, Ashton?"

He kept walking, without saying a word.

"Ashton, what's going on?"

Still no answer.

"You just come in and cause all kinds of chaos the minute you arrive, and I know it's so in character for you, but I need to know—"

He came to a halt and pivoted to face her. "What the hell do you need to know? You want to know why I am blasting off to the bank?" He was mad now, looking right at her—or through her.

"Yes!"

"Are you sure you can handle the truth?"

"Yes," she replied, trying to find her resolve.

"I wouldn't have to worry if Grandma wasn't blindly stealing from people," he snapped, as he got into the vehicle, then slammed the door shut, rocking the whole truck.

"What?" She hopped in beside him. "I don't understand. That can't be true. I sure as hell hope you're wrong."

"Yeah, you better hope I'm wrong," he snarled.

Crystal didn't know what to say. As they drove to the bank, she kept trying to talk to him, but he was furious beyond anything she'd ever seen from him.

He finally spoke. "Seems like an odd place for her to be when her husband is missing. A little too convenient for me."

When the tic in his jaw slowed, she finally asked, "Are you serious?"

"Very serious."

"She wouldn't have had anything to do with, … with Grandpa's disappearance. You know that. She loves him."

"No, I don't know that," he argued, "because a woman with an addiction like hers, … I don't know what all she might have done."

"You used to love her."

He looked back, and she realized her tone was harsher than she intended. "I'm not saying I don't," he clarified, "but I can tell you one thing. The reason I left so long ago is because of her."

"What?" She stared at him in shock. "No. … No way. I mean, all she ever talks about is how she wants you home again."

"Only to cover up the shit she's been pulling."

Crystal was downright devastated to hear this.

Ashton continued. "She was supposed to have stopped her stealing, and Grandpa was supposed to make sure all his clients' funds got paid back. So Grandma better not be involved in Grandpa going missing. I also wouldn't be shocked to find out that John is involved too—especially when suggesting that Grandpa's mentally incapacitated."

"Look," she cut him off. "None of that makes any sense.

Maybe we should start at the beginning because I don't understand."

He tossed her a look. "Yeah, I get that. That's because you were never involved in the business aspect of it."

"Well, you aren't either, at least not anymore."

He shot her a look. "I am 100 percent still in the background of *all this*," he spat, followed by a snort. "And don't ever think that will change."

She just blinked. "But John—" Ashton shot her a look. She shut up as her mind tried to process all this.

"What did John say exactly?" Ashton asked, his tone kinda scary.

"It's John," she replied, with a helpless wave of her hand. "I mean, he talks a lot, but he never really comes out and says things clearly."

"No, and that's part of the problem. He wants you to believe that he's in control. He wants you to believe that this is all his now. And, sorry to burst his bubble, but it's not." He glared at her and asked bluntly, "Are you still engaged to him?"

"No. … I was *never* engaged to him." He shot her a dark look, and she pursed her lips. "Look. He asked me," she shared, exasperated, "and I declined. He told me it was a great way for me to stay part of all this. But I didn't want a marriage that would keep me *a part of* whatever this is."

"Why?"

She choked out a laugh. "You'll think I'm being silly."

"What's wrong with being silly?"

She rolled her eyes at that. "I wanted to be married out of love. And, so far, that hasn't happened either," she muttered.

He just nodded and didn't say anything.

She shook her head. "Christ Almighty, please tell me that you're joking and that none of this is true."

"I'm not joking," he stated, his tone hard.

She realized he really was telling the truth. She just didn't know what the hell the truth even was. "So, if you're still dealing with family, what is John doing?"

"I don't know. But believe me that I'll figure that out. And I really need to know where Grandpa is because that completely changes a lot of my world."

She hesitated at that. "Meaning that you'll take everything over?"

He glanced at her and nodded. "Something like that."

"But you're already in the background."

"Yeah, I sure am." He hit the gas, seeing the wide-open road, and then looked back at her. "No way I couldn't be, not now, not with all this crap. Believe me, if I could have gotten out of this, I would have."

"Why? I don't understand. I mean, … they said you left, and you got cut out because you didn't want to be part of the family business."

"When the family business was cheating investors out of their money and stealing from the family, I surely *did not* want to be a part of that," he shared, his tone curt.

She gasped. "There's no way." He once again gave her a hard look. She sank back and whispered, "Dear God."

"Yeah, *dear God* is right," he snapped. "Now, I don't know how much you know—"

"Obviously not a whole lot." She cut him off curtly, not helping to reduce the sting.

"Then I need to tell you that things are not always as they seem. And, from here on out, they won't be anything like you once knew."

CHAPTER 2

CRYSTAL WATCHED AS Ashton hit town and now drove with almost exquisite slowness, as if trying very hard to get himself under control. Meanwhile he continued straight up to the bank, where he parked with a sure fierceness to his movements that had her reaching out. "Look. Maybe you need to calm down first."

He glanced at her briefly and gripped the steering wheel, his knuckles white as bones. "Yeah, that's a great idea," he snapped. "But first I need to make sure she hasn't done something completely beyond repair." And, with that, he hopped out, Crystal trailing behind him as fast as she could, as he walked into the bank. He scanned the area quickly, while everyone seemed to be busy with clients.

But then he saw Grandma and strode toward the older woman, sitting in the bank manager's office, leaning in to say something with an earnestness that Crystal had seen from her many times. What was happening here wasn't clear at all, but obviously it was major. Crystal just didn't know what it could be.

She was also unsure of this new version of Ashton, when she thought she'd known him very well. Now he was walking forward as if ready to slay dragons. And not in a good way. She grabbed his arm as he headed toward the manager's office, even as other people also came to him to see if they could help. "Ashton, slow down. Maybe this isn't the best time to be doing what you intend to do here."

He looked at her and muttered, "There is no good time."

"I get it, but you don't know what this is about."

"But I can tell you that *she* does," he noted, "and if she sees me—"

"There'll be all hell to pay," she interjected. By the expression on his face, he knew that too.

He got to the door and pushed it open. Crystal stepped in front of the other employees, who were trying to stop him. With an apologetic smile to those she had blocked, she stepped in behind him, just in time to hear Johanna Nelson, thanking the manager, before she looked back and gasped in horror.

"You!" she cried out, bolting to her feet. She backed up to the windows, as if looking for an outlet. And there was none, at least nothing open. Grandmother looked from Ashton to Crystal, her face pale.

Ashton asked the bank manager, "How far did she get?" When the man didn't immediately speak up, Ashton asked again, his tone angry, "How far, Roger?"

The bank manager sighed. "Not far, not for the lack of trying," he added. "She's been in here for the last forty-five minutes, trying to get me to release the money."

Ashton just nodded at Roger. Then he faced his grandmother. "Out … now."

Johanna frowned at him, shaking her head. "No. … I'm not leaving." And then she turned to Crystal. "I'm not going anywhere—"

"Yes, you are," Ashton declared, his tone bitter. "Otherwise we're calling the sheriff."

She paled at that and stared at him. "How dare you come back like this?"

"Yeah, well, we'll talk about all the potential *how dare you* scenarios soon enough, Grandma," he spat. "But right now you decide whether you're coming peaceably or I'm calling the sheriff on behalf of the bank." He turned to the manager. "Sorry, Roger."

"Maybe you need to do a little bit more in this instance," Roger admitted, with a meaningful look.

"Oh, I'm working on it," Ashton declared. "Do you have any update on my grandfather?"

Roger frowned at him, then glanced over at his grandmother, who was staring at Ashton sullenly. "Update? Johanna just told me how he was at home and just not feeling well."

Crystal turned to her. "Why would you lie about that?" she asked.

The older woman glared at her and stated, "This has nothing to do with you."

Crystal winced because being reminded of her place was something she was well accustomed to. *Know her place, sit and be pretty, mind her* Ps *and* Qs. She was adopted after all, not even formally at that, according to everybody who thought it mattered.

That attitude was a major part of her plan to leave this year. She'd been trying to complete her education, looking to set up her own business, so she had someplace to call her own. And every time she turned around, it seemed like there was hell to pay from somebody.

She turned to Ashton, who even now glared back at Johanna.

"Crystal's family. Don't speak to her that way. Now

make up your mind right now—leave or the sheriff?" He pulled out his phone and presumably proceeded to call the sheriff.

Johanna flushed. "Fine, I'm leaving." She glared at Ashton. "But you haven't heard the end of this. I have a lawyer now."

"Good," he replied, bitterness in his tone. "You'll need one. And your husband has a lawyer too, but first we need to find him."

Roger gasped.

Crystal nodded and shared, "Grandpa's been missing for better than three days now."

Grandma stared at Ashton for a long moment. "Surely you don't think I had something to do with that?" Apprehension filled her tone.

He looked up from his phone and studied her intently. "Maybe you need to convince me that you didn't," he replied, staring at her, "because what I'm seeing here is a woman trying to clean out the accounts of a man who has been declared missing."

"But *missing* means I can't access anything or have him legally declared dead," she snapped, "for like seven freaking years."

He nodded. "Guess you should have thought about that first then, *huh*?"

She blinked at that. "I don't understand," she muttered innocently.

"But you do understand," he argued, "and it's all part of the act you're putting on for our friend Roger here. Now"— Ashton looked from Roger and back to Johanna—"if you're leaving, we're going now."

She looked at him defiantly, and then her shoulders

slumped. "Fine, we're leaving." She turned to the bank manager and muttered, "I won't forget this."

He gave her a resigned expression. "I'm sorry, Johanna, but there are legalities that I won't bend or break, not even for you."

It was the *not even for you* part that had Crystal staring at him. "I hope that means you wouldn't do it for anybody," she stated, frowning at him. "I'm really not sure what's going on here."

"And you don't need to know," Johanna snapped. "It's none of your business."

She sucked in her breath at that and stared at her grandmother. "Yeah, you've made that abundantly clear. Thank you very much," she snapped, her tone bitter, despite not trying to antagonize her. "Just so you know. I came here thinking maybe *you* would need, I don't know, some help with mediation or *protection* even."

Johanna rolled her eyes at that, then sniffed, scrunching up her nose. "I don't need protection from you. And, if Ashton has any sense, my grandson will see himself on the other side of the law on this one."

He sighed and quipped, "*Right*, like last time?"

"Well, it worked, didn't it?" she stated briskly. "I got rid of you for what—hasn't it been six years?"

"Yeah, you did," he agreed, "but yet you didn't. I've been in the background the entire time. Then, of course, maybe Grandpa didn't tell you that."

She stared at him in shock. "What?"

He nodded. "Did you really think that we would let you take over and destroy the entire place, our home and Grandpa's business, with your gambling debts?"

Crystal stared and tossed a quick glance over at the bank

manager, who was trying hard to school his face, to make it not react the way it wanted to react. She was shocked as well.

Johanna hissed at him. "That's just BS, and you know it."

He shook his head. "Nope, it sure isn't, and the real question is whether we're going to keep you on this side of the jail cell or whether you're going inside one," he spelled out, eyeing her intently. "Either you leave now or I call the sheriff, and we'll just deal with all this right out here in the open."

She paled quickly and marched out.

"I'll see you at home," he called out behind her, as she exited the manager's door.

She looked back at the door and shrugged. "No, you will not."

He nodded. "That's fine. I'll just call the sheriff and have you picked up if you aren't home in an hour."

She froze, turned at the doorway, and stared at him in shock.

He grimaced. "Yes, *that* is where we're at."

She took several slow attempts at calming her breathing, glaring at him still, then turned to the bank manager and asked, "You heard him threaten me, didn't you?"

He looked at her with sympathy. "No, not at all. That's not a threat," he stated. "It appears that some legalities have been ignored. And, if that's the case, those absolutely need to be straightened up. I would highly suggest you deal with them." His tone was stiff, also edging on outrage that she would have involved him in whatever she had going on.

She stared at Ashton and then threw a fit. "This isn't fair. This is abuse."

"*Right*," Crystal snorted. "Ashton hasn't even been here

for six years. Give it a rest, Grandma."

"You can see what kind of trouble he's causing me right now. He's rude, inconsiderate, not to mention nosy. He just rides into town as if he owns the place."

He looked at her with a quiet smile and shrugged. "Because I do."

ASHTON DROVE BEHIND his grandmother, making sure she was fully aware that he was right there on her bumper, about to fulfill his promise to her that she needed to behave herself *or else.*

He was sorry that he had blurted that all out in front of Crystal. She was shocked, if nothing else. As they drove home, she finally broke the silence.

"I don't understand what's going on here."

He nodded. "No, and you won't like the truth," he began, "but it's damn well time the truth came out. I didn't want it to come out like it did, but it's not just you who needs to know. … Grandma also needs to know that all her dirty laundry is now out in the open. God knows that Grandpa wasn't enough to keep her in line." He glanced at Crystal, wishing he could see her expression, but she had her mask on. "Has she always treated you that way?"

She sighed. "Yes, and it's been getting worse. I don't really understand why, but, somewhere along the line, she's become verbally abusive like that," she noted. "She used to be the sweetest grandmother ever."

He nodded. "She was."

"But she's changed. And I don't know how much of that is some mental condition—some element of dementia or whatnot. I don't know what's going on."

"From what I saw at the bank, she's still as wily and conniving as ever, no dementia at all." He heard Crystal suck in her breath, and he added, "I know. That's probably a shocking thing to say and not what you expected to hear."

"No, didn't expect that," she confirmed. "And you seem very sure of yourself." Then she hesitated and asked, "Do you really own everything?"

"Yes. I own it all. The property, the houses, Grandpa's business, all of it. Grandma was in the bank, trying to make a withdrawal without my permission. She fully intended to go around my back, maybe even forge my signature," he suggested in frustration, "and I had already forewarned the bank manager and the lawyers that she was up to no good. So, we'll just have to see what she tried to do. I couldn't ask Roger in front of her, but I need to have a private phone call with him and find out exactly what she wanted to happen."

When no response came from Crystal, he turned to her. A stunned expression covered her face.

She asked him, "Do you want me to leave?"

Her tone was formal, and his eyebrows shot up. "Why?"

She just stared at him.

He glanced over to catch sight of her face again and saw the confusion on it. He frowned. "I have owned it for a very long time. I didn't kick you out before, and I'm not planning on kicking you out now."

"So, Grandma knows—"

"Oh, she knows all right," he muttered, with a chuckle, "but she was attempting to access more money."

Crystal frowned.

Ashton sighed. "She didn't used to be full-on malicious," he shared, "but her behavior just now, the way she spoke to you, makes me wonder if she always was this selfish, and I just wasn't aware of it."

"I don't know about malicious. She's certainly gotten worse. And, since Grandpa went missing, I've seen almost a panicked side to her that I hadn't noticed before," she told him. "I'm glad to see she's upset that he's missing, but—"

"But?"

"This isn't the kind of behavior that would necessarily be … normal for a supposedly happily married couple, who have a good understanding of what's been going on for a long time," she noted cautiously.

He didn't say anything and just watched as Grandma headed down the driveway, and he followed intently behind.

"What about Jenny?" she asked.

"What about Jenny?"

"Does she know?" Crystal asked.

"I don't know how much Jenny knows. She's certainly been here a long time. Why?"

"Because Grandma tried to kick her out recently, and Jenny just stared at her and declared how she wasn't going anywhere."

He barked out a laugh. "Well, good for Jenny. I mean, that's hardly what I would consider normal Grandma behavior either," he noted.

"No, and I was really surprised. But, as I said, Grandma's been pretty vicious with me recently. So, I didn't know if maybe I just wasn't seeing something."

He didn't comment on that part. "I'm worried about Grandpa's going missing and the fact that nobody even has a clue where he is."

"I tried phoning the deputy earlier, but he hasn't got back to me yet."

"What's the latest information?

"Grandma said that Grandpa went out for a walk and just never came back. We've all gone out riding, looking for him. The deputies organized a search party for him, but, so far, there's been no sign of him."

He frowned at that. "What was the weather like that day he first went missing?"

"Normal, and that was three, four days ago," she replied. "Grandma told everybody *three* days ago." He swore at that, and she nodded. "And when I said four days, correcting her, she just glared at me and basically told me to toe the line or else."

"Ah," he snorted, shaking his head.

Crystal asked, "You think she's got something going on?"

"She absolutely has something going on. I just don't know what it all entails. And what she doesn't know is how loyal anybody will be once they too find out whatever she's got going on."

"But she didn't …" Crystal sighed. "Look. I get it. As far as you're concerned, what she was trying to do there at the bank was criminal. I just don't know what she thinks is the point of this."

"Yeah, and that is something else I need to figure out and fast," he grumbled. He watched as his grandmother pulled up to the front of the house, got out, slammed the car door shut, and stalked inside.

He smiled at her antics. "She really has a temper."

"What do you expect?" Crystal said, with a shrug. "You embarrassed her in front of Roger and threatened to call the sheriff on her. Everybody in the whole bank probably heard everything, as you did get loud for a bit." She glanced at him sideways. "Would you have gone through with it? Calling the sheriff, I mean."

"Absolutely. And I still might have to," he stated. "Believe me that you don't even know the half of it." He snorted. "And I already am worried as to *why* Grandpa's gone missing. Frankly he may not have gone missing on his own. If that's the case," he vowed, shaking his head, "then we've got a much bigger problem." He got out and slammed the truck door.

Crystal exited his truck and asked, "I don't suppose you would care to fill me in on those details."

"Maybe, but not right now because I need to get set up for a whole lot more. Are you living in the house?"

"I live in one of the dower cottages," she said and stopped to point.

He nodded. "Good, I'm going to ask you *not* to come inside right now. And, if you see, my, … my lovely cousins, maybe keep them out too."

"If that's possible," she muttered, rolling her eyes.

"Well, if they get aggressive, let them in."

She stared at him with a hint of surprise. "I've never seen Glenn or John aggressive."

He smiled at that, but it wasn't a pretty smile. "I've seen both of them go bat-shit crazy, so just keep that in mind."

She let out her breath in a harsh gust.

"I know. This is a lot, and I'm sorry you have to know, but this affects the whole family. You will be a party to probably a whole lot more family secrets than you ever considered before."

"I thought *I* was the family secret, until it was made very clear to me not all that long ago that I'm not," she shared, her tone casual. "So, right about now, nothing surprises me, except maybe the speed at which you just seem to have come in and destroyed whatever Grandma was trying to do."

"Good. Hopefully I did. Believe me that a big family meeting is still to come and not just with her. I guess I need to talk to Jenny too."

Crystal frowned at him.

He nodded. "Jenny knows some things. She just doesn't know it all. And there have been a lot of problems between Grandma and Jenny for a very long time."

"I see that," Crystal agreed. "And you're right. I suddenly feel as if I don't know anybody here."

"Look. Let me go in and confront Grandma. Then I'll talk to Jenny. Afterward I will come to your cottage and explain things a little bit better."

She nodded, and he could tell that she was a little frazzled and upset.

"It will be fine, Crys," he whispered, as she flinched at the use of her nickname. "I'm not kicking you out. Just remember that. I didn't have any reason to do it years ago, and hopefully there isn't any reason to even think about something like that now—unless all the money is truly gone," he added. "In the meantime, a hell of a fight will soon start inside."

And, with that, he walked into the house alone to find his grandmother waiting for him. He nodded and smiled sweetly. "You're still up to your old tricks, aren't you?"

"No," she snapped, glaring at him. "And you had no business interfering today."

"Well, that depends on exactly what you thought you were doing. And how much of any of this has to do with Grandpa being missing?" Her bottom lip trembled, and he nodded. "How much trouble did you get into? And how much of it was Grandpa trying to bail you out of this time?"

She closed her eyes and collapsed onto the kitchen chair.

He saw the tears forming, but he already knew what her crocodile tears were like and how often she used them to get what she wanted out of Grandpa.

"I don't know."

"I don't believe you," he stated.

She opened her eyes and glared at him.

He nodded. "Yeah, I know you thought that, whatever this was, you would do it all on your own, and there would be no fuss about it. And I don't know whether you were trying to get the money and book out of town or what," he admitted, "but that's obviously not happening. I also don't know if you know something about Grandpa's disappearance, but I would like to think that you were trying to help the poor man."

She kept glaring at him.

"Yet I know all too well that you were more likely trying to just help yourself."

She stared at him for a moment longer, and her face flushed. "I forgot what a bastard you are."

"Yeah," he chuckled, "and I forgot what a conniving witch you are. But it's all coming back to me now."

She stared at him. "I'm not a bad person," she muttered.

"No, you didn't *used* to be a bad person. I know that. However, you do have an addiction," he declared. "A serious addiction that you won't get help for. It's already cost you your property, your home, Grandpa's business, and God-only-knows what else. I could throw you out on the street right now, and you wouldn't have two cents to put together."

Silence filled the room.

"The question is, … who is waiting for me to do just that?"

She blinked at him and frowned. "I don't understand."

"Yeah. You say that," he replied, "but what were you trying to do at the bank today?"

She shrugged. "I just need a little bit of petty cash."

"Yeah, sure you do." He scoffed.

She stood up, clearly irate, and announced, "I don't have to take that behavior from you. This is my house."

"No, it's not," he said, raising his voice. "This is *my* house, and I am not tolerating any of the crap that you've been pulling. So, if you think you're getting *more* money out of this place, you're wrong. And, if you think you'll be spinning more lies to cover your tracks or … if *you* had something to do with *Grandpa* going missing—"

"I would never hurt him," she wailed, staring at Ashton. "I don't know why you're being so mean to me."

"Because you're past seeing what is normal and what is right here," he snapped. "Honestly I think you've been past that point for a very long time, but Grandpa didn't want to make you mad. He didn't want to upset the apple cart. So, he was apparently okay letting you ruin everything that everybody else built, just so you could keep up your gambling habit."

He took a moment, staring at her. "The question is, did your gambling have anything to do with Grandpa's disappearance?"

She stared at him, and he watched as the color slowly faded from her skin, as she finally took in what he said. "They wouldn't do that," she replied frantically.

"What do you mean, *they wouldn't?* Have you already been warned by your bookies?" he asked her.

She stared at him, looked away, and then back.

He could almost see the wheels spinning.

"I've never been in that kind of trouble," she stated. "You know that."

"No, I don't know that," he argued. "As I'm looking at you now, I'm not sure I know anything about you anymore. The woman who used to love her husband would never have done anything to put her family under this kind of stress or would force her husband to sell off parts of the land to repay her debts."

She stared at him. "Isn't that how you got the place?" she asked in a nasty tone. "You waited until he was vulnerable, then took advantage of him."

He stared at her and smiled. "We know that's what *you* intended to do."

She flushed at that. "I did not. It's my money as much as his."

"Not your money. Not his money either. You stole the family funds dry, then decided to steal from Grandpa's investment clients. That stolen money is what you're giving to loan sharks," he clarified for her, as if she didn't already know. "Then you're losing it at the gambling tables. So it's never been *your* money. Let's not forget that part."

She sniffed and pouted. "You don't know anything about it."

"Unfortunately I know way more than I should. And, when I think about it, I realize I should have just pressed charges when I was here six years ago."

She looked at him, steeling her gaze. "What do you mean?" Her voice shook.

"You think I don't know?" he asked, his tone bitter. "Do you really think I didn't have a clue what you were doing?

Do you think I didn't know how long you've been stealing money from Grandpa's business, his clients' investment accounts, to pay your gambling debts?"

She paled ever-so-slightly, then sniffed and said, "So what? It's not like they care. It's not money that they need. It's not money you need either."

"It's not *your* money at all," he repeated.

"Well, I've been very good. I've won back lots of it," she declared. "So, … obviously I can continue to keep winning it back."

"Until you hit that next bad streak and the next," he reminded her, "and then you found out that getting more money wasn't so easy anymore, like today at the bank."

"I've been putting the money back," she snapped. "So I should be allowed to get some more to, you know, clear the debts again." She sniffed. "I mean, that's how it is. Some days you win, and some days you lose."

He nodded. "And some days you just don't get access to the money." He gave her a knowing smile. "And, by the way, your contractual agreement was to deposit money to cover your theft. That contract doesn't allow you to then withdraw the same money you just put in. Those deposits you make into Grandpa's special business account, I then move them to pay back the people you stole from."

She stared at him, and then her face flushed. "And you also removed my access to those accounts?"

"You're damn right I did. Grandpa promised me that he would take care of it, … if I didn't press charges."

She snorted. "Well, he did take care of it. I got into it again because he's just … unavailable."

He stared at her. "*Right.*"

"Yeah, and, if it will cool you off, at this point in time,

most of the accounts have been paid back."

"*You* paid them?"

Her eyes widened at that, and she nodded enthusiastically. "Of course—"

"No, you did not. The accounts are paid but not because of you. *I* paid them back. I had to buy out and sell an awful lot of stock in order to get that done, and there was a price to pay for that too."

She frowned and asked, "What was that price?"

"His portion of this place is now mine too," he declared. "And Grandpa was fine with that arrangement."

A shock wave took over her expression.

"So, now the question is, who decided that Grandpa was doing something they didn't like and decided to do something to him?"

She stared at him in shock. "You can't honestly think that somebody would have hurt him?"

He snorted. "We already know that you would because, as far as you're concerned, this place is just a cash cow for you to bleed dry. And it doesn't matter who suffers for it."

She shook her head at that. "You should talk. You got a big chunk of your great-grandparents' money, and that was never supposed to be yours."

"I'm not even talking to you about that," he replied, with a smile. "That is my personal business and definitely *never* included you."

"Well, it should have," she declared, with a huff. "I mean, I was their daughter-in-law. I should have been given something. And you know very well how upset your grandfather was when he didn't even get any of that."

"He knew perfectly well why he didn't get any cash," he stated, looking at her, "and so do you. Do you think your in-laws didn't know what you were up to with your growing debts? They already knew about your gambling habits and stealing family business money long before they were gone. They changed their wills accordingly. And they couldn't trust their own son to do the right thing either, as Grandpa has been covering for you for decades. *That* is why Grandpa got no cash, just part of the land. And they told him well beforehand, so he could make plans accordingly."

"Well, they didn't know you. They didn't know anything."

"Actually they knew a lot about me when I was younger," he stated, with a smile. "We spent quite a bit of time together. Like it or not, you remember that very well."

She sniffed at that and declared, "They were old."

"Yeah, well, guess what? Now you're old."

She stared at him in horror. "That's a terrible thing to say."

He laughed with a shrug. "If you tried living in the truth instead of whatever fantasy world view you weave for yourself, you would probably do a lot better—inside your body and outside."

She blinked and then sagged back down onto the kitchen chair. "I need money," she stated, resignation in her tone.

"Well, that's too bad," he replied, "because you're not getting any. Not from any of the sources you've been tapping into up until now."

She stared at him, long and hard. "You don't understand, Ash. ... I need the money." Hearing that old nickname from the past was a new low and meant she was truly desperate and pulling out all the stops.

"You'll have to explain exactly why you need the money and what's going on before you get the time of day from me.

No more lies. You've gone way too far for way too long, Grandma."

She looked at him, her shoulders sagging. "They're holding Alexander hostage."

CHAPTER 3

WHEN A HARD pounding came at her door, Crystal opened it up to find both John and Glenn standing there, glaring at her. She smiled and said, "Hey."

"Yeah, hey. What's going on over there?" Glenn asked animatedly.

"What do you mean?" she asked, turning to look at the main house.

"The doors are locked. We can't get breakfast," Glenn replied. John stood there impatiently, about to jump out of his skin. "And apparently our long-lost cousin has arrived to save the day or whatever the hell he thinks he'll do this time."

She winced at that. "I don't know what he's got planned, but let's just say that he is home and that I don't know anything."

"Of course you don't," Glenn scoffed.

She stared at him and asked, "What does that mean?"

He rolled his eyes and said, "We all know you're sweet on him."

She frowned and tried to understand where that was coming from. "*That's* what's on your mind?"

"Sure," he snapped, "we all know it. Everybody's known it, especially when you turned down John."

She just blanked and shook her head. "That had nothing

to do with it."

"Right. Of course it didn't," Glenn said, with a sneer.

"If you want to know what Ashton's up to, go ask him yourself."

Glenn yelled, "You better tell us what's going on in there. Otherwise we'll start breaking down doors."

"You do whatever you want, but I'm not going anywhere near that house because Ashton already told me that we weren't allowed in."

"And what the hell does that mean?" John asked, his tone deep and dark as ever.

She shook her head. Everybody was taking a turn playing their parts in some crazy Godzilla movie. "As I already told you buffoons, I don't know." She raised both hands. "So, when you figure it out, you can tell me."

The twins exchanged a glance between them.

"For real?" John asked sweetly, his tone completely changed.

"Yeah, for real. I don't know anything about any of this," she repeated. "so take your nasty comments and leave." And, with that, she slammed the door in their faces.

It was the first time she'd ever done that, and she wasn't sure whether they would take it to heart and leave or pound on her door again—in which case she would have a heck of a time getting them out of her hair.

But they did leave, much to her surprise and relief. She watched as they walked down her front steps, staring over at the main house the whole time. She could understand their confusion, but they were also takers, always expecting the rest of the world to provide for them.

While she didn't quite know what was going on, a part of her felt like maybe it was a damn good thing that Ashton had come home. It was also a good thing, as far as she was personally concerned, but way overdue. But, if this much trouble was going on in the family, maybe her hope for his return visit was *not* the reason he had come home.

And that was a thought she had never once entertained. It was also a little disconcerting that her two brothers, stepbrothers, or whatever they decided to call themselves at various points in their life, had decided that she was interested in Ashton, assuming that was why she had turned down the proposal from John. It wasn't the biggest part, but it was certainly a consideration.

She'd always had a bit of a crush on Ashton, but it was also obvious that he didn't return it. So, she had quietly killed it during one of her therapy sessions. She'd struggled hard to get decent counseling help that understood the problems related to being adopted in a family. The reactions to her alternated between ribbing her about it, then acting like she was part of the inner circle of the family, only to rebuff her later, yet again.

It was such a weird feeling to know what they thought of her right now or at any moment in time. She glanced around the Nelson property, realizing she really did need to pull up stakes and to find another way to make her way in life, even if her business wasn't up and running yet.

It was past the point where she could justify staying here, particularly with the problems she saw now. Clearly she didn't understand what was going on here, and obviously way too many more problems were yet to come.

It would not be easy for her to relocate, but, with that in mind, she walked to her tiny office and sat down with her laptop, wondering if she could board the horses anywhere else, until she got herself set up. That whole physical infrastructure part of starting her business had stopped her up until now.

Grandma had given her six horses, and she worked and trained with them all the time, but, with Grandpa not here, she had no idea what that would look like for her and her business model, … if there even was one to begin with this time.

That caused her so much pain, but nobody else seemed really bothered about it. She contacted several of her neighbors, asking about boarding the horses until she could get set up somewhere.

She didn't get any replies right away and continued to fire off a mass of emails, until she heard a knock on her door. Instinctively she knew it was Ashton. She got up, checked to make sure through the window, and opened the door to him.

He eyed her intently. "Is there a reason why you're checking the window to see who it is?"

She flashed a smile and shrugged. "Well, the other two were here earlier, and they weren't very happy that I didn't have answers for them."

He just nodded in understanding. "Of course they would come to you for that."

"Well, I guess they tried to get into the house, and no one would let them in."

He smiled and chuckled lightly. "No, I wouldn't be at all surprised about that."

She hesitated. "Is Jenny part of the inner circle?" she asked.

"Not really, but she has always been extremely loyal and very aware, I think, of Grandma's *problem*," he shared, with emphasis. He looked tired and worn out.

"Do you want a cup of tea or something?" she offered.

Surprised, he nodded. "Thanks, that would be nice. I'll have to face my cousins soon enough, and that won't be terribly fun."

She nodded. "So earlier, … you said that you weren't kicking me out."

He looked at her. "Honestly, even if you were looking at moving, I would really appreciate it if you could stay for a bit," he admitted. "I need some stability to get to the bottom of this."

"You do know that I don't understand any of this, right?"

He smiled. "I'm not sure anybody does right now, but I can tell you that my grandmother—" He sighed and shook his head. "She's got a very ugly gambling habit," he began, "and she's cost my grandfather basically everything. In fact, she's cost all of us basically everything."

She stared at him, too stunned to even say anything.

"I know it's a shock to you," he stated, "because, for a long time, my grandfather wanted to keep it private, thinking that nobody would understand. It was not only her addiction problem but his humiliation, not being able to do anything about it that really got to him. It bothered him greatly because he's a righteous man."

"And did you say something about other people's money?"

He stared at her and nodded. "I'll explain some of this," he began, "but I don't want any of it going anywhere, okay?"

She nodded. "I don't really have anybody to talk to anyway," she noted, "so that's not hard to promise. However, your cousins will quite likely have something to say about it."

He shrugged. "They will all find out soon enough, but Grandma's gambling problem has spread to Grandpa's investment firm, and she's been taking money out of his clients' accounts and using that to feed her addictions."

Crystal's jaw dropped, and she couldn't quite comprehend what he was saying, though he had made it very clear. She tried to speak several times, and he just smiled grimly.

"Yeah, believe me, that's partly how I feel. Last time I was here, Grandpa swore he would make it right. So, against my better judgment, I didn't press charges, but I told him that they had to fix it, or I would have no choice. We managed to sever her ties to all company assets, even the household funds, and they were putting money back in those affected client accounts, trying to repay it, but always held a little back.

"And then I guess on a whim, being generous or something, she put in a fair chunk, and who knows what happened. I had already stopped her ability to take money out. She could put money in because I was hoping she would do the right thing and give back all the stolen money, as she had sworn she would do."

"So, you knew all along?"

"Yes, I had to know because I was the financial advisor this whole time. Plus, I do own the whole Nelson property, only because I bought Grandpa's portion to keep him from selling the place to some stranger, after the mess that Grandma made. So, back to the point, as soon as Grandma put money in, she immediately wanted it back out. Yet she couldn't get it back out again. I had set it up so I would be notified of all the deposits," he added and then shook his head.

"And obviously I also made arrangements to be notified

if someone tried to make any withdrawals. I wanted to make sure that Grandma didn't continue her theft pattern. I'm not sure what happened, but, when she couldn't get money out and needed it for God-only-knows-what, that's when she went to the bank to try and force Roger to give her the money, implying that she owned the business—"

"Which is not hers?"

"Nope and hasn't been for some time," he stated forcefully. "She was also trying to get money out of the household accounts, which do have money in them because I have to pay for everybody to maintain this place." She looked up, surprise in her gaze. He continued, "Jenny has some control over that. When Jenny wouldn't give Grandma any money, Grandma went to the bank manager. You can tell that's caused a certain amount of problems with Jenny."

"Good God," Crystal muttered, hanging her head. "So, you trust the money with Jenny but not with Grandma? How the hell did all that happen, and how come I never noticed?"

"Jenny pays the bills," he explained. "And she's resourceful, resistant to all threats. Something that Grandpa was not. I have spoken with Jenny many times over the last few years, and she knows perfectly well that this place is mine. She also knows that I have been supporting everybody, but I'm sure you can understand that's something I won't continue to do."

She winced and nodded. "If that's the case, your cousins are about to become a problem."

"They have always been a problem," he stated, "and none of that has anything to do with why I came."

She stared at him. "What do you mean, why you came?"

He smiled. "Friends of mine needed help tracking down

the whereabouts of a retired K9 War Dog that disappeared from somewhere in this town. They run a program to monitor the status of these dogs for the War Department. This particular War Dog was reported missing, and they asked me to look into it for them."

She blinked, dumbfounded.

"Yeah, I know," he muttered, "hard to imagine. But these people are friends of mine, plus I am and always will be an animal lover, particularly of the K9 dogs that spent their military lives keeping American soldiers alive," he shared. "I have no intention of not doing what I can to help them, so, if you have seen a Malinois-shepherd cross in this area, about eight years old and quite well trained, let me know. It's probably running loose at this point since it's apparently gone missing, or at least that is the rumor."

"What will you do to find it?"

"I'll need to track it down while I'm here." When she just stared at him, he sighed. "I know, things are as convoluted as ever."

"How?" she asked. "How is it that you can show up right in the nick of time, yet have your own damn problems to deal with?"

He looked at her, surprised, then a smile broke across his face. "We always have our own problems to deal with, Crys," he noted. "That'll never change. The trick is to solve them without making everybody else pay for our mistakes. And hopefully get away with whatever you need to get away with until you can make it happen."

Crystal grimaced. "So, now the question is, did Grandma's mess have anything to do with Grandpa's disappearance?"

He looked at her and smiled. "I just found out that

part—*supposedly*—as to why she was extra desperate to get her hands on some money. She needs to win back a whole pile of money in the hopes that she can get Grandpa *released*."

Crystal sank down to the couch, all thoughts about tea completely gone. "I'm sorry?"

"Yeah, you heard me," he said, nodding at her. "Grandma got herself in too deep with her gambling debts. She wasn't just borrowing from us, from the company, she was borrowing from, well, … certain lenders in the gambling scene. She got in too deep and couldn't get any back out to pay up the bookies. They don't like somebody playing with their money who apparently doesn't have a way to pay it back. I don't know who it is, but they apparently grabbed Grandpa, at least according to Grandma."

"But he's not the one who's responsible," she protested.

"Well, he's responsible enough," Ashton pointed out, "because he would never stop her. And, while Grandpa and I have both been working to pay back all the money she stole, there is still an arrearage on Grandpa's investments accounts, as well as Grandma's bookie account."

"But is that really on you?"

"My inheritance, my issue. I need a little bit of time to verify where everything stands and to figure out how much is still missing."

"What did Grandma say about all that?"

He sighed. "She's adamant that, if I just gave her a little bit of money, she could go gamble it into more and could resolve this problem … *again*."

"Jesus," she murmured, as she stared at him in shock. "I feel as if I've been right here and have never understood all the undercurrents going on around me."

"Maybe that's a good thing," he stated, "because some of these undercurrents are rough to navigate. I had quite the blowup with Grandpa over it all when I came back six years ago. He was struggling to make some payments to clear her troubles and to pay out money to some of his investment clients, who wanted to withdraw funds from their accounts. However, Grandma had stolen from them without anyone suspecting anything. That's when I realized that he still hadn't taken away her access to those client accounts."

"So—"

"Back then she hadn't taken very much more, but she had certainly taken some more. So I put a lock on all Grandpa's client accounts, so she couldn't get any more money out. At least I thought so, but she just told me that she got it from Grandpa anyway. God knows what extortion scheme she'd come up with to get him to do it."

Crystal swallowed back her tears and her fears as she thought about how horrible and completely irresponsible Grandma had been and how all of it fell on Ashton's shoulders. "Well, not to ask an overly personal question, but I presume it wasn't a whole lot of money if you were capable of paying it off."

"I haven't paid it all off," he replied, his tone grim. "Part of the problem is that, back then, she had taken out a lot of money. Now we were very close to getting it paid off. So it seemed to be a good thing when she put that big chunk back in, until she went to take it back out again.

"That's when she realized she couldn't take money *out*. So, for four years, she had been good, relatively good, abiding by her agreement, a written contract which she signed, all wrapped up in a confidentiality agreement. No one knew about it—except her, Grandpa, me, and the attorney who drew it up. She abided by her obligation to put money back in and to never trigger any withdrawals, until …"

"Until she broke that agreement, so the question would be why."

"She says she broke it because *they* are holding Grandpa hostage."

She blinked at him several times and then whispered, "Oh my God, he's been kidnapped by loan sharks?"

"Something like that," he muttered. "At least, that's what she says. I can't trust her. So, yeah, I don't really know what to tell you."

She just stared at him, not sure what to even say. "What can you do?"

"What Grandpa should have done a long time ago," he said. "A deputy is on the way."

She closed her eyes and whispered, "Oh, hell."

"Yeah. Oh, hell, it is," he agreed in a bitter tone. "I have no problem moving the money around and paying off the ransom—if Grandpa truly is being held for ransom—but now we're in a completely different scenario. There is no guarantee that any loan shark kidnapper will hold up their end of the bargain and let him go, … alive and well."

She nodded. "I agree totally, but wow."

"Oh, I know," he muttered, with a smile. "Believe me that I know. What is worse is that I don't think Grandma's bookies have Grandpa. I just hope and pray that it's not an inside job."

"Oh my God," she whispered. "You do understand that Glenn and John will be all pissed off and angry, thinking that none of this is true, right?"

"Yeah, but Grandpa *is* missing." He looked at her with a

meaningful expression, and she knew what that meant too.

"*Right*. They've been happy enough to just let the old man *wander off*."

"Meanwhile, he's stuck somewhere, and Grandma's getting desperate, trying to figure out how to get some money so she can go gamble some more and make enough to fix everything. At least I hope that was her intent and not something totally selfish. And the bank manager, of course, wouldn't let her get more money."

"Thank God for that," she said.

"Yeah, thank God for that," Ashton repeated. "I still owe him a phone call and an explanation, plus a plan going forward because she'll continue to try to access the accounts."

Crystal nodded. "That's what addictions do. They drive people to do whatever they can do for their next fix. You had already informed the bank, right?"

"Yeah, I did, but we are dealing with a financial institution. Plus, she was loosely considered part owner of Grandpa's investment firm as his wife, so it can get confusing. Roger's been with the bank for a long time, and he's certainly willing to help, but the bank will not take on the liability for Grandma's thefts."

"And she has proven herself to be a real problem."

"Exactly, so this is the explanation for the grumpy homecoming you experienced when I first got in."

She closed her eyes and whispered, "I don't even know what to say." He laughed that deep rumbling tone, and it brought back so many memories.

"Yeah, how do you think I feel?" he asked.

She looked at him, unable to hide the admiration. "And you've been paying off Grandma's gambling debts and outright theft of Grandpa's client accounts?"

"I've been paying off what I could because I inherited a lot of money from my great-grandfather," he explained. "Still that inheritance wasn't meant to pay for all this. That's why my great-grandparents wrote Grandma and Grandpa out of their wills, at least any cash inheritance portion. Grandpa only got land, just in his name too. They couldn't trust their own son to keep his gambling wife in line. Yet, here I am. Doing it myself. So, to keep Grandpa from selling off parts of the ranch, I've been taking parts of the property in exchange for those repayments I'm making."

"But you would have inherited everything anyway."

He smiled. "But … you only inherit if anything is left at the time that they pass."

She shook her head as she understood it better. "Which means there isn't anything left."

"Well, there wouldn't be. Not once Grandpa's been declared dead, and everything comes to light," he clarified. "So, yeah, *no*."

ASHTON MADE HIS way up to his room, more than tired and worn out. Rather than getting into bed, he sent off a million texts, some to Badger, some to Kat, some to Roger, and some to the local lawyer who handled the Nelson family business. All of them were people whom he knew and trusted.

And, in each case, they knew what Ashton was up against. Yet the deputy had been here and gone, telling Ashton that it all appeared to be another tall tale his grandmother was telling in a desperate act to get more money out of Ashton. The sheriff's office had absolutely no proof that anybody had kidnapped his grandfather. Deputy David Hale was new to the town but seemed competent enough.

When Deputy Hale left, Ashton couldn't deal with his grandmother right now. He made his way upstairs, just wanting to crash. As tired as he was, he still quickly sent a message about the missing dog to everybody as well.

No way he would forget that, even though Kat told him that it wasn't his top priority, not if he needed to spend the time with his family and sort out the rest of it. He understood why she mentioned that, but no way he would not help out with the War Dog as well. Kat and Badger had been instrumental in helping Ashton too many times—particularly back when his grandmother had made it very clear that he wasn't welcome home anymore, especially not now that he was a cripple.

His grandpa, on the other hand, had been very understanding, stating that was complete BS and that he would have a talk with her. And, if nothing else, he would control the money aspect so she would have a change of heart. Ashton and Grandpa had talked several times on the phone since then. According to Grandpa, he had things well in hand.

Except he didn't. Ashton sighed.

He had already planned on coming back home within a few months, but his grandpa's disappearance had completely changed that. Even now, as he sat here, wondering how crazy this would all get, he fully realized it would get bad, seriously bad.

When his phone buzzed, he looked down to see a message from one of the deputies, somebody he used to know too. But, when he read it, he was confused. So he just called him. "Hey, Timmy."

The man on the other end laughed. "I don't know anybody else who calls me Timmy anymore," he replied, with a note of humor.

"Yeah, sorry about that. … Old habits. That was just an instinctive response," he shared, with a chuckle.

"I couldn't believe it when I heard you were back again."

"Just a sucker for punishment apparently."

"Yeah, Deputy Hale had a lot to say about that. I also heard that your grandfather's gone missing. And then I just heard something about your grandmother—how her gambling frenzy may have had something to do with it."

Recognizing his tone, Ashton realized that Timmy knew Grandma well enough to see through her lies. Timmy had known her as long as Ashton had, so Timmy's skepticism was not all that far-fetched. "None of your colleagues seem to believe it though."

"Well, she has become a bit of a problem in town," he began, "to put it delicately."

"Right. And, *delicately* speaking, just how much of a problem has she become?"

"It's kind of bad for some people," Timmy shared, his tone very cautious. "She stopped paying for things in grocery stores and tries to walk out with them. She's become a shoplifter, skipping out without paying bills at restaurants. So, now people refuse to serve her."

"Anything else?"

"It's … weird, man. She wasn't like that before, but she's turned a corner. They're all thinking she's got some klepto form of dementia or something like that."

"Okay. I'll make amends with the merchants. I need to call her doctor anyway. I'll take a look at that too."

He noted cheerfully, "Better you than me."

"Yeah. Thanks for the heads-up."

Timmy laughed. "Are you staying in town?"

"Uh, maybe." And then he gave a short laugh, not able to wrap his head around the growing mess he would have to clean up. He'd known it was a mess before, but now it was dragging him deeper than he'd ever imagined. "Honestly I've got a hell of a mess to clean up here right now. And then? Then … we'll see."

"Good enough," Timmy said. "So maybe coffee when you get a free moment?"

"Coffee would be great," Ashton stated, "but I do need to find out what's going on with Grandpa though."

"Yep. You do. … I don't really have anything to tell you. Everybody is keeping their eye out of course, and they did a twenty-four-hour search in the woods, but nobody saw anything."

"Which is why I thought it was possible that my grand-mother spoke the truth for once."

"Well, if it's possible, we need more proof," he pointed out. "She has not been exactly …"

Ashton knew what Timmy was holding back. "Just say it, Tim."

"Right. … Well, she has not been very forthcoming with information."

"Yeah," Ashton muttered. "Agreed, and that's the way of it. And you probably know better than I do that she has a gambling addiction, right?"

"I've certainly heard rumors around town, but apparent-ly that's not something anybody has put on record," Timmy shared. "Nobody really seems to understand how bad it is."

"No, because my grandfather has done a good job of hiding it," Ashton revealed. "So, give me a few days to figure out what's going on, and then I'll take you up on that coffee." And just as he went to hang up, he asked, "By the way, do you have any information about a Malinois-shepherd cross, a K9 War Dog in town? It's apparently gone missing, so it could show up at odd places if he's been lost or abandoned. Have you even heard it's gone missing?"

Tim asked, "Are you're talking about Sean's dog?"

"Yeah, maybe so. I think that's the name of the guy who owned Khan when the dog went missing."

"I don't know what that has to do with you," he noted, "but you need to proceed with caution. Sean is, well, let's just say, he's got some issues."

"Sure," Ashton said. "He's a vet, and we do tend to come home with issues."

"I'm not trying to insult you because I know that you're, you know, you're home yourself, but, Sean's generally not somebody who anybody believes. So, when he told people he was missing his dog, I don't think anybody … I hate to say it, but I'm not sure anybody believed him enough to care." And, with that, Timmy ended the call.

Ashton stared down at his phone and started swearing. This was not what he needed, and he hadn't even had two seconds to figure out where he was and what all he had to deal with. He'd literally hit the ground running, and it didn't look like it would ease up anytime soon.

As soon as he updated Kat and Badger with this latest info, he headed for a shower and a chance to unwind. He hadn't had any food either. About the time he got out of the shower, he heard a knock on his door. Wearing only a towel, he quickly grabbed a robe hanging by the shower, then answered the door to find Jenny there. He looked at her and smiled. "Hey, is everything okay?"

She nodded. "Things have been very difficult today, but I came to tell you there's food in the kitchen, if you want a hot meal."

"I would love a hot meal," he admitted. "I just need to get dressed. I was desperate for a hot shower and a minute to clear my head. It's been quite a day."

"You didn't even get a chance to settle in," she noted, with a sad smile. "I'll see you down in the kitchen."

"And what about my grandmother?"

"Johanna generally doesn't come down at all in the evenings," she shared, with a careless wave of her hand. "So I can't be sure what she's up to right now."

He winced at that and nodded. "Give me five." He closed the door and quickly grabbed some clean clothes.

Wearing fresh clothes and feeling like he might make it now, he headed downstairs. He walked into the kitchen just in time to see Jenny serving up a plate with a homemade meat pie, some hot potatoes, and a green salad. He sat down with a smile. "I forgot what it was like to have some of your cooking."

She chuckled. "If you would come home more often, you might remember easier." She left it at that, and he nodded.

"Well, I'm here now," he declared, taking in the delicious smell.

"Are you staying?" Jenny asked.

"I think so, at least for a time. I'm not sure I can afford to leave right now," he shared.

"So, the answer to that question is yes, but with a little bit of a warning in it," she noted, with a light chuckle.

"Yeah."

She sat down across from him, nursing a cup of tea. Lost

in his thoughts, he looked at her and asked, "What is it you want to say?"

She sighed. "I'm just hoping Alexander is still alive."

"So am I," he whispered. "I can't seem to trust anything that comes out of my grandmother's mouth anymore."

Jenny stared off in the distance, then looking down at her hands, still nursing the cup, she nodded. "I heard some of that today."

"I figured the deputy would speak to you to ask about Johanna's mental capacity."

"No, he didn't talk to me, but she's not well. I'll be honest about that. And, since your grandfather's gone missing, everything's kind of unhinged in a way. I know that's not a fair thing to say, but that's how I feel."

"You are entitled to how you feel," he said, eating at a fast pace. "And we need the truth. Grandma's been pulling way too many tricks here, and I don't know how much of that is her supposed health or mental condition and how much of it is panic, with Grandpa gone, that she won't have the money to keep up her gambling. I just don't know."

Jenny nodded. "She's won some big amounts but then just loses it again. Win or lose, she never seems to stop. It's always about chasing after this big score, that big score."

He nodded. "And the trouble with the big scores is that she's taken the money out of other people's accounts." He looked at Jenny, and she stared at him in shock, and he nodded. "She's been stealing from Grandpa's client accounts."

She sat back and shook her head, dumbfounded.

"I've tried to keep a lid on it, so a part of me gives some weight to her comment about somebody expecting her to pay that money back before they'll let Grandpa go."

"That can't be possible," Jenny whispered. "Surely she wouldn't do something so …"

"*Criminal?* That's the word for it," he declared. "She's been doing it a long time, and that's one of the reasons Grandpa and I have had all kinds of set-tos about her because he wouldn't or couldn't curtail her. When I came back six years ago, I just wanted to confirm that everything was signed, sealed, and secure. So Grandma wouldn't have access to anybody's money. Plus she agreed to continue to pay it back, which she has been trying to do," he conceded. "But, in six years, you can only hope that people don't need their money."

"And of course they did." Jenny sighed.

"Some people needed it rather quickly, and I am pretty broke myself at this point from trying to keep everything afloat."

She stared at him and asked, "You're paying her debts?"

"Well, I had a cash inheritance from my great-grandfather," he shared, "which was supposed to bypass Grandma and Grandpa because of her gambling and his inability to control her. Yet I'm still using that money to pay off her gambling loss and her outright theft from Grandpa's investment clients. He's paid me back by transferring over his part of the land and homes here—into my name only."

"But it's yours already, or it will be. Why would you do that?"

"Sure, but, as I explained to Crystal, you only inherit if something is left to inherit. I didn't want some stranger swooping in to buy up this place, especially with Grandma's gambling becoming more and more public. Yet Grandma sure seems hell-bent on making sure nothing is left for anybody, even herself," he muttered. "So, yeah, I've lost a fair bit of money on this place, which is part of why I came in the way I did, more than a little irate that Grandma was trying to steal even more money from the household account."

"So, that's what she was doing at the bank?"

"Yes, that's what she was doing."

She closed her eyes and shook her head. "I am so sorry."

"Me too," he replied. "I've spent the last however-many years shuffling around as much of the money as I could to keep this place afloat, while Grandma's out there stealing, then trying to pay back as much as she could, only to then turn right around and take more. Because, of course, once a gambler has a win, she's just emboldened to gamble some more, hoping the lucky streak never ends."

Jenny nodded. "She kept coming to me for money, but I didn't have any more to give her."

He just stared at her and groaned. "Don't tell me that she's into you for money too?"

She smiled. "Well, I didn't give her much. I don't have much. It was a couple hundred bucks." He snorted at that. Then she winced and added, "Does that mean you're paying my wages too?"

He nodded. "I've been paying for all this. Some of my inheritance money I still have invested, and I'm hoping I'll be allowed to keep some at the end of the day, but the reality is, we may lose it all. That's not being dramatic about it. It's just a hard fact of life."

"Good God," she whispered, as she stared around the kitchen.

"Yeah, I know," he muttered. "That's what happens when you have an addict in the family." She turned to him and winced. "So, how has her attitude been toward Crystal?"

Jenny frowned and stared down at the table.

"I already heard some pretty disturbing things," he shared, "so the unvarnished truth from you would help a lot."

"Somewhere along the line, she decided that Crystal should pay rent, and it should go directly to her. Oh, and that the twins should be doing more around the place."

"Well, that's true. The twins should be pulling their weight." Ashton snorted. "I don't know what they're doing or not doing, so that's a conversation for tomorrow." He shook his head. "How did the whole rent discussion with Crystal go over?"

"I think she was okay to pay rent. It was the way it was done. It's like Johanna has lost all her filters, and she's just making life hellish for people," Jenny told Ashton. "She's changed a lot, and your grandfather disappearing has made her even worse."

"Do you really think it's been worse since my grandfather's gone missing?"

"Yes," she replied, "I would say so. There's been the odd occasion otherwise where she's said something completely unwarranted, but, for the most part, I think it's been somewhat okay, until Alexander went missing. But that's just me talking. You'll have to ask Crystal yourself."

"Maybe I will." He sighed. "I talked with her earlier this evening, and she also went to the bank with me, so she certainly found out what some of the problems are, but she doesn't know all of them."

"I don't think anybody does," Jenny pointed out, "because your grandpa's been trying to keep a lid on things for a long time."

"Yeah, he has, and not very successfully," Ashton grumbled. "At least not the part about keeping her spending reined in. If his going missing has something to do with her gambling, that will be a whole different ball game. And honestly, once this all blows up, I don't know if anybody out there can save the business or the property. I'm in danger of losing everything too."

When she stared at him in shock, he nodded. "That's what happens when you end up with criminals in the family who don't care," he stated. "They destroy it for everybody."

She swallowed hard. "Look. You don't have to pay me wages for the next while." She had a look of fear in her eyes. "Obviously you don't have the money for it."

He smiled, understanding where she was coming from. "Everybody deserves to be paid for the work they do," he told her, "but thank you for the offer. It's not that bad right now."

"You sure about that?"

"For the moment anyway. I do need to speak to the lawyer and see how much exposure we have with all of Grandma's stealing. That's something I'm still not sure of," he noted, "and I'm working my way through it. That'll be yet another *tomorrow* headache. I'm hoping to find *something* than might keep our heads above water for now."

She winced and nodded. "What do you want me to do about Johanna? How can I help?"

"I don't want you to spy on her per se, but, if you could keep me abreast of any weird behavior, for example, if you hear her talking to anybody or things like that? She's not in a space that I recognize at all, and, since I don't know quite what she's up to, if you can keep an eye on her, it could help."

"I heard her on the phone earlier," Jenny shared hesitantly. "She was talking to somebody, saying that she just needed a little more time."

He looked at her. "And how did she sound? Anxious or afraid?"

"She sounded very anxious, almost panicked. So, fear had to be a part of it. When I asked her if she was okay, she was pretty ugly about it. She told me how I shouldn't be listening in on conversations. And, let's just say, she had more to say about it all."

He sighed as he stared at her. "This family has been quite a trial to you, hasn't it?"

She smiled. "I have been part of this trial, as you put it, for a very long time. I just hope that Alexander is okay and that his absence has nothing to do with her ... shenanigans. I've always known she had a problem," she shared, as she shook her head, "but I didn't realize the extent of it."

"Yeah, me too," he admitted. "Nobody ever really wants to know the extent of it either. Everybody here just wants life to continue as it is. The cousins and Grandma have enjoyed a free ride and get to just take care of their own stuff without any consequences or contribution to the place." He looked around, then focused back on her. "However, there are consequences now, and an awful lot will change. That's another problem for tomorrow." He smiled and, with a shrug, added, "I'm also supposed to find a missing dog."

She blinked.

He laughed. "I know. In a way, it's something a little more normal for me to stay focused on, although I recognize that everybody else thinks it'll send me one step over the brink when I even mention it. But I'm doing this as a favor to friends of mine who helped me so much in this last little while, after Grandma told me how I shouldn't come home if

I wasn't whole."

Jenny stared at him in shock.

He nodded. "Grandpa told me to come here, to my house, my home, back where I belong, but Grandma had a whole different opinion about that one. So, I didn't come home, when apparently I should have."

She stared at him. "She said that to you?"

He nodded. "Yeah, that happened again more recently. Looking at it now, she probably thought my being here would cramp her style where the gambling money was concerned. But I'm home now, and I'm working on all kinds of things, one of which is this missing dog. It's a K9 War Dog, … a dog who spent the better part of his life saving soldiers like me," he explained. "So, if he needs a hand, I'm here to provide it."

"But how will you find it?"

"That's the question. Do you know a guy by the name of Sean Keaton?"

She frowned and shook her head. "I don't think so."

"He's an older vet, disabled, reported the dog missing from his home to the locals, but the deputies didn't believe him. Yet he wants Khan back. So my friends who follow up on missing War Dogs sent me to help him find Khan. So, now I'm here to deal with it. And again, at the risk of sounding like a broken record, I'll deal with that tomorrow."

She looked at him with a silent acknowledgment. "Sounds like your tomorrow is going to be a hell of a lot like your today."

"I hope not," he muttered, "because the last thing I want is to go back to the bank and haul my grandmother out again. I still have to deal with that fallout." He sighed. "But I had a great meal, and I appreciate that. And, if you come up with anything on the dog, I would appreciate hearing it."

She looked at him, a twinkle in her eye, and asked, "What's that now? You sound like you almost think the hired help knows things?"

"Oh, the hired help always knows things," he confirmed, with a smile. "That's not a mistake I've ever made."

She chuckled. "No, you never did. However, it's a lesson Johanna never seemed to learn." Then she sighed and added, "I should be a better Christian than that."

He looked at her and chuckled. "All you are is human, Jenny. Just like the rest of us."

"Well, in that case, I'll just say that I hope she gets a come-uppance," she declared smartly, "after everybody has been saving her sorry butt all this time. And now poor Alexander," she muttered, with a headshake. "I sure hope we can get him home again. He's always been kind to all of us here."

"I hope to get him home soon," Ashton stated. "That's the goal." And, with that, he got up. "I'm going to head off to bed because, as you know, tomorrow—"

"Is looking like one hell of a day," she added, laughing.

He smiled, headed up to his room, and crashed.

CHAPTER 4

WHEN ASHTON WOKE the next morning, he knew the list of what he had to get through today was long and arduous. Yet the War Dog was one of today's priorities, along with a search for his grandfather. The thought of Khan and Grandpa suffering because Ashton wasn't on top of things was completely unacceptable. He headed downstairs, made coffee, and quickly fried a couple eggs and put them on toast. He was already sitting here, eating, before Jenny wandered in.

She stopped and frowned at him.

He smiled and chuckled as he greeted her. "I'm still on early morning military time," he explained. "So don't get yourself riled up about me cooking my own breakfast."

"Well, I should at least be here to look after your meals," she snapped, glaring at him.

He laughed. "Maybe you can do that tomorrow then," he suggested. "Today has already started, and, as you know, I have about a day and a half to get through in the next twenty-some hours." He tossed back his coffee, refilled it, brought out his phone, and started setting up what he needed to do.

"Surely there isn't anything you can do at this hour," she muttered.

"Not just yet," he said. "I've got appointments at eight

with the lawyer, at nine with the banker, at ten with the sheriff, and, after that, I'll search for Grandpa and Khan and go from there."

"You'll have to adjust your schedule as you go," she pointed out, "because one hour won't be enough in some of those places."

He frowned at her, double-checked his schedule, and groaned. "Maybe, but I may not have much of a chance to change it either. Things are pretty tight because everything is a top priority."

She didn't say anything, just nodded. She poured herself a cup of coffee.

He asked her, "Will you look after Grandma?"

She looked at him and raised one eyebrow. "I always do."

"I know," he confirmed, "but *you* also know that we have a bigger problem than many of us thought we did."

She nodded. "Yes, you're right there," she agreed, with a shrug. "You do need to talk to Crystal though."

"I do—and also John and Glenn." She didn't say anything to that. "Have they caused any trouble?" he asked.

"Not *caused* trouble, but the twins don't really do anything helpful either," she shared. "So, I don't know what that'll look like if you're planning on shifting things."

"Well, I have to," he stated, "because the place cannot keep going as it is, particularly with too many people taking with no intention of giving back. Something has to give, or we can't remain here."

"And, of course, people don't like change," she pointed out.

He smiled. "I know that, and I've already told Crystal that she's welcome to stay."

"She's trying to get out on her own and has been for a while. You should know that Johanna has been … just snarkier and meaner to her, which has made her very uncomfortable."

Ashton sighed. "I do know that."

"Your grandmother will come in for breakfast pretty soon—or maybe not now that you're here," she corrected. "The twins, however, rarely miss breakfast."

"And why do they come in here?" he asked her curiously. "Aren't they in one of the suites?"

"They are, but they don't cook for themselves," she said. "I still do that." He just stared at her, and she nodded. "I get it. Changes need to be made."

"Yeah," he muttered, "they definitely do." He got up and added, "I don't know quite when I'll be back."

Just then, the back door to the kitchen opened, and Crystal walked in. She looked at him and then frowned.

He frowned right back. "Good morning."

"Good morning," she replied. Then she saw the coffee and smiled. "If you don't mind, I could use a cup of coffee."

He stared at her and shook his head. "Of course I don't mind. Why would I?"

She shrugged. "Well, things are obviously changing, and I don't quite know how much."

"They're going to change, yes," he confirmed, "and in a big way. But that doesn't mean you're not welcome to coffee. And, if you need to talk to me, I am about to walk out the door because I have multiple things I need to do today."

"Right." She nodded. "Didn't something in your day have to do with a dog?"

"Yep, I'm going to see Sean Keaton this morning."

She frowned at him and repeated, "Sean?"

"Yeah." He turned to her and asked, "Do you know him?"

"Yeah, I volunteer with the seniors' groups here," she shared, "and he's one of the people I work with sometimes."

"When you say, *work with*," he asked cautiously, "what does that mean?"

She smiled. "He doesn't need care, per se, but he's old, lonely, and he's really suffering right now because of his missing dog. We find that if we spend some time just keeping people company, they aren't so isolated. Plus, it provides the opportunity to identify other issues quickly when they arise."

"Which is also why I'm trying to find the dog. It's not good for either of them to be separated," Ashton noted, with a shake of his head. "I need to talk to him."

She stared at him for a moment and added, "Sean doesn't do very well with strangers."

"I don't know if he would consider me a stranger after a few minutes," he replied, "because we're both veterans, and generally that helps clear the air."

"Yes, though he's not been treated that well either," she added. "Some people here? … Honestly they haven't been terribly welcoming."

He stared at her for a long moment, his gaze going to Jenny, then back to Crystal. "Are you telling me people in this town have been hassling a veteran?"

She didn't know what to say, but she glanced over at Jenny, who spoke up.

Jenny began, "Listen. After you went to be bed last night, I had a talk with Crystal, and we agree that you are likely to find that the twins aren't terribly welcoming of anybody who is different."

He stared at her for a long time and muttered, "We're going to have lots of fun coming up, aren't we?"

She winced and nodded slowly. "Yes, so you probably need to be prepared for that."

"*Great*," he muttered, his tone calm. "So my cousins find me different too and will likely be difficult when I speak to them about the upcoming changes, is that it?"

"Maybe," Jenny noted, "but let's not go in that direction yet."

He laughed at that. "Right, and you say *yet* because …?"

"Well, your grandmother is quite partial to them."

"So, are they enabling her? Or is she enabling them?" Jenny winced and didn't say anything. He just nodded. "Got it. So, they think the cash cow will never die? So they're just staying on her good side, hoping that they get this place, is that it?"

"I don't think anybody really understands how the finances sit," Jenny pointed out, cautiously looking at Crystal and then back at him.

Crystal clarified, "We spoke at some length last night, and it's obviously that various issues have been compartmentalized. Now that we're seeing the larger picture, things are becoming clearer, and we feel the potential is there for people to make assumptions about what they might gain in ways that just aren't true."

He let out his breath slowly. "So, Grandma's really done a number on them, hasn't she?"

Jenny didn't say anything. She just lowered her gaze and stirred her coffee.

"Right," he muttered, turning to Crystal. "So, to answer your question, there will be a lot of changes—a lot more than I care to admit. However, that'll have to wait because I have a full day. So, if either of you need me for something, text me, and I'll get here when I can. Or wait until I get home. I just don't know when that will be."

"I could come with you," Crystal suggested, "and help break the ice when you talk to Sean."

He hesitated and looked from Crystal to Jenny, then back again. "Is that really going to be an issue?"

She took a deep breath and nodded. "It might be, yes."

"Well, in that case, get ready to go because I'm heading out now." She hesitated and he nodded. "My day will not get any easier. So, I fully intend to get as much done as I can before I run out of energy," he explained, with a small smile.

Crystal nodded. "Be right back." And, with that, she turned and bolted out the back door.

He turned to Jenny and asked, "Since when has she done volunteer work with seniors?"

Jenny smiled. "Crystal does a lot of volunteer work. Seniors, people on welfare, single moms, the women's shelter. She's kind of all over it."

"And does she also work another job to make money?"

"I don't really know, but she's mentioned trying to set up her own business."

"And is that going okay?"

"I have no idea." Jenny shrugged. "I can tell you that, out of everybody here, she at least works to help out, and she does the chores."

"While great on its own, it doesn't bring any money into this place."

"Right."

"Something to keep in mind then."

Jenny grimaced. "I get the idea and can see the problems you're facing, but not everybody is the same here."

He smiled, leaned over, and gave her a hug. "That I do know. When Grandma gets up, tell her that I'll be home a little later, and I need to talk with her."

Jenny rolled her eyes at that. "Which will guarantee that she'll run to the country club or somewhere else in order to avoid you."

He smiled, his face beaming. "Yeah, that country club membership has to go as well. Yet not today, so hopefully she'll stay out of trouble in the meantime."

"Don't count on it," Jenny muttered. "Johanna has an unending ability to get into trouble." Then she sighed. "She really isn't a bad person, you know?"

He looked back at Jenny and smiled. "I remember how she used to be, and she wasn't a bad person back then. But what she's doing now is very wrong, and she's putting the whole place and the whole family at risk."

CRYSTAL RACED BACK to her little house, grabbed her wallet, keys, and a sweater as a second thought, then headed back over to the vehicles. "I'll take my own truck," she called out, as she neared his truck.

He shrugged. "Okay. Any particular reason?"

"Yeah, because I need to come back and feed the animals," she explained, trying to get the vehicle unlocked. "This is way ahead of my normal schedule," she noted, with a quiet smile. "And I don't want to … put you out of your way, having to bring me home when you're in the middle of something else."

He just nodded, and she hopped into her truck, trying to figure out everything else that she needed to do while she was in town anyway. She pulled out, watching as he followed her, wondering at how quickly everything here would be changing.

He seemed to be somebody in charge already, and that surprised her. She didn't think the twins had even the slightest clue that their world was about to flip over.

She worried about Jenny too, who was almost a family heirloom in her own right. Jenny had been here for decades serving the family. Crystal had to wonder at what point in time even Jenny's tolerance for the BS going on at home would come to an end. Although, given how close Jenny was to Ashton, she may know a lot more than even Crystal did. Particularly if there wasn't any more money, which Crystal wasn't sure was much to begin with. It seemed that Jenny knew by now, dealing with the household bills and orders and such. Her grandmother too, for that matter.

But Grandma's strange behavior was an issue in itself. More than once Crystal had overheard Grandma berating Jenny in an over-the-top way, wholly unacceptable. Jenny never said anything, never pushed back, probably trying to avoid exacerbating Grandma's outbursts.

Crystal headed down the main highway and took the familiar route to Sean's place. She turned off onto the gravel road and drove carefully as the truck bounced over the uneven surface. When she parked right at the front door, she noted it was a little bit open. She hopped out and walked forward, calling out, "Sean? Sean, are you okay?"

Ashton's footsteps were rapid behind her. To stop her, he grabbed her hand, which she quickly took back. "I presume this isn't normal."

"No," she replied, frowning at him. "This isn't normal."

"Stay here."

His words were direct, not quite an order, but no mistaking his tone of authority. She stopped where she was and watched as he stood in the doorway and called out several times. Then, with a look back at her, he stepped inside. In that moment, she realized what kind of a military life Ashton must have had, fully prepared for something godawful to be going on in there, yet stepped in without hesitation anyway.

She didn't even know what she would have done. She probably would have gotten to the doorway, then stopped, hoping everything was okay. Beyond that, she didn't know. She didn't have any experience with something like this.

When Ashton reappeared at the door again, he shook his head. "Doesn't seem anybody is here, but the place also appears to be tossed."

She frowned at him and then bolted forward.

He let her go inside. "Don't touch anything," he called out behind her.

She realized he was thinking more along the lines of somebody having broken in. "But Sean doesn't have anything."

"No, but not having anything isn't the same thing for you as it could be for somebody who's not quite in the same financial situation."

"But Sean doesn't do drugs, so that's not here either. He's just a lonely old man who is rather desperate to get his dog back," she shared, trying hard to not let the tears spill. "He was suffering pretty heavily over that," she added. "I know the deputies were sick and tired of hearing about it, but they didn't have anything to offer. Nobody has seen the dog, and there were just no answers as to where it could have gone."

Ashton didn't say anything. He walked back inside,

around to the bedroom, and checked the phone without touching it, then hovered around. "Have you been to his place before?"

"Yes, yes, of course. Several times."

"And did it look like this?"

"God no. Sean's quite neat, organized, and all. I think it's part and parcel of his military training. So this is very unusual," she stated, as she stared around.

Ashton huffed. "Honestly, it's criminal."

"Yeah, yeah," she agreed. "I would think so. It looks like somebody has literally tossed it. Now, that doesn't mean that they did it on purpose though," she noted cautiously.

He shot her a look.

Crystal took that to mean how Ashton was probably thinking the same thing she was. He knew something too. She pointed out, "I'm just saying that, if they came upon this cabin, and nobody was here, they may have just decided to look for drugs or something because it was an opportunity."

"Maybe," Ashton conceded, "and maybe it's something else altogether."

He dialed a number, and she asked, "Who you calling?"

"The deputies."

She heard him talking to somebody as Ashton wandered around Sean's place. When he rejoined her, he shared, "They'll send somebody out. They think Sean just wandered off."

She frowned at that. "You know, people like to say things like that when someone gets old, but neither Sean nor Grandpa would have just wandered off. Sean would, however, have gone looking for his dog."

"And would you, ... would he have had any idea where that dog is?"

"No, not that I know of, but I didn't see him very often," she said. "I came to talk to him once in a while just to make sure he was doing okay." She frowned and added, "Now I feel like I should have been here a whole lot more. I mean, this"—she stared around the space—"is not normal."

"My concern is whether somebody did this, looking for something other than normal petty cash. Something they could pawn off to get drugs. My next concern is whether a bigger, uglier motivation is behind this."

She cast him a quiet look. She wasn't sure whether he was expecting an answer or not because this wasn't her world. "I don't think I like the world you've lived in."

"Right. You wouldn't have liked the military world I lived in. Unfortunately it's not all that hot at home just now either."

She flushed at that. "Yeah, Grandma's gambling. I have to admit she has been off lately."

"Yeah, she's off all right," he confirmed. "And now I'll have no choice but to corral her on a permanent basis. And that won't be fun."

She stopped and stared. "Are you talking about putting her in a home?"

"I don't know what I'm talking about," he admitted, "but I need somebody to give me an idea of whether what she's doing is part of a medical condition or a mental condition or an addiction, or just plain selfishness. But lying to the first deputies about Alexander just walking off, then lying to Deputy Hale that her bookies are holding Grandpa for ransom over her gambling debts?" He shook his head. "Either way, it's not normal behavior, and I need somebody to take a more serious look at her."

Crystal frowned. "Grandma won't go for that. Plus, this

is addictive behavior, whether drugs or alcohol or gambling."

He looked at her and shrugged. "I do know that she won't go willingly to the doc. And of course, the *willingly* part is the issue."

She winced. "Yeah, she really won't go if she thinks you'll commit her or something."

He shook his head. "That's not what I was thinking. I just need a medical consult."

She felt a sense of relief over that, not much, but it was something.

"But paranoia? … It can also be a sign of dementia. Her actions are definitely off the wall and not normal. And whether that's completely understandable in the realm of an addiction, I don't know either," he admitted. "That is not in my wheelhouse, so I really do need an expert. Surely you won't get mad at me for getting an expert involved to see if Grandma can be treated with medications to help her in some way?"

"No, not mad," she clarified, "but I also know that she's traumatized because of Grandpa. And you can't get her to speak to a shrink any more than you can get her to speak to a medical doctor—at least not honestly."

"Yeah, there is that," he muttered. "But then, is she traumatized because of Grandpa? Or because of what she did that brought this to him?"

"I don't know," she said, shaking her head. "I just don't know. I wish I did."

"So do I," he muttered. "And you can see me as the bad guy all you want. But this?" he noted, with a wave of his hand. "It all must be taken care of, and you don't even know the half of it. So, just hold off on the judgment, please."

She threw up her hands, horrified that he thought of her

like that. "Look. I am not judging you," she snapped. "But Grandma spent a lot of time raising me. And gave me a good start in life. While she's been *different* lately, I just don't want to see her in trouble for nothing."

"She's already in trouble, and it ain't *for nothing*," he declared. "*Major* trouble and I don't even know if I can keep her out of jail." With that, leaving Crystal gasping in shock, he turned and walked to the door. "You might as well go home because the deputies will be here soon. So, here's your chance to not be involved in this mess."

"What will you tell them?"

"I'll just tell them this is what I found."

"Well, no point in *not* telling them that I was here," she remarked. "I work with them sometimes too. It depends on the situation."

He glanced at her and nodded. "Did you ever think about going back to school and getting a degree in social work or something?"

"Yeah, I've thought about it, but I went the veterinarian route," she replied, with a careless shrug. "I've thought about getting another degree a few times, but it takes more money, more time, more effort. And none of those things appear to be something I really have anymore." He shot her a look, and she just shrugged. "I'm fine. Don't worry about it."

"We'll talk about that later," he vowed. "I don't hear *fine* in anything you're saying."

She groaned. "And I haven't had a chance to see who you are in the last many years either," she pointed out, "but you've stepped in, and it's as if you've taken over."

He nodded. "Yeah, but there's a damn good reason for that."

She studied him, a questioning expression on her face.

"Nobody else has stepped in to date, and meanwhile the place has gone to pot. So again, hold off on the judgment. Give me a chance to sort through things and to see where we're at."

"And how much time will that take?"

"I need a day or two," he replied.

"I'm not against giving you that day or two," she noted, "but I do need to know that Grandma will be safe when this all ends."

He gave her a wry smile. "I can't promise safe. I can almost surely promise jail time." At Crystal's gasp, he added, "She brought this all on herself. Yet it's really nice to think that you still care that much about her because I'm really not sure many people do, not after the way she's been treating them."

"I know Jenny does."

"Yet Jenny is more concerned about Grandpa, at least at the moment." He sighed. "Probably because Grandma's been burning a lot of bridges lately, and that's pretty painful for the people involved."

"I know Grandma's been pretty rough on Jenny."

"Yeah, and Jenny doesn't deserve that," he said. "Neither do you. So, give me your honest opinion. Do you think there is a chance that some medical reason could account for the change in Grandma's personality?"

"I don't know," she muttered. "I hadn't really considered that."

"Well, I am here now, and I have to consider it," he stated, "because it's also highly possible that she'll wind up in prison. I need to know whether that's something that will get her committed to some mental hospital or wind up in general population? She would be safer in the mental hospital, in my mind."

She stared at him, shell-shocked. "You're serious, aren't you?"

"Hell yes, I'm serious," he snapped, looking at her. "I've shared more than enough with you that I would think you could easily see the criminality here. So, where among all this crap did you think I *wasn't* serious? And if you think I'm doing this out of spite or something like that, you're wrong. I really want to find Grandpa, and I'm hoping he's still alive. But, either way, Grandma has her own issues that will have a *very serious* impact on what happens to her. It was bad enough when Grandma was stealing from the household money. She was effectively stealing from all of us. But now Grandma continues to steal *other people's* money in the form of Grandpa's investment clients. Did I not make that clear enough already?"

"You have proof? Real evidence?" she asked. "Not just theories?"

"Hell yes, I've got proof. I've got money trails. I've got bank documents on each end. What the hell, Crystal? Do you not remember my own college degree was in finance?"

She closed her eyes, trying hard not to panic. "Dear God, I don't know what she's done, but surely it can't be that bad."

"Well," he began, slowly turning to face her, "what is the absolute worst thing that *you figure* she could have been involved in? Playing bingo? Hell no. Gambling. Stealing other people's retirement funds. That's prison time for her, maybe even for Grandpa for enabling her."

She frowned and didn't say a word. She gave him a hesitant wave and took off in her truck.

CHAPTER 5

ASHTON WALKED THROUGH Sean's property, waiting for the deputies, looking for any sign of what could have happened to Sean. He texted Crystal, asking if Sean had a vehicle, and she quickly responded.

No vehicle. His nephew used to come by occasionally and deliver groceries, but it didn't seem very consistent.

He thought about that and frowned because *occasionally* wasn't exactly helpful for somebody like Sean, in a wheelchair with no car. His wheelchair was also missing, which was potentially a good thing, meaning he was off in it, looking for Khan. He sent Crystal another text, asking for the nephew's name.

Charlie Nester.

He stared at the name, tweaking something in his brain, but he couldn't quite place it. He quickly did a Google search, but nothing came up. When he heard a vehicle, he turned to see a deputy cruiser pulling up.

He went out to greet the two guys, whom he hadn't met before. He explained what he had found and that he had sent Crystal back home again, but they could talk to her if they felt it was needed. He led them through the place. "There's no sign of Sean, and he's disabled and a senior," he shared, "so that's not a good sign."

The deputies just looked at him, and Ashton smiled, thinking they were trying to place him. "I'm from around here. I've just been away for the last several years. I'm Ashton Nelson."

The two deputies nodded, seemed to recognize his name. One said, "You're the grandson who's been off in the military."

"I am, and I'm home again."

The same one noted, "Your grandmother has been making all sorts of accusations."

"I'll bet, so in what way are we concerned about her accusations?" Ashton asked. "My grandmother is obviously in a state about a lot of things."

"She's making accusations about you trying to steal her home out from under her."

He smirked at them and then chuckled. "You're more than welcome to address that in a separate investigation, if you like," he suggested, "but, right now, I am more concerned about Sean's disappearance."

"He's probably at his nephew's place," said the same deputy who did all the talking, adding a shrug.

"So, he's probably at his nephew's place, and you don't care, is that it?" Ashton asked, frowning.

The deputy flushed at his tone. "We don't really know you, do we?"

"So, because you don't know me, you're not worried about Sean? So, just contact Charlie then and ask him when he last saw his uncle."

"Look. This is hardly a major case."

Ashton stopped to stare at both of them. "So, Sean's place has been tossed, the door's found open, and a disabled senior citizen is missing, and you're saying it's not important?"

One deputy flushed again, while the other deputy glared at him.

Ashton nodded. "I can see how this will go."

"Oh, you're more than welcome to talk to our sheriff," said the glaring deputy.

"Oh, don't worry," Ashton replied, calm and cool. He pulled out his phone and called the sheriff. "Hey, Richard. How's the town treating you?"

The two deputies froze right where they were.

Richard chuckled. "I see you've been causing all kinds of chaos since the minute you got here."

"Yeah, well, here's some more. I've got two of yours here, and they seem to think that Sean going missing isn't even worth writing a report on." Silence came on the other end, and Ashton added, "They didn't identify themselves to me, but I sure was shocked to hear them say that. I can't tell you who they are, but I can give you the license plate off their vehicle."

At that, one of the deputies protested, "Hey, that's not fair."

"What's not fair?" Ashton asked, turning and holding up the phone. "This is your boss, and you yourself told me that I was free to lodge a complaint against you if I wanted. So, I'm taking you up on that and lodging a complaint, which is why I have phoned the sheriff."

A roar came from the other end of the phone call, and one of the deputies winced.

Richard yelled, "Ashton, I'll talk to them."

"Yeah, you better," Ashton said. "I don't know what the hell's happening around this area, where gossip has become evidence, but your deputies all but accused me of stealing *my grandmother's property*. And you know better than I do what that accusation really means—*defamation*, and all that goes with it."

Dead silence came for a moment on the other end, and then Richard sighed. "Yeah, I'll *really* be talking to them," he declared.

"I'll be stopping by the station later today to see how all that goes." And, with that, Ashton disconnected and looked at the two deputies, who both looked stomped. "If you guys aren't prepared to do what's right by Sean, who's *missing*," he emphasized, "then I'm wondering just exactly what the citizens in this town are paying you wages for."

The two deputies remained silent, then shared a look at each other. "Look. We didn't say—"

"Yes, you did," Ashton corrected. "Yes, you absolutely did everything I complained about to the sheriff. So just to be clear, I expect *this* missing person's case to be taken very seriously. I understand my grandpa has already been reported as missing, so I trust that you will give *that* missing person's case your full attention as well. I'll be stopping in town later today to talk to the sheriff on both these matters. I do not, however, have time for it right now. Therefore, you've got some time to redeem yourselves, at least a little bit."

And, with that, he returned to his truck, hopped in, and drove away, without even giving them a second glance. He didn't get very far down the road when his phone rang. It was Richard. He answered it and asked, "What the hell kind of a shop are you running these days?"

"Yeah, your grandmother's done a hell of a job on you."

"Well, that's nice. She doesn't own jack shit and hasn't for many years. Oh, and besides stealing from the household account, she's graduated to stealing from Grandpa's invest-ment clients," he explained. "So, maybe you need to think about that one too."

After a brief silence, he came back, "Are you serious?"

"Has everybody forgotten I am a finance major? Hell yes, I'm dead serious. I talked to Timmy yesterday, and I figured he would fill you in on the details."

"Maybe you better fill me in," Richard suggested.

"Grandma's been embezzling for years. I've been trying to pay back the money to buy some time for them to get it straightened out. I came back six years ago to make sure she didn't have access to the family's household checking accounts *and* Grandpa's investment clients. I set them all up so she could only put money back in, deposits only. In the meantime, I've been trying to cover all the gambling losses and outright thefts," he shared. "And now that my grandfa-ther has gone missing, my grandmother has gone crazier than normal and has everything pretty spun up."

"You never thought to let me know any of this?" Richard asked.

"Believe me that I thought the legal agreement from six years ago, that Grandpa's attorney drew up, that Grandpa and Grandma both signed, was a stop-gap measure to prevent any future thefts and would correct the theft issue, forcing repayments, given enough time that is. So far Grandpa's clients have been covered, when asking for distributions. Grandpa definitely didn't want to advertise any of that, and I surely didn't want Grandma's addiction to destroy Grandpa's business either. It was one thing when she was stealing from the family, but it's gotten way worse. Hell, I'm the financial officer over all this mess, and I'm pretty damn worried right now."

"Look. You need to come in, so we can go over this from top to bottom."

"Yeah, that would be nice, *except* I got a really close look at your crew today," he pointed out. "So, if gossip and innuendo and sheer ineptitude and laziness and lies are what I'm looking forward to, believe me that I'll be speaking to my own attorney first."

Richard groaned. "Look, Ashton. We go back a long way, and I will deal with my deputies. I'll remind them that's not how we operate around here. At least I didn't think it was, until I heard what they did today." He sighed and added, "I promise I'll handle it better."

"And remember that my grandfather is also missing too." And, with that, Ashton ended the call.

Ashton headed into the lawyer's office. Even though he was a few minutes early, his lawyer, Anderson Moore, was there, and the coffee was on.

Anderson smiled at him and got up to greet him. "How much chaos have you already caused?"

"A lot." He then explained just what had happened this morning so far.

Anderson's eyebrows shot up, and he asked, "You do know Richard, don't you?"

"I do and for a very long time," he replied, "so I was a little unprepared for his guys and their piss-poor attitudes."

"Well, the gossip about you stealing the place from your grandma they'll just have to stuff because that place is yours free and clear. The fact that you told him that she's been stealing money from your grandfather's client accounts is a whole different story. That contract, signed by both your grandparents, was also an NDA."

"Which contract was broken in the last couple years, *by*

my grandparents. So, I'm a little fed up with everybody acting like I'm the big bad wolf being hard on this sweet little old lady and her poor missing husband."

Anderson nodded. "In the last few years, Johanna has been anything but discreet, so that should help discount any rumors she's spreading." Yet Anderson had to laugh.

Ashton shook his head. "Yeah, I've heard about her not paying the local merchants too. I am sick and tired of trying to keep the lid over the mess that Grandma's created herself, as well as paying back her gambling losses and outright thefts. She stole more and more from all of us, with Grandpa just letting her. I'm the only one who sees the handwriting on the wall, and having to explain to everybody that the place may no longer be ours soon won't be received well because my family doesn't own up to its problems."

Anderson nodded. "Yeah, you're right. The twins will be shocked that they have to find employment. Now I didn't go through official channels, but I did hear from somebody, whom I know privately, that your grandmother has opened up another account and has put a fair chunk of money into it."

Ashton put down his coffee cup, leaning forward. "We need to put a lien on that and get an injunction or whatever you need to stop her from accessing it."

"I can't get the account number," he shared, "and the channels I used are obviously not official. So, you'll need to find that account or get it out of somebody. We've got to put a stop to her shenanigans really quickly, or you won't have much left in that place."

"What the hell has she gotten into now? This goes way beyond *little old lady* shenanigans into plain old selfish cruelty from a bitchy old woman who is running all of us off our own land."

Anderson suggested, "You want to talk to her about it? I doubt she would give you the truth, but you could start with her, at least put her on notice."

Ashton shook his head. "Don't want to give her a heads-up. She'll just go pull out that money before I can stop her. I just had *the talk* with her yesterday, after causing a scene at the bank." He groaned. "And believe me that I've got no end of headaches over that one too."

Anderson nodded, a commiserating expression on his face. "Sorry, this won't be easy for anybody. You'll have to be prepared for a fight."

"No, it sure as hell won't be easy, but I also don't know how I'll access that new bank account info. I'm on my way to the bank right after I'm done here anyway, so just another item to talk to Roger about."

"Right, so you can find out from Roger what you need in order to freeze the accounts, but having already told Richard that this is going on might be enough to freeze access to the account."

"Not if I don't do something officially," Ashton muttered. "I need that new account number, which you just told me about yourself. My God, how much more of this crap is going on that I don't even know about yet?"

"Yeah, Johanna can be secretive when it serves her, so that new account will be a bit harder to find," he agreed, as he shook his head. "Plus, we don't necessarily want a big nightmare with a bunch of publicity over all this."

"No, we sure don't, not yet. I have limited funds to pay back what Grandma stole. I can't have Grandpa's clients all up in arms, with *everyone* demanding their money back today, for God's sake. All of it hasn't been recouped yet,"

Ashton explained. "I mean, if my calculations are anywhere close to right, lawsuits will cripple Grandpa's investment company that is on unsteady ground already. And, personally speaking, I've already lost everything to this property and his business." Ashton sighed. "So, short of my grandfather stashing away some money—"

Anderson held up one hand. "Your grandfather did set up another account," he shared, "for emergencies. He told me, if there was absolutely no other way, to give you this." Shuffling through paperwork, Anderson handed over an envelope. "It's his rainy-day account."

Ashton took it and nodded. "I'll need that so I can have Roger look it up today. Will I need anything else paperwork-wise?"

"You already have power of attorney, don't you?"

"Yes, I do," he stated, "unless something's changed."

"Just give me a second to check." It didn't take long for Anderson to find the most recent documents. "No, you've still got power of attorney," he confirmed, looking away from his computer. "I don't know that your grandma even knows about that."

"She doesn't," he stated. "We can't trust her." He hesitated, then asked Anderson, "Can you give me your professional opinion? Is my grandmother doing this on purpose, or is there some medical or mental decline that I'm not seeing?"

"I don't know," Anderson admitted. "I don't know of any medical decline that would allow her to do all this without being aware of what she's doing—cognitively, I mean. She's probably panicking because you're here, and she wants to continue to gamble and to steal. So she must have access to money to do both. Your being here puts a dent in her plans."

"And that new account of hers that you mentioned, where did she get the money for that?"

"I don't know," he said, "but, as per the agreement she signed six years ago, any money that she's made has to go back into the business to replenish funds she's taken and losses she's created, plus pay you back for the money you have put in yourself. Therefore, it doesn't matter wherever she got it from."

"So, if it's hers, then it theoretically isn't hers? It belongs to all the people she's defrauded?"

Anderson nodded.

Ashton let out a big sigh. "It's all going to come out and will get really ugly, won't it?"

"Yeah, it will. If you can't pay back that money fast, it certainly will."

"I'll need my grandfather to make that happen," he noted, "and he's disappeared."

"What? When the hell did that happen?"

"It's been four days, four and a half now, and nobody's seen him or heard from him. Nobody seems to have any idea where he is."

"That's bad, Ashton."

"Yeah, tell me about it." He snorted, rubbing his face. "Do you happen to know Sean, the older disabled veteran in town here?"

He thought about it and nodded. "That description sounds familiar. What's his last name?" Then he stopped and said, "Never mind. It's Keaton, Sean Keaton. He just came in here, like a couple weeks ago, wanting to get his affairs in order. So, yeah, if it's the same guy—older, in a wheel-chair—yeah, I know him. He's a client."

"How did he get here, do you know?"

He stopped and stared at him. "I don't know. I never even thought about it."

Ashton asked, "Did he come in alone?"

"He did, wanting to establish his estate docs, like a will and that sort of thing. Why are you asking about him?" he asked, looking puzzled.

"Because he's also gone missing, and his place was trashed."

Anderson sat back, an odd expression on his face. "Damn it. You know, he as much as told me that he was afraid. Not like afraid for his life, he didn't say that. Yet he was afraid what would happen to his dog if something happened to him. People do love their pets. However, he did look a little nervous. I asked him if he felt threatened in any way, but he never answered me. I pushed, but he's a stubborn veteran, thinking he can take care of himself."

Ashton snorted. "Yep, you got that right."

Anderson continued. "So Sean insisted we get it all done before he left. He literally sat here in my office while we drafted up the documents, then waited until everything was finalized and signed."

"And did somebody witness it?"

"Yes, my receptionists witnessed it. I had two here at the time. They do a job share and were changing shifts, so both signed off as witnesses." He frowned, his fingers tapping his desk impatiently in a staccato movement. He glanced over at Ashton, a worried expression on his face. "Do you think something happened to him?"

"I really hope not. Who was the beneficiary to Sean's estate? His nephew?"

Anderson chuckled. "Nope. Crystal."

"Didn't see that coming," Ashton admitted. "The other thing is, I'm looking for a War Dog that Sean adopted. The War Dog's a tracker. So, if I can get a hold of the dog, I could start finding some of these missing people," he muttered.

"Dog, dog, dog," Anderson muttered, frowning.

Ashton eyed him and asked, "Did you hear about the dog?"

"I think so." He shuffled a bunch of paperwork and mentioned, "I heard something about a dog just the other day."

"Who was that?"

"Another client, checking on zoning for boarding horses, *dogs*," Anderson replied, frowning.

"What did they say about the dog specifically?" Ashton asked.

"They picked up a shepherd in the bush, tracking around. It resisted getting picked up. It sounded like it was pretty upset and angry, but then it calmed down, or gave in, but it was already on a leash, so there wasn't anything it could do. I guess they're keeping it locked up as they try to find the owner."

Ashton stared at him. "I need the name of that person because there's a good chance that is my missing War Dog out there, trying to find Sean, its owner, who is also missing."

Anderson immediately pulled out his phone and brought up the number. "Don't mention where you got this number from."

Ashton nodded and keyed it into his phone. "I'll tell the Wilfords that the chip in the dog not only IDs the dog but has a GPS locator, and I found them that way, via the US

War Department."

Anderson frowned. "Wow. Impressive."

Chuckling, Ashton shared, "I just made that up. GPS requires an antenna, so *no go* with a dog."

Anderson added, "Let me draw up another couple documents here to try and get you out of being liable for everything your grandmother, even your grandfather in his neglect, are currently doing, because believe me that she's doing something way worse now than what we already knew about."

Ashton nodded. "You do what you can, and I'll check over everything at the bank to make sure we've done what we can do there, since she seems hell-bent on destroying everything."

"Yeah, better you than me."

"I just don't know whether she's hell-bent on destroying what I'm doing or something Grandpa was doing. Or she's really just off in her own little world and living as if it were twenty years ago."

Anderson winced.

Ashton held up a hand to stop whatever Anderson was about to say. "I know. I've already mentioned to a couple people the idea of taking her in and getting her assessed, and they're dead set against it."

"Of course, because then, as both power of attorney and medical attorney," his lawyer noted, "you would have the ability to lock her up, if need be."

"Well, somebody needs to stop her somehow," he muttered, "because, while I've been able to stop her from accessing any of the client accounts in the last six years, she doesn't have everything paid back yet, and that was the agreement."

"It was," Anderson confirmed. "So, if you want to bring her in, we can go over that agreement again. I'm sure a clause or two in there could allow you to detain her lawfully."

"She's stolen so much from the company, from the family. and from me. I literally can't afford to give her a free pass anymore," he shared. "I've already talked to Richard about it, so we need to move fast to minimize any further damage."

"Well, she doesn't have access to these accounts."

"That we know of today," Ashton pointed out. "After all, she created her own account under our noses, as you mentioned. Just something else to deal with."

"Yeah," he replied, "that'll be fun."

"Hopefully not too much fun. I'll call the Wilfords and see if I can see them now. I was supposed to go to the bank and the sheriff's office after speaking to you, but I may get the dog first. Regardless, I'll stop back by here today or tomorrow to sign whatever you've got for me." And, with that, he got up and walked out, leaving Anderson staring after him, more puzzled and more worried than ever.

CHAPTER 6

CRYSTAL WALKED INTO the main house at lunchtime to hear Jenny on the phone. She was about to back out and give her privacy, but then she realized Jenny was speaking to Ashton on the other end.

Jenny looked over at her and nodded her in. "Ashton needs a bank account number that Johanna has set up. Do you know anything about it?"

She stared at her and frowned. "I don't know anything about the financials."

"Well, he wants us to try and find the account number."

She winced. "That feels very much like we're going against her."

Jenny ended the call and looked at her, her gaze stern. "And I don't know that you realize this, but she had been stealing money from your grandfather's clients, a lot of money, and Ashton's rather desperate to pay it all back before he loses everything. He invested absolutely everything he had into saving this place, and now we have a big problem because Johanna wasn't supposed to have access to any money, and everything she could come up with over the last few years was supposed to go back into the business to the repay those client accounts. But apparently, just in the last few days, she's managed to open a personal account and put a huge chunk of money into that, probably thinking it would be hers and hers alone."

Crystal stared at her, miserable to find out that Ashton had been right all along. "Are you serious?" In her mind, she knew it was the beginning of the end for them all.

"Yes, I'm sadly very serious," Jenny muttered. "And, no, I don't like talking about family issues, but Johanna's also come to me for money over the years."

"Me too," Crystal shared. "I didn't know what for, but I didn't ask. I just assumed Grandpa didn't give her very much to run with."

Jenny snorted. "Johanna always had plenty to run with. She was just never very good at not spending it on her gambling."

Crystal felt everything inside her give way. "So, Ashton was right about all of it?"

"Yes, that's why he's moving so fast on all of this."

"That bad, *huh*?"

"Yes, it's really bad right now, and he doesn't even know whether he can save the house or anything else because Johanna's pretty-well blown it all and left what may be an insurmountable challenge," Jenny explained.

Jenny sat here, looking older than Crystal ever remembered seeing her.

Jenny had tears in her eyes. "I'm supposed to live here my whole life, and, if I don't even have that? … I have no place to go. I was supposed to get one of the small dower houses that everybody is currently living in until I die. That was always the agreement, but, if there is no house, no land, … well, my own future at this stage is in question too."

"Good God," Crystal swore. "No wonder Grandma has been so very odd lately."

"She's been panicked is what I would call it," Jenny

snapped, her tone bitter. "I've known that woman since she was young—when she first married into the Nelson family—and I've seen her through both thick and thin. I've seen her through some times where maybe she could have been a better person and times where she was really trying." She snorted and added, "There was a time when she truly loved Alexander, and that's always been an easy way to forgive her."

Crystal nodded in understanding. "Of course. As long as she was happy to look after Grandpa, then—"

"Exactly," Jenny interrupted, "but then she started gambling, and Alexander's life shifted in a horrible way. He too spent everything he had over the last several years just trying to save the family home and the business," she told Crystal. "The people working in the offices in town have no idea, but, in the background, it's always been Ashton and Alexander, trying desperately to keep everything going, to pay back Johanna's theft. Working to pay off everything they could, before any harm was passed to the family or to one of Alexander's clients."

Crystal frowned in shock. "Only to find out now that Grandma has stashed a big chunk of change for herself? Doesn't sound like Grandpa helped her with that, not now that he's gone missing."

"Yeah. Probably so she could continue funding her gambling addiction, and that's a huge issue," Jenny stated.

Crystal glanced around. "She's not even out of bed yet. And I don't know how to help Ashton. I mean, where would Grandma keep that bank information? In her office, maybe?"

Jenny shook her head. "Johanna doesn't do much in the office anymore, and I haven't even seen her go in there in a very long time."

Crystal whispered, "It feels very much like we're sneaking around into her personal affairs."

"I know," Jenny agreed, "so I won't involve you in this. I don't want you to do anything that goes against what you feel is right. However, I'm thinking about all the people she has ripped off without a thought, and the reality that they'll find out what she's done, potentially rather quickly, and that the savings all those clients have worked their whole lives for is potentially all gone? That's just wrong."

"Jesus Christ," Crystal muttered, "do we have any idea how much money is at stake?"

"No, I don't. I just know that Alexander and Ashton have been constantly funneling money in, and that's why Ashton now owns this place," Jenny shared. "He owns it all, so don't kid yourself. No matter what the twins say, it is all Ashton's. The land, the barns, the houses, the business, it's all his. Even after all he's put in, he knows perfectly well he's in danger of losing absolutely everything he ever had."

With that, Jenny got up, and, with the movements of a woman three times her age, she headed into Johanna's office, leaving Crystal sitting in the kitchen, coffee cup in her hand, wondering how the hell something like this could even happen, and yet how does it *not* happen when somebody with issues over money gets access to more money?

They should have stopped Grandma's access way the hell before she got this far. For all Crystal knew, maybe they tried. There had been some comments about that at some point in time. Crystal just didn't understand how Johanna Nelson, the woman she knew, could continue do this when she knew it was destroying the family. Then again, did she even care as long as she could keep feeding her addiction?

Crystal had thought about various addictions a lot because of the work that she did on a volunteer basis, seeing how addictions destroyed families. This just seemed to be yet another example, only one very close to home, and that was hard to take.

She heard footsteps and looked up to see Grandma coming down the stairs, with the same regal *queen of the manor* air that she'd always had, but now that Crystal knew more of what was going on, at least part of it, this behavior was hard for her to accept now.

Johanna frowned at her and sniffed. "Don't you have something to do?" she asked, with a wave of her hand, as if dismissing her.

"I do," she replied. "I also was thinking I needed to go to the bank. Do you need to?"

"No, I was just there," she declared, a smug look on her face. "I won't ever get to the point where someone needs to take me to the bank. I handle my own affairs."

Knowing what Johanna had done, and the problems Ashton now faced, Crystal couldn't even look at her grandmother in the same way anymore.

Johanna poured herself a cup of coffee and turned, staring at Crystal. "I thought you had things to do," she snapped, glaring at her.

She sighed. "Of course, as you command, my queen."

"Watch that lip, young lady," she snapped again. "I don't have to take that from you."

Crystal just stared at her, saw the old lady living in some fantasy world that only contained herself, and nodded. "Do we have any update on Grandpa?"

"No, I don't," she stated, with another wave of her hand. "He's probably off canoodling with some young thing somewhere else."

It was such an incredible thing for her to say that Crystal stopped and stared.

Grandma glared at her. "I'm pretty sure you should be doing something."

It was as much of a dismissal as she had ever received, and Crystal slowly walked out. She texted Ashton about what Grandma just said.

He called her afterward. "Really?"

"Yes, I don't know what's going on."

"I'm not sure I do either," he admitted, "but I'm trying to get to the bottom of it. I've just left Anderson's office, and I have to delay my meeting with Roger at the bank, plus getting an update from the sheriff about Grandpa and now Sean. However, I am about to speak to somebody who picked up a dog, and I'm hoping it will be Sean's."

"That would be good."

"Did you know the dog?"

"I've been around it several times, sure."

"Good, because I'll probably bring it back to the property. So, it would be good to see his reaction if he sees you, and it might help him to adjust. I'm hoping I can use him to track down Sean, even Grandpa. The War Dog apparently was picked up in the woods and was acting very erratically, so I'm thinking Khan had already picked up Sean's scent and was trying to find him in the woods."

"But … he's in a wheelchair," Crystal pointed out.

"I know," he replied, "but my boss just had another case not long ago with somebody else looking after a K9. In that case some severe elder abuse was going on, and I'm really hoping this won't be the same thing."

"Good God," she muttered, "I would hope not. If anything, Sean would have gone out to do something to help somebody else."

"Maybe that's what he did do. Did he and Grandpa know each other?"

"I don't know. … You know, I think they did."

"Yeah, that's what I'm wondering myself," he noted. "Anyway, I'll let you know"—he had to laugh—"or you'll see me when I show up with a K9."

"I hope so."

"As far as Grandma goes, just avoid her if you can. I've already spoken to the deputies who came out to Sean's place, and that was an eye-opener for them as well, so we'll see where all this goes."

"Did you tell them what's going on?"

"Yes, I set their asses straight, called the sheriff on them too. Grandma told them that I was stealing the homestead from her."

"Oh God," Crystal muttered, "that's not good. No matter, she won't handle that well that you set the deputies straight."

"No, she won't, but I keep hoping she'll wise up. This is beyond serious, and she's broken many laws. Every bit of profit and every bit of extra money that Grandpa and I have made over the last however many years has been funneled back into his clients' accounts, to cover *her* thefts. But they're not completely repaid yet, and, if she's now put money away for herself, it's to continue her gambling, not to pay back these clients for all the money she stole. That won't go over well, so she doesn't get to continue this scot-free living, while she makes the rest of us suffer."

"What are you thinking, Ashton?"

"Nothing that's not right, Crystal. I'm not out for revenge, but I will not allow her to take even more money to feed her gambling addiction. If she's got money, it needs to pay back what she's stolen." With that, he disconnected, leaving Crystal staring in shock at her phone.

"How does a family come to this?" she murmured to herself.

MEANWHILE, ASHTON DROVE up to the address in question. It was a decent-sized property, not quite a ranch, maybe a hobby farm. He hopped out of the vehicle, walked up to the front door, rang the doorbell, and got no answer.

The Wilfords were expecting him, so he was hoping that they were hanging onto the dog and were doing it for the right reasons and would be helpful. He rang the doorbell again and heard a shout from the back. He walked around to the rear of the house and saw an older couple, standing with a couple horses. They looked over at him. He sauntered closer and introduced himself. "I'm here about the dog."

Mr. Wilford frowned. "Well, you're going to have to prove it's your dog," he began. "We ain't just handing it over to anybody."

He looked at him and nodded. "Sure enough. If it's a War Dog, it should be chipped, with the registered name of Khan. We can go to any vet clinic and confirm it immediately. I do believe it's Sean's dog."

"And when you say, *Sean?*" Mr. Wilford asked.

"Sean Keaton, a disabled vet. He's gone missing, and his dog has also gone missing." The two looked at each other. "And that's why I need to know where you found the dog, in case Sean's out there as well."

Mr. Wilford still frowned. "Well, if he's on a disability,

he's not likely to be out there."

"I don't know where he is," Ashton replied. "I did, however, just come from his place this morning, only to find that he and his wheelchair are missing, and, for all I know, he's out there looking for his dog. This dog is a retired K9 War Dog, so it's not a dog that people can just pick up and keep on a whim."

Mr. Wilford flushed. "We're not trying to do that," he protested. "Obviously we picked it up because it was in trouble." His voice was stiff, as if he had taken that personally.

"I appreciate that," Ashton noted, "but you also are implying that, if it's not my dog, that you won't let me see him. I need to see the dog so I can identify him, and we'll go from there."

The couple again shared a look.

Mr. Wilford started to speak again, and his wife just tapped his arm, shaking her head.

He glared at her. "Well, it's a good dog, and we could use a watchdog."

"Come on. It's not our dog," she told him, "and he won't stay if he belongs to somebody else anyway." She glanced over at Ashton.

He nodded. "Can I see the dog now?" Ashton asked.

She glanced at her husband, who was still glaring at Ashton. "Come on, dear. Let's get the dog."

Mr. Wilford pointed at Ashton. "We don't even know who he is. I'm not going to let the dog go just because he *says* he's got some sort of claim on it."

"I can give you my boss's name. He works for the US War Department. They are the ones interested in finding the lost War Dog." He pulled out his phone to show them the number to call.

Mrs. Wilford continued to speak to her husband. "Come on now. We found him, but you know that he won't stay, and we'll spend all this time keeping him locked up."

Ashton snorted. "That's not a life for a dog, not to mention the fact that it's not your dog," Ashton declared, frowning at the two of them.

Mr. Wilford glared at him and added, "It's not your dog either."

"That's true," Ashton agreed, "but I am here representing the War Department, and I need to know that this War Dog, who has spent the better part of his life protecting and saving our GIs overseas, is safe and sound with the person assigned to legally adopt the dog."

Mr. Wilford flushed at that, and Mrs. Wilford seemed nervous. "We'll go get him," she said, as she looked at her husband. "You need to go get him. Now." He just glared at her, but she didn't relent.

"Fine," he muttered, then headed over to the barn in the background.

She turned to Ashton and apologized. "I'm really very sorry. He's not usually this difficult, but we once had a similar-looking dog who was the love of his life. So when this one showed up out of nowhere," she explained, "he took it as a sign that he was getting his beloved animal back."

"And did the animal take to him?"

"No, not at all," she admitted, "and that's been a bit of a challenge."

"That's because the War Dog already has somebody, and he knows and wants to be reunited with Sean," Ashton told her. "Also I have two missing seniors, and this War Dog is a good tracker. I'm hoping I can use him to find them both, so

I can get everybody back home again."

She stared at him in shock. "We didn't know any of that," she cried out. "We were trying to find the dog's owner."

"How hard were you trying?" he asked shrewdly.

She flushed. "My husband is definitely connected to this dog."

"Yet the dog is not connected to your husband."

She winced. "He's just been lost without his dog, that's all. He's very concerned and wants the best for the dog. That's all."

"And where have you kept the animal since bringing him home?"

She stared at him and then glanced at the barn.

"The dog is locked up in four walls? He's a big animal, and he's used to being outside, and yet you've got him contained? Did you take him for any walks? Did you feed him? Did you do anything with him other than lock him up and try to keep him as your own?"

The woman flushed. "You must understand, he's, … he's really—" She looked miserable, turning all shades of red.

Ashton nodded. "I do understand wanting a dog, but I also understand that *this* is not your dog."

"Maybe it's not even the one you're looking for." A note of desperation filled her tone.

Ashton asked, "How long should it take your husband to get the dog?"

She grimaced and stared at the barn.

"I suggest we both go to the barn," Ashton noted.

She looked at him and whispered, "You just have to understand."

"I heard everything you said to me, and what I'm also

hearing is that this dog may not be safe here."

"No, my husband wouldn't hurt him," she whispered. "He would never hurt him."

"I'm glad to hear that," Ashton declared, moving at a fast clip as he headed to the barn. He opened it just in time to see the old man trying to put a muzzle on Khan, who was fighting him at every turn. Ashton hurried inside and stopped him. "A muzzle is not needed."

Mr. Wilford shot back, "You don't belong here."

"Yeah, well, watching you put a muzzle on a War Dog that doesn't want or need to be muzzled, a dog that isn't yours in the first place, when you were supposed to be bringing it out to me, makes me wonder if you had something to do with this dog going missing in the first place."

The wife gasped, a silent cry of distress.

Ashton turned to her and asked, "That's what happened, isn't it?"

She closed her eyes, but the husband just started yelling at her.

"Don't you say anything, don't you dare!"

But Ashton already knew. "So, what happened to the old man whose dog you stole? A disabled veteran, a senior citizen in a wheelchair? A man who isn't where he belongs and whom nobody seems to know what happened to him?"

She shook her head. "We … we didn't hurt him."

Shocked, Ashton turned to her. "Are you telling me that you two stole this dog from an old man who needed him, just because you wanted him?" he asked, staring at her, struggling hard to hold back the disgust, but she saw it anyway.

She closed her eyes and muttered, "You have to understand."

"I think the time for understanding has passed," Ashton announced, as he walked over to where Mr. Wilford held the leash tightly. Ashton looked down at Khan, and the dog looked up at him. There wasn't a note of desperation, but there was almost a stillness, a quiet.

Ashton gave him a short, sharp whistle, Khan stood at attention, had followed through with no hesitation. Ashton looked back at Wilford. "Either let him go or I'll command him to pull on that leash, dragging you along if need be. So, just in case you think you're keeping this animal, you're not. From what I see, you probably shouldn't have any pets. I worry about what happened to the poor dog you did have," he shared, "because this is not how you treat animals."

When Wilford refused, Ashton gave another sharp whistle, and Khan separated from the old man, taking his leash with him to come and stand at Ashton's side, with absolutely zero hesitation.

Ashton looked over at the wife and called out, "Do you have any further doubts?"

She shook her head and whispered, "We didn't know."

Ashton shook his head. "You didn't know, and you didn't care either. You were totally okay to steal an animal that belonged to somebody else, whose heart was bonded to somebody else, but again, you didn't care, just as long as you got what you wanted. I will report this to the sheriff."

Tears filled her eyes, and her shoulders slumped.

Ashton was being hard on her, but he was pissed. Then again, since he'd come home, he'd seen a steady stream of selfish entitled people taking what they felt was theirs, even though they had absolutely no right to it.

He shook his head. "Where did you find Khan, or did you take the War Dog from Sean's home?"

She looked over at her husband, who was still glaring at Ashton, but tears were in his eyes as he stared down at Khan, standing at Ashton's side.

"We saw them out walking," she began, "and they got into a confrontation about it. My husband may have acted a little foolish."

He stared at her and asked, "What do you mean by *a little foolish?*"

"He threatened him, threatened to take the dog if he didn't turn it over to us. I told him to stop and that it wasn't our dog, but he …" She hesitated, looking back at her husband. "My husband got very angry at me. The other man—Sean, as you called him—also got angry, and then this dog also reacted in the wrong way. So, in the kerfuffle that followed, my husband knocked over the old man."

"Hang on a minute, he knocked over Sean?" Ashton snapped. "Was he not in his wheelchair?"

"He was using walking sticks," she added, "something about wanting to keep up a certain kind of exercise, so he wasn't wheelchair-bound all the time. Anyway, it got ugly." She sighed.

Ashton was disgusted. "And you just let it happen?"

She flushed. "What was I supposed to do?"

"I don't know. … Call the deputies, report your husband for abusing a senior citizen. What do you expect when you take something from people? What right do you have to decide whether a man gets to keep his own dog or not?" he asked, looking at her in disgust.

She shoved her hands into her pockets. "You don't have to judge us for this."

He shook his head. "I don't know why the hell not. Didn't the man you knocked over have any rights to not be assaulted? To not have his dog stolen? So, what happened? Did the deputies not come and question you?"

She paused, then nodded. "Yes, they did."

"So, you just lied to them?"

She stared at Ashton, then started to reply, "You have to understand—"

"Don't say that again. Do not tell me that again. Sean Keaton is now missing, probably out trying to find his dog, which is a big part of his heart and his life," he told the Wilfords, "and you *stole* Khan from him. You knocked down Sean, and you stole a dog that's not yours. That's assault and theft."

She whispered, "It sounds bad when you put it that way."

"Yeah, it sounds bad because it is bad," he snapped. With Khan at his side, he picked up the leash, and he added, "I hope you realize this dog can never be yours. It will never be yours, and now we have a problem."

"What kind of a problem?" she asked, as she trailed behind him.

He turned to her. "Do you really think I'm not going to contact the War Department too?"

She turned fifteen shades of pale, and then a red flush came over her. "You can't," she stated, sounding more mad than afraid.

"Why not?" Ashton stopped to stare at her. "What kind of compelling reason could you possibly come up with that would make me think I shouldn't?"

She stared at him and replied, "You'll destroy my husband."

Ashton sighed. "I'm hearing that a lot lately. I'm not sure at what point in time those who are enabling this kind of abusive behavior should be allowed to get off scot-free either," he shared, looking at her. "I understand why he may have wanted the dog. I understand his own pain and sense of loss, but to take an obviously bonded dog from a senior, a disabled veteran, who is barely able to get around as it is, and to knock him to the ground?" Ashton just shook his head. "I suppose you told the deputies that you didn't attack Sean either."

She nodded, shamefaced. "My husband … may have, and I didn't contradict him." She nodded. "You understand he's not been himself."

"I get that. But since when is *not being himself* an excuse for hurting others? How well would that work before a judge and jury, much less the US War Department?" he asked, looking at her.

She didn't have anything to say.

He walked back toward his truck, pulling out his phone as he went. When he got there, he called Richard. "I know we've already spoken today," he began, "but I've just found yet another scenario where your guys either messed up or, at the very least, didn't follow up on."

"Now what?" Richard asked, with a heavy sigh. "Believe me, since you came back into town, the shit seems to be hitting the fan."

"Yeah, you're not kidding. Remember Sean, the disabled vet, who I told you was missing this morning? And Khan, the K9 War Dog that I was sent here to find, was Sean's dog?"

"Yeah, what about them?"

"Well, I found the K9," he stated.

"Where?"

"At the Wilfords' hobby farm. Apparently Sean contacted you guys, reporting that his dog had been stolen, describing the couple who took his dog from him, who knocked him down. I assume the deputies came out to talk to the Wilfords, the couple Sean accused of taking his dog."

"Yeah, and they didn't have the dog."

"Yeah, that's where the problem lies and where your guys messed up … once again. The Wilfords did have the dog," he declared, disgust filling his tone. "Now I have the dog, and they admitted they lied. Not only that, they attacked Sean, knocking him to the ground, just to get Khan away from him."

He heard Richard swearing on the other end.

"So, the War Dog is now in my possession, and you need to do something with this couple. I plan to report them to the War Department, as well as to the local zoning committee. That man should never have animals in his charge. Plus, now we really need to find Sean," he added.

"Just hold on. Stay where you are. I'm coming."

"No, I'm not staying here. It's bad enough that I'm having to do all this shit to begin with," he stated, "and I don't have time to do clean up everything going around this shithole. You need to come out here and sort it out, and, if you think I don't have proof, you're wrong," he snapped, "because it's all recorded. I'll be happy to send you the recording because I don't trust either Mr. or Mrs. Wilford to tell the truth again."

"Hang on a minute, Ashton," Richard said, swearing heavily.

"I'm not staying here. All you need to do is take their statements. Put some pressure on the wife. She's trying to protect him, and he, well, I hate to say it, but he's lost. Meanwhile, I have two missing people to track."

CHAPTER 7

CRYSTAL CAME OUT of the barn when she heard a vehicle approach and instinctively knew it would be Ashton. Since he had arrived home, it had been nothing but chaos. She hadn't even seen the twins since this morning and knew they would be much less than happy to see him. But, at some point time, that needed to happen too.

She wasn't sure how to make it less confrontational because those two boys loved conflict. As a matter of fact, they lived for it, and they had an awful lot of their grandmother's taste for drama too. She couldn't imagine how this would all go down, and she didn't want to be around when it happened. Yet she had no place else to go.

As he pulled up, she realized he had a dog with him. She walked over, and the dog took one look at her and got incredibly excited. She laughed as the door opened, and Khan jumped out and jumped all over her.

"Khan," she cried out, as she bent down, greeting him. "Oh, my goodness, you found him!" She tried to hug him, but he was a wiggling mess. By the time he finally calmed down enough for her to put her arms around him, he went off on another wiggle session.

Ashton smiled over at her. "Well, at least I know I've got the right dog."

"Oh, absolutely," she declared, with a smile. "He's always been a great cuddler. Where did you find him?"

When he gave her the basics, she stared at him in shock. "What? The Wilfords knocked Sean over and took the dog, and they didn't expect any repercussions?"

"Because Sean was a veteran, disabled, and not in very good shape, they told the deputies how Sean dreamed it all up, and they didn't have anything to do with it. They were *sorry for his mental state* and all that BS. Yet I have their admissions on tape. So, anyway, I've already sent Richard over there to deal with them, and I've already updated the War Department too, even the local zoning council, as I got word that the Wilfords may want to start boarding horses or dogs. No way in hell I'm letting that happen. Everybody involved has a copy of their confession tape," he shared. "But the bottom line is, and I've said as much to Richard, we now have two old men missing, Sean and Grandpa."

She shook her head. "Surely it's not connected." She watched Khan sniff the area all around them, his ears forward inquisitively and his tail high. A happy dog.

"I don't know what's connected at this point," Ashton told her.

She saw the fatigue in his expression and in his body language, along with a certain amount of anger. "You were pretty hard on them, weren't you?" He shot her a look, and she raised both hands. "And I approve. I'm sure they're both in a hard place, and, once they committed the act, they couldn't get out of it easily."

"Hell no. You do the crime, you do the time. These are grown-ass people who won't just fess up that they did something wrong." Ashton groaned, shaking his head. "Does nobody do the right thing anymore? At the very least, somebody needs to be aware that Mr. Wilford is dangerous and has no problem knocking people over to take whatever he wants, and his wife just enables him," he pointed out. "What the hell is it with people enabling this damn behavior? I don't get it."

"Love," she said simply.

He snorted. "How is it love when you know the person you love is hurting others? How is that love?" he asked, anger still in his tone.

"I guess I don't know what it is either. But it also shows the depths to which people go to when they have a spouse who's out of control."

He stopped and looked at her. "Now *that* I understand."

"So, nothing new on Grandpa?"

"No, nothing that I know of. Richard doesn't have anything. But now that I have a tracking dog," he noted, with a smile down at Khan, "I will head out soon and take a good look at the lay of the land."

"I can go with you," she offered.

He frowned at her, his gaze searching.

"I've been searching the property, looking for him, ever since he went missing."

He hesitated, studied her closely, and asked, "Can you promise me that he went missing *from here?*"

She looked at him in shock, offended even, until a sudden realization hit her. "No, I guess I can't." She sighed, shrinking back. "That's just what—"

"Grandma told you, right?"

He was right about that but had no need to say it. Yet Crystal was beginning to see a pattern here.

"I will, however, start looking from here," he conceded, "because that is the easiest, but it's not necessarily the truth."

She took a deep breath and asked, "You don't think

Grandma had something to do with this, do you?"

"I no longer know who and what has had anything to do with anything," he admitted. "So, pardon me if I don't have the same trust that you guys have in her." He whistled, and Khan came running to his side, more than happy to be with him.

She looked at him, unable to contain her surprise. "You haven't even known him very long."

"No, but he recognizes somebody who has been training animals, K9 dogs just like him," Ashton explained, his gaze following Khan. He greeted Crystal's two dogs, who'd given the new arrival a bit of space, but had now come over to say hello. A moment later all three bounded closer together.

"He knows his own commands, and he'll never forget those," Ashton added, patting down Khan. "Anybody who had any kind of K9 training or military experience with these animals can get Khan to do what they need. But what I need him to do now is help me find both these men. We'll start with Grandpa this afternoon, even though it's a little bit late. But I want to get the lay of the land because I haven't heard from anybody specifically where he went missing from."

"I was told he went out for a walk from here," she shared, looking at him. Then she frowned and added, "But why would anybody give me incorrect information?"

"I don't know," he acknowledged, with a shrug. "Believe me that I don't. Yet something is going on here that I don't like, and I need to get to the bottom of it. I'll grab a sandwich and make a couple calls. Then I'll get on my riding clothes and head out." He called Khan over and headed toward the house.

"Meet me at the barn," she added, "and I'll go with you."

ASHTON JUST NODDED and walked inside the front door, Khan eagerly going with him. Ashton quickly threw together a couple sandwiches and then sat down to eat, while making his phone calls. The first was to Roger at the bank. He asked if Grandma had opened an account there, and Roger snorted. Right, her pride wouldn't allow her to do that. So he asked Roger about his father's special account. Roger admitted how he really wanted to tell Ashton about that, but he had been sworn to secrecy by his grandfather and by the lawyer. Roger was happy to tell Ashton what the balance was of that account.

Ashton felt bad about what he had been saying about Grandpa enabling her, then taking no responsibility to stop her. In his own way, he had done both. Ashton was pleased to hear enough money was in Grandpa's rainy-day emergency account to not only pay back the rest of Grandpa's clients but to save the Nelson estate.

Well, … depending on Grandma not stealing more money, plus Ashton getting that newest account of hers frozen, the one with the big chunk of change in it.

Still, Ashton would rather have his grandpa back. He would dip into that account, using his power of attorney, if he needed to.

Chowing down on the second sandwich, he now called the sheriff. "Richard, any word on Sean and Grandpa?" He got no good news, except that his deputies had not yet been out to see Grandma about Ashton spilling the family secrets. "Give them the day off before they interrogate her. I'm gonna scour the property and see what I can dig up, now that I have a tracking War Dog with me."

Richard didn't like that idea, but Ashton reminded him, "Your lazy-ass deputies would never have followed up at all, if not for my pressuring you. So what does one more day do?" Richard eventually agreed, giving Ashton until tomorrow before the useless deputies started asking some hard questions of Grandma. "Don't let her run roughshod over your guys," Ashton added, then disconnected.

CHAPTER 8

As Crystal headed back to the barn, she didn't even want to think about somebody from here being involved in Grandpa's disappearance. She walked into the barn, saw John up ahead, leaning lazily against a stall, giving her a side-eye. John didn't like horses—or work—so why was he here?

"So, he really has returned, *huh?*"

She asked him, "Haven't you talked to him yet?"

"No, don't want to either."

"Why not?" she asked. "He's your cousin." She almost added how he owns the place, but she couldn't imagine John would be happy about that.

He laughed. "Hell no. He's always been one of those workaholics, where everybody pulls together and gets the job done, that kind of BS." He shuddered. "Yeah, that's not happening. Let me know when he leaves town." He sent a smug smile in her direction. "That's much more my style."

She shook her head. "I don't understand that. He's family."

"Yeah, well, he's not any family that I want anything to do with," he declared. "He's always been a bit arrogant, that *gone to war, did something to be proud of* type. That doesn't sit well with me. He acts like the rest of us are just lazy slugs."

She didn't want to get into an argument, but it was on

the tip of her tongue to ask just what did John do for work because, as far as she understood, he didn't do anything and was part of the problem Ashton was dealing with here. And to a certain extent, so was she.

Dismayed at that realization, while totally ignoring John, she set about getting two of the horses saddled up.

John came closer and asked, "You taking him out riding?" Something in his tone she didn't recognize.

"Yeah, he wants to look for Grandpa."

He laughed at that. "Well, that'll be fun."

She turned on him and stated, "We should *all* be out looking for Grandpa every day."

"We did look the first day," he noted lazily. "No way that old man survived anything after that, and you and I both know it. So why should we waste our time on that? I got better things to do."

"Like what?" she asked, raising her hands. "What exactly do you do?"

He glared at her. "I do lots of things." He was flushed, his temper flaring, but, unlike Glenn, John was never one to show his anger lightly. "Don't go getting smart and snippety with me."

She stared at him and smirked. "Right, of course not. I mean, I'm just the hired help after all."

"Well, you're an adopted cousin who's living here on borrowed time," he clarified, with a sneer. "Best you remember that." With that, he turned and walked out.

She stared after him, and, when Ashton called out to her, she was still standing with the horses.

"What was that all about?"

She turned around to see Khan racing toward her as if he hadn't seen her in days and not just a short hour earlier. She shrugged at Ashton. "I don't know," she muttered, her voice quiet. "That's the first time he's ever said that."

"Said what?"

"That I'm the *hired help* and that I am living here on *borrowed time*. He's implied it many times before, but this is the first time he's come out and told me so directly."

"He's a lazy entitled ass. Just another symptom of things going on under the radar here," he pointed out, with a smile on his face, "more things that we won't like. You'll need to have a thicker skin than that if you want to survive out in the world."

She closed her eyes and whispered, "Please don't tell me that they're involved too."

"I don't know whether or not they're involved because I don't know what all is going on here *yet*, but you can see why I'm concerned."

She nodded. "Here," she said, as she handed him a set of reins. Khan stepped forward confidently and exchanged sniffs with the big gelding. "I was hoping you could handle this guy. He hasn't been out in a while."

"Well, I haven't been out in a while either," he quipped, "so we'll make a good go of it together." He smiled up at the gelding. "I haven't ridden Mirage in, what, six years?" he asked, with a laugh. The horse nickered and nuzzled his hand. "Yeah, I remember you always liked your treats beforehand too, didn't you?"

"No, he just likes treats," she corrected, "before and af-ter."

With a smirk, Ashton swung up on the horse's back with ease.

That made her feel better. "I guess you haven't forgotten anything, have you?"

He smiled at her. "I haven't forgotten a thing."

Enough of an innuendo was in that statement for her to realize he hadn't forgotten something she wasn't sure she ever wanted to remember—a blazing hot kiss they'd shared six years ago, when it felt like it was completely wrong, as if they were truly related. She had to remind herself that she had been adopted and not born into the family. His comment just brought it all right back.

ASHTON PROBABLY SHOULDN'T have made that comment, but seeing Crystal here in the barn with the horses just brought back so many feelings. Then there was everything else, simmering under the surface—so much intrigue, nonsense, and entitlement. It was making them both angry and depressed, and—at least for him—wanting to blow the lid off everything, just to have it all come to light and to hold people accountable for their actions.

The fact that John had come right out and said what he did to Crystal was a huge concern. In Ashton's mind, he was *encouraged* now that Grandpa was out the picture—or now that Grandma had promised him whatever. Add that to the fact that the twins hadn't come forward and even said anything to him? They were definitely hiding something too. Like Grandma, like cousins—at least Ashton's male cousins.

What were they up to in the background?

And did it have anything to do with his grandmother? His missing grandfather?

It wouldn't surprise him at all that the twins were helping Grandma, as she'd always favored those two among the four cousins. After all, Glenn and John and Ashton and

Crystal were cousins, whether blood relatives or adopted. They had lost all four parents within a short time frame, and all the cousins had lived here together, raised by Grandma and Grandpa. The losses were a blow that almost took out his grandfather. His grandmother had been affected, of course, but it was almost like she blamed Ashton, maybe even wishing Ashton had died, instead of Grandma's own son dying.

Grandma had never been very easy on Ashton, even after his own father's death, but then he'd never been easy on her. She probably was well aware that Ashton was the one fighting her constant gambling, whereas John and Glenn probably didn't care, especially if she had some money for them. The new reality here at the Nelson estate would be eye-opening for them at some point.

Ashton didn't expect to say anything to Crystal about that kiss they'd shared a few years back. Well, six years back, to be honest. He'd left soon afterward, and there hadn't been a word shared between them since. He'd been injured in the line of duty not long after that. Ashton had been busy, trying to heal and to push through rehab and to adjust to his new life. So he had chosen to let that opportunity slide, thinking Crystal would probably have found a better partner on her own.

But then he'd come back, only to discover that she wasn't hooked up with anyone. He glanced at her and asked, "How come you're still single?"

She looked over at him, a blush on her cheeks. "Because I haven't found anybody. Why are you still single?"

"Because I spent the last six years trying to save this place," he replied. "Not to mention the obvious injury too. There was no time for socializing, no time for dating or anything else while I was on the job. I took on as many extra shifts and missions as I could, doing the only thing I knew how to do."

"And yet you were already a financial planner, an investor," she noted.

"Yes," he confirmed, "and I still do that, and, for the most part, I've done well. However, this place has been sucking me dry, mostly because of our dear beloved grandmother."

"What do you want to bet that your cousins think they'll inherit all this?" she asked.

He nodded. "I wouldn't be at all surprised. The surprise is going to be when they realize there's nothing for them to inherit."

"And yet they're likely to fight for possession," she suggested.

"They can try," he muttered, slowly navigating as he rode Mirage. "And, yeah, I'll go to court over it, but they've done nothing here in the way of supporting the farm, have they?"

She shook her head. "No, they don't help at all. I look after all the animals. I do the shopping as needed. I arrange for the hay and stuff," she pointed out. "But I guess you're paying the bills, aren't you?"

"Yep, I sure am," he said, as he smiled and reached down to rub the horse's neck.

"Some of these horses," she began, not sure how to say it, "they've been here a very long time."

He nodded.

"Will you keep the place?"

"I don't know yet," he muttered. "It's a little too early to sort all that out."

"I'm sorry," she replied. "That has got to be hard."

"It is, but not as hard as it'll be when the deputies come to interrogate Grandma," he added. "I already told Richard about Grandma's gambling addiction and taking money from the investor accounts. I've got to get access to that secret bank account of hers before Grandma finds out that I know about it, before the sheriff spills the beans too. I don't know anything about it yet. And where the hell did she get money from? And a *big chunk* of it?"

"Why does that affect you?" Crystal asked.

"It affects all of us. If the twins have access to that *big chunk* money, that's even worse. That's three people who can possibly withdraw that money before I even find out where it is," he explained. "If I can't recover that money, I can't replace the remaining balance on the stolen investment money that is *still* unpaid. So far, I've somehow managed to stay ahead of it all, putting in money before the client gets a withdrawal, but it's not been easy. It's about to wipe out the last of my savings and my own investment portfolio."

She grimaced. "I'm so sorry, Ashton. It all fell on you."

He nodded. "Not your fault. Given enough time, I could take care of this. But with Grandma's antics getting worse, I had to call in the sheriff. So I'm outta time. I wish Grandpa was here. As for me, I'm on disability from the military, and it's just the financial and advisory money that's keeping us going right now." She sucked in her breath, and he sighed. "Yeah, confusing so far, I'm afraid."

She shook her head. "I just don't get it. How did it all end up on your shoulders?"

"Well, if Grandpa could be found alive and well," he replied, "then I could possibly get more answers, but I'm not at all sure just what's going on here."

They rode on in silence for a while, until Crystal spoke up.

"Let me tell you where I've looked," she began, as she pointed off in the distance. "I rode that section on the first day. I rode that section, north and onto the other forty, and there was nothing. I mean, I feel like I've covered every inch of the place, but there's been no sign of anyone out there. And nobody, outside of that first day, cares to even ride out anymore."

"Who went with you on the first day?"

"Everyone. Me, Glenn, John, and two deputies. The twins were out here riding, but they don't ride much," she shared. "So, they were complaining constantly the whole time, but I wouldn't listen to it. It was all about making sure everybody was out looking for Grandpa."

"And did they go one direction and you and the deputies went another?"

She nodded. "Yeah, … they did, over toward the neighbors. The twins checked those acres to the south," she explained, frowning as she tried to recall where they went.

"And have you been back over where they went since then?"

She seemed surprised at the question.

A sinking feeling took over his gut.

She frowned, shaking her head. "No."

He nodded and turned the horse. "Then that's where we'll start."

CHAPTER 9

CRYSTAL AND ASHTON rode quietly, her mind spinning with the implications. Khan walked, ran, raced out and back again, as if half enjoying himself and half working. She'd never seen a working dog, so wasn't sure what that would look like in action. So Khan's antics didn't look serious enough, except when he would stop, sniff the air, and take off after something.

She looked over at Ashton a couple times to say something but then just didn't bother. What was there to say? She could only hope that his suppositions were completely wrong about one of the family doing something to Grandpa. But Ashton had brought Khan, the tracking War Dog, so something was on Ashton's mind. At the same time, she had not gone back over the same ground as her good-for-nothing siblings had, and, for that, she was castigating herself.

"What purpose would they have?" she finally asked. "The cousins, Grandma, to get rid of Grandpa?"

"I don't know yet," he admitted. "We need to sort that out. The fact of the matter is, if you haven't checked that property line again, then I don't know for sure it's clear. From what you told me, everybody stopped searching for him after a day, a day and a half."

"I didn't," she declared, exasperated, "but I don't know what else to do. I've been out here every day, even yesterday for several hours."

He nodded. "And now we're out here looking. I should have been out here earlier," he muttered, as he swore.

She frowned at him and asked, "When would you have done that? It's been chaos since you arrived, and you've had multiple issues just trying to get to this point."

He gave a big sigh. "What I needed was this guy," he said, pointing to the dog on the ground, who was walking ahead, running, jumping, and having a grand old time. It was as if he was aware that he was finally free and was running with unexpected joy.

"And you think he'll help?" Crystal asked.

"He sure won't hurt our search," he noted. "I have a lot of faith in these animals."

"Yes, but it's not as if we have anything of Grandpa's to show Khan to track."

"I already did that," Ashton explained. "I had him in the house and went through Grandpa's bedroom. Thankfully Grandma hasn't cleared out his stuff yet," he muttered, with a note of irony.

She winced at that. "God, can you imagine someone doing that at a time like this?"

Khan stopped up ahead and sniffed. Then barked. He looked back at Ashton, then kept going.

She watched as Ashton didn't say anything, just turned Mirage ever-so-slightly to follow Khan's lead. She stayed close to Ashton. She had no idea what was up ahead, but nothing in this instilled confidence.

"Unfortunately I can imagine that. I have a feeling that Grandma's thinking, with Grandpa gone, she's the lady of the house now and can do whatever she likes."

"Of course but she doesn't know any different, does she?"

He smirked at her. "Not really, but that's an awakening she'll deal with soon enough."

"And yet you already phoned the sheriff?"

"I had to," he said. "We have insurance for embezzlement, and I need to pull on that in order to pay clients the restitution due to them. I don't want to make a big thing out of this and lose our company name and our family name, much less the Nelson farm and everything on it. However, if I have to in order to give people their money back and to save the company's reputation and our reputation—or at least repair those reputations—I will," he declared.

"And all of Grandpa's work, his life, goes down the drain because of this, which would be devastating."

"It will be devastating to him. I don't know that it's devastating to anybody else," he noted. "And that's part of the problem here. Does anybody in the family even care about him? Care that his hard work has been stolen? Care that he will lose his good name over something Grandma did? Or, in the minds of our family, does Grandpa already have one foot in the grave? If that's the case, what the heck, might as well just—"

"What?" she interrupted. "Just what? Push him, so he's got both feet in the grave?"

He just stared at her and didn't say anything.

She sighed. "Okay, the twins are bad, but are they that bad? I'll accept the fact that it's not looking all that great at the moment, but I really, really don't want to think that these people who I've known all my life are like that."

"And yet how much abuse have you endured from them?"

She flushed. "I've never thought of it as abuse," she hedged.

"Well, it is," he confirmed. "It's verbal abuse, plain and simple. To me it's psychological abuse too. Look at what John told you just this morning."

She nodded. "I was surprised at that," she admitted. "Most of the time, I don't have anything to do with him. I've always just worked here for my room and board. At least, that is how I've always looked at it. But I guess that's probably not enough."

"Are you kidding? You're the only one who takes care of the animals," he stated. "If it wasn't for you, would any of these animals even exist on the farm? Of course not. That's a salary owed to you, not room and board to be collected from you. Crys, if I can make that right, I will. I promise you."

She looked over and gave him a small smile. "I was hoping you would see it in a more favorable light."

"Sure, I do. I've just got to get to the bottom of what's going on here. With all the new escapades of Grandma's popping up, it may take me a couple weeks instead of a couple days. But first, we need to find Grandpa, and I'm really, *really* hoping he's alive."

She stared off into the wilderness and asked, "How could he still be alive?"

Ashton grumbled, shaking his head, "I don't think he went missing on his own."

Just then Khan, farther up ahead, turned and let out a sharp loud crisp bark.

Crystal was shocked into silence at Ashton's words but also didn't question him as they trotted toward Khan. The dog was sitting and waiting for them. At a command from Ashton, Khan took off toward the fence line. She rode beside Ashton, looked at him occasionally, but he remained quiet, obviously lost in thought.

Finally she asked, "Who do you suspect did this?" He glanced at her, as if surprised that she was still on the same topic. But she stared at him and added, "I have to admit, you've shocked me pretty badly over this one."

He nodded. "That's a good thing. I would hate to think something like this would have even been on your radar."

She shook her head. "No way I could ever make that leap to have such a thing make sense or even seem possible. Grandpa has always been there for me."

"I understand, and the thought that anybody in the family is involved in his going missing is just too horrific to consider, and yet it's quite plausible, considering the circumstances."

"What circumstances?" she cried out. "I mean, why would you even think that?" He turned to her, seemed to be weighing the idea of telling her the truth. "It feels like the family that I thought I knew has been slowly disintegrating. And maybe not even slowly," she admitted, looking at him. "You haven't been here for six years. Now you've come back like a thunderbolt and basically blown everything I thought I knew out of the water. And, even at that, I'm not sure how much of everything you've told me is even believable."

"Believable?" he repeated, and then he chuckled. "Well, if you don't think it's believable, then you can't handle the rest either. Look. I'm not trying to push you into believing anything either way. It would be nice if you could come to your own conclusion based on the evidence. But I do realize this is your family, people you absolutely love and want to protect."

"But that does not make me blind," she interjected.

He looked at her approvingly. "No, it doesn't. Except in this instance, it might make it a little harder to wrap your head around just what's going on."

She let her breath out slowly, glancing around, realizing they were still a good couple miles from where they expected to be. "So you think somebody kidnapped Grandpa?"

"Yes, I absolutely do."

She closed her eyes and asked, "Somebody from our family?"

He nodded. "While I don't have that evidence yet, I'm not tossing that idea in the meantime. Isn't that why you keep searching for him?"

She nodded. "I have hope to find him. I was out here last night," she shared, turning to him briefly. "And I was out here again first thing this morning."

"I only got in yesterday," he said, with a note of humor, "and I get it. For an old man in his condition, that could mean everything in terms of his not making it."

"I don't even want to think about that," she muttered. "To think that he might not make it is bad enough, but, if somebody in our family is behind this, it's absolutely criminal."

"Oh, it is criminal all right," he declared. "I have no doubt about that at all. The question is, who is the criminal, and how much involvement have they truly been aware of, and how much have they been a dupe for?"

"What possible reason would there be for anybody to hurt Grandpa?"

"I'm not sure they want to hurt him as much as cause an early demise," he clarified. "In case you don't know, he's had a number of questionable health reports recently, but I haven't made it to his doctor yet to see if they're true or false."

"False?" she repeated in shock. "You're saying that people are falsifying his medical records now?"

His lips twisted up. "I come from a world where everybody's a suspect and where everything is suspicious. You come from a world where nothing is gray," he explained. "I understand that, for you, the idea that anything is shady or underhanded about what's going on here would be really hard to accept."

"Yeah," she grumbled. Her gaze searched for Khan but saw no sign of him. Until she heard a bark ahead, as if Khan was saying, *Over here and hurry up.*

"I'm not asking you to accept my suspicions willy-nilly," he began, as he followed Khan. "However, I am asking you to give me a little bit of time to prove it one way or the other."

"You haven't asked anything of me yet," she pointed out. "And, honest to God, in a way it would be easier if you did."

"Then I ask you to suspend judgment," he stated. "Let me do what I need to do, and then we'll go from there."

"As long as what you *need to do*," she clarified, "isn't causing anybody harm." The look that he tossed her way would have made somebody weaker crumble, but she was made of sterner stuff, at least she hoped so.

"Does it look like I'm hurting anybody?" he asked.

"No, not yet." She swore. "And yet maybe—because I'm not exactly sure what's going on with Grandma."

"Yeah," he agreed, "that's a big one. And because you haven't witnessed that part of her shenanigans over the decades, because she wanted it hidden and because Grandpa wanted to protect her—this seems all brand-new to you, making it seem like no big deal because it's not the truth to you yet."

"Well, it is a big deal if she has been stealing money from clients," she acknowledged. "How the hell is that even a thing?"

"I don't know. And that's part of the problem with Grandpa because he's always just trying to keep her out of jail, and I suspect enabling her habit. I, on the other hand, don't give a crap anymore and think that jail might be what it takes to get her attention."

Crystal wanted to say that she was willing to give Grandma the benefit of a doubt, but he raised a hand.

"Yeah, I know. I hear you. … Why would I feel that way when she's family?" He shrugged. "She's had multiple chances to fix the mess that she caused. Instead she keeps getting herself deeper and deeper, and that's what addicts do."

She nodded slowly. "I have seen several addicts," she shared, "and they definitely have a challenge when it comes to changing their behavior."

"Yep. It takes those around them to have the strength and the character to make them stop doing what they're doing because, whether they're hurting themselves or not, they *are* hurting other people. And when is that the priority?"

She could see his point. "How is it that I wouldn't have seen it?"

"Well, you can thank Grandpa for that," he added. "He's been hiding everything, and unfortunately he's lost almost everything he had because of it."

Such fatigue filled his words, as if he had been dealing with this all on his own for a very long time. And she realized that he probably had, and nobody was likely on his side over it. And it appeared he had been fighting family members for a very long time too. "Do you think the twins know?"

He looked at her and nodded. "The boys definitely know."

She winced. "Okay. It's a little depressing that everybody knew, but I didn't."

"They probably wanted to keep you out of it. Too many cooks can spoil the broth, or whatever that saying is," he said. "And, if you were to know and told somebody, that could put whatever they're up to into danger as well."

"What do you mean by *whatever they're up to*?" she asked, her voice faint. "You can't think they had anything to do with this? With Grandpa going missing?"

"I don't know who had anything to do with what, but they've been living here free of charge, not lifting a finger, and acting like they own the place for a very long time," he pointed out to her. "But the fact is, they don't own it and their *free-of-charge* living is about to come to an end."

"Oh, that won't make them very happy."

"No, and I notice they've also been avoiding me."

"I saw Glenn and John yesterday, and John again today, but they asked if you were here for sure, and I told them, yes, and that they should go talk to you. They both gave a mock shudder, like, no way in hell were they doing that."

"Interesting," he noted.

"Why? What's interesting about it?"

"I'm trying to figure out who's involved and who's not in a lot of issues," he shared. "So, from my perspective, anybody *not* willing to step up and talk to me is suspicious as hell."

She winced. "I didn't mean to make it sound like they were guilty in any way."

"No, but do you see their behavior, their actions, as upright, stalwart, and honest?"

"I think they're just lazy," she replied. "They don't want to work. They don't have jobs, and they don't really do anything."

He just looked at her and laughed out loud. "And who's covering all their living expenses?"

As she stared at him, she realized that hard truth too. "You are, aren't you?" Oh Lord. Ashton had been dealt one ugly blow after another. Ahead she scanned for Khan, reassured when he was running back and forth sideways in front of them, as if hunting for something. And she knew what that was. She both wanted it and now was petrified of what they'd find.

Ashton asked her, "And you want to tell me why I should continue to pay for those lazy slugs to remain on this property?"

She didn't have an answer for that. "I don't know what to say to that."

"You don't know what to say because why would I? After all this time, why would I want to continue to pay them to sit on their butts and do nothing? Tell me that." She swore softly, then he continued. "I was going to deal with it quite a few years ago, and Grandpa asked me to leave things status quo, saying he would handle it."

"And I gather he didn't."

"Does it look like he changed anything with those two?" Ashton quipped. "Anyway, I got injured not long afterward, which stopped me from following up on that sooner." He urged Mirage closer to Khan. "The accident wasn't all that long afterward. And, of course, Grandpa hadn't dealt with it. Not with Grandma. Not with the lazy-ass cousins. At that point in time, I was no longer physically capable of coming and storming the gates and retaking what was mine." He glanced at her. "So, believe me, it's been *fun*."

"No," she argued, "I guess it hasn't been at all."

"Hasn't," he agreed, shooting her a sideways look. "What do you think?"

She winced. "I promise I will get out."

"No," he said, "I've already told you that's not an issue. And, if anything, you should have been paid wages for all the work you've been doing."

"The horses are mine," she blurted out, before it became awkward or before she started overthinking herself to death. He stared at her, and she frowned. "You didn't know that?"

"No, I sure didn't," he began. "I have all the receipts and bills of sale on record. They are under my name," he shared, "and I sure as hell didn't sell them to you."

The color faded from her cheeks as she stared at him, wide-eyed.

He glanced at her several times and noted, "But you obviously believe they are yours."

"They—" She stopped, feeling like a fool. "Oh my God. Oh my God." She didn't know what to say, but she needed to try and get something out. "Grandma told me that they were mine. That, as long as I looked after them, they were mine."

Ashton asked, "So, did she give them to you or did she sell them to you? Did she transfer their ownership to you?"

She looked at him, his words sinking in slowly, and she shook her head. "No, she did not," she whispered, and she doubted he even heard the words.

He nodded. "That's because she can't. They are my horses. They aren't anyone else's to be handed out."

"Holy Hell." She didn't even know what to think.

He suggested, "That is something you and I can work out, but—"

"No, no, no," she wailed. "Oh God, oh my God—"

"I'm sorry," he said. "They aren't hers to dispose of any more than anything else on this property is. Even with proper titles on this property right now, I'm worried that this place will even survive this shitshow. If I can't get together enough money to cover this latest set of client withdrawals, I might be able to save the Nelson homestead but… I might not."

She nodded, understanding what he said, but still in shock over what she thought were her animals. "Jesus, if I had moved out and taken them with me before you got here, I wouldn't have had a clue what was going on."

"And I would have come after you, asking for proof of ownership," he replied. "Listen. I'm not here to take the horses away. But, as you may remember, several of these horses were my pets."

She nodded. "I know that, and I was surprised when Grandma told me that I could have them all. But I wasn't going to look a gift horse in the mouth." He gave her a wry look, and she frowned. "Yet you're right, I shouldn't have believed her."

"Honestly, whatever her reasoning was, it could have been simply to get back at me. Or to try and get you on her side."

"Maybe. I'm so confused, I don't know what to think."

"I don't know either," he said, "but the horses weren't hers to give away."

Crystal felt like her whole world was crashing down.

He glanced at her and whispered, "I can see that this has been more than a bit of a shock to you. And I'm trying to explain to you that I'm not here to take them away, but obviously there's a whole different question involved here."

She just nodded, realizing she had been a fool to not ask for any proof or a bill of sale or something. Yet, even if she had, it wouldn't have held up, which is probably why Grandma hadn't given it to her in the first place. "I don't even know what to say," she cried out. "Everything in my world has become a complete con. And I, … I didn't even know."

"It's not that it's been a con," he corrected, "but it's definitely been fraught with smoke and mirrors, and you didn't know enough of the family situation to understand how bad it was. Did Grandpa tell you that the horses were yours?"

She looked at him and shook her head. "No, only Grandma."

"And you know that she's never had anything to do with the horses, right?" he asked. "She doesn't ride, won't even go near them, and has always made it clear that she hates them."

"I know, and I guess that's why I thought she was okay with my having them, since she really doesn't like them." When he didn't say anything, she snorted. "Christ, I've been such a fool."

"No," he said. "You believed in someone you love and thought loved you."

"And did I—I don't even know what to say at the moment. It's a little more of a shock than I can bear. I don't even know what to feel right now." She stared blindly, not even seeing the gorgeous scenery as the horses kept walking. "I had an entire future planned out, and I've been working toward getting a place big enough where I could take the horses with me." She gave a bitter laugh. "I guess I don't need to be worried about that."

He sighed and suggested, "How about no hasty decisions until I get to the bottom of this?"

"No decision to be made apparently," she muttered, feeling numb right through her heart. She glanced down at the horse she rode. Bessie had been with her for a decade. She reached down and scratched the mare's neck as she tossed her head in response. "She's been with me a long time."

"And I'm willing to look at that," he repeated. "I'm just saying—"

"I know. I know what you're saying," she snapped. "I'm so sorry, Ashton. I didn't even stop to consider that they weren't even hers."

"Of course not. Why would you?" he said. "I mean, she's got everybody thinking that it's all hers, but that's just wrong."

"And if the land and houses and horses were anybody's, it would be Grandpa's, right?"

"Part of it, at one time at least. You may not remember, but my parents owned all this. They are the original Nelson owners. When they passed—this would be Grandma and Grandpa's son and his wife, my parents—their wills set up a trust with Grandpa in charge of my inheritance until I became of age. So he and I inherited the Nelson farm. Once I turned eighteen, Grandpa had my part legally transferred into my name only hoping to bypass issues with his wife. Little did he know, right?"

He shook his head. "So, while it may look like Grandpa and Grandma owned all this, it was legally owned by me and Grandpa—until Grandma stole everybody's money, and I had to pay back those stolen monies. Then Grandpa transferred his share of the Nelson holdings in repayment to me. ... I've been the sole owner of Nelson farm for more than a decade now."

"But nobody knows that, right?" she asked.

"Just me, Jenny, Grandpa, the attorney—and now you."

Crystal frowned. "But, like me, then Grandma and the boys would think, of course, when it comes to a marriage," she suggested, "possession of property is a thing, but, … oh shit, … only if he's gone." She froze and stared at Ashton, her eyes widening.

He gave her *that* look.

"Please not that, please, please not," she cried out softly.

"I don't know," he shared, "but it has to be considered."

"Dear God," she muttered. "You have to be wrong. I cannot let myself even begin to think that is happening here."

"And I don't have a clue," he told her. "I'm just trying to find Grandpa, and then we can go from there."

She nodded, but, for her, it was not so much *going from there* as it was trying to distance herself from the shock and horror of the possibilities. It was just too unbelievable to be true.

He asked her, "Did you finish school? Your vet school?"

"Yes," she muttered, hanging her head. "I'm about six months away from my license and was trying to get to that point. I wanted to set up my own center, my own clinic, but I'm, … I'm pretty well run dry money-wise, just with the school fees and all."

"Of course," he noted. "Was Grandpa helping you at all?"

She wasn't sure if he was asking for his own interests or for another reason, but he did ask, so he deserved an answer. "He did initially, and then told me how he couldn't afford to help anymore. I believed him and could tell he felt bad about it. Now it makes more sense, and I realize it was because of Grandma and her gambling."

He just nodded and didn't say anything.

"It's really hard for me to understand how all of this could go so bad so quickly."

"Yeah, I hear you. I've been dealing with this for a while and not only is that hard to understand, it's also hard to understand how Grandpa couldn't stand up to her. And that's a huge part of the problem. I made the mistake of trusting him to do it, then I ended up sidelined when I got injured, which led to a long series of surgeries and rehab. It was a bad scenario that I just had to face and deal with. Meanwhile, things at the family homestead just got worse."

"And you really think Grandma's been withdrawing money from the client accounts still?" she asked.

"She was under an agreement to deposit repayments for the money she stole, and she wasn't to have access to any of the accounts. But recently, according to what the lawyer found and what the banker told me as well, she did get back into one of the accounts, using Grandpa's login, and has removed a substantial amount of money."

"And when you say a substantial amount, how much is that?"

"Over one-quarter million dollars," he stated in a clipped voice.

She stared at him in shock. "Oh my God, that—"

"*Yeah*. And *that* is separate from the additional almost half-a-million dollars that she socked away into this new personal checking account that I need the account number for. I have no idea where she got that money from." He shook his head. "If we can't freeze both accounts and access that money before Grandma takes off with both, that will cripple us, even with Grandpa's emergency fund that the attorney just told me about. I know you don't want to believe it, but the numbers don't lie. So hear me on this. … Don't misunderstand me. The houses and the land and the horses will all have to go."

Her heart sank even more.

Ashton continued. "Maybe I can mortgage it, but it's not as if I'm a solid bet right now. I do have money, and I've been paying for everything to keep the status quo, but that doesn't mean anybody will give me a loan, unless I have the wherewithal to pay it back."

She couldn't imagine what he must be feeling, as her own heart slammed against her chest with the shock. She thought about the little old lady who, for the most part, had treated her well but had recently shown a completely different side of herself. "Grandma has been very different lately," she stated, "and I don't, … I don't even know quite how to describe it."

"Right, but I have a pretty good idea what you mean."

She winced. "I would like to think that she is doing everything to help Grandpa and the property that she says she loves."

"She loves it, no doubt about that, because it's been a source of money for her," he stated bluntly.

She winced. "I really, *really* hate that I see her in a completely different light now."

He smiled and then sighed. "You don't have to. I mean, everybody else has turned a blind eye to it, so you could just join the pack."

She shook her head. "I can't do that now, can I?"

"Everybody else has, including your stepbrothers."

She just stared at him and asked, "Do you think they

know? About this part?"

"I not only think they know but I think they're probably finagling how to get it out from under us or how to come out on top of all this somehow. I just don't know what that looks like."

"You don't have a whole lot of love for them, do you?"

"Not once I realized they were enabling her, no," he admitted, with a dry laugh. "Sorry, but fairy tales were never a thing in my world. Maybe for other people, but I never had the ability to just let everything go and be something other than what I am."

She knew what he meant. After she had been adopted by his uncle, her life had been thrown completely out the window too. "I understand that much," she replied. "It's hard when everything in your life blows up and when the people who should be there just aren't anymore."

He nodded. "Did you ever look into other family members, your birth parents and such?" he asked her.

She shook her head. "No. It occurred to me every once in a while, and I wondered and thought I might like to know, but then I chickened out, realizing maybe I didn't want to know after all."

He nodded. "Information like that, once you know it, changes everything," he noted. "But still, if it's something that you're interested in, maybe you should."

"Grandma made it clear that she wouldn't appreciate if I took that route."

Surprised, he looked at her and asked, "Why is that?"

"I don't know, but now I really don't want to know," she muttered, followed by a hysterical laugh that sounded odd, even to her. "It seems like everything has been tossed on its head, and I don't really understand anything that's going on. So, I can't really answer that."

They rode at a decent clip as their gazes searching the fields and woods.

Then, without warning, the words popped out of her mouth. "Do you know anything about my adoption?"

"No, only that it happened."

"And then within about, what, four years, six maybe, my aunt and uncle were killed."

He nodded. "Yeah, that's what I remember."

"So, I lost my birth family, then got adopted and gained two stepbrothers, who absolutely love to bug me, and then we lost their parents as well," she noted.

"Yeah, too many losses in one family and not far apart either. As to Glenn and John bugging you, brothers in general love to bug sisters," he shared, "and I'm not even sure I would blame them for that." Ashton gave her a wry smile. "But I can see that, for you, they probably weren't the easiest to get along with. Yet you have been very resilient, so kudos for that. I'm just sorry that your life has been so ... difficult."

"Yet I didn't think it was all that difficult," she shared, with a dry laugh. "Lots of work, sure, but honestly it felt like I was doing okay. Until I realized that not only was I not doing okay at all, but I had also been sucked into drinking the Kool-Aid. Nothing is okay with what you've been telling me."

"But none of that has anything to do with your adoption," he noted. "I know my aunt and uncle really wanted a daughter. They were absolutely delighted to have you. So don't ever think any differently about that."

She smiled. "That much I do believe, and I do remember them, as my adoptive parents. They were with me during some of my most formative years, so I don't think I could ever forget them." She added, "I felt appreciated and loved, so I can't let go of those memories. And the fact that they died so soon after I was adopted was another big blow for me. After that, I just never felt like I really had a home."

She gave half a laugh. "That's why I was so determined to have a place where the horses could be safe, knowing they had a home for the rest of their lives, instead of being shipped off for meat, because nobody gave a crap about them anymore."

"That whole meat industry is …" Ashton shook his head. "I'm not a fool, and I certainly appreciate the market raising beef for food. Yet it hits me wrong to think about horses being butchered for just that reason."

"I know," she agreed, "and yet it happens."

"It happens everywhere," he stated, with a nod.

She sighed. "I just find it personally difficult to fathom. It's also one of the reasons I wanted to become a vet," she explained. "I was hoping I could have a rescue in the future and could bring in as many animals as possible and let them live out their days in peace. Does that sound insane?"

He smiled. "No, that sounds like you."

She laughed. "I always was kind of animal crazy, wasn't I? In many ways, coming to live with your family, under such terrible circumstances, I found all the animals were a saving grace. I was shocked when your aunt and uncle first brought me to the Nelson farm, and I saw what my new home would be like. That was pretty impressive, especially for an animal lover."

Khan set up a series of loud sharp barks. Ashton urged Mirage into a faster pace in Khan's direction. Moments later, he suddenly pulled up and looked around. "Would you say you covered this area?"

She nodded. "I would have, yes." Then she frowned. "I didn't ride along this section though. The deputies and I were over there." She pointed a little bit more to the north. "I rode along that line and came back around behind here, and I've been repeating that search pattern for days." She groaned. "You don't think Grandpa could possibly be lying on the ground out here or anything?"

He looked at her and said, "No, not at all."

Not sure she understood, she noted, "Then I don't understand what we're doing here."

He smiled, as they rode forward a little bit. "Any *other* vehicles coming through here?"

"*Other?* No. Vehicles are not allowed through here at all. You know that."

"I do know that," he declared, "but look." Then he pointed just ahead, where Khan was lying on the ground, waiting for them. "Whose tracks are those?"

ASHTON KNEW HE'D thrown an awful lot at Crystal in a very short window, but he didn't have time to play games right now. It would really help if he had somebody on his side, somebody other than Jenny, who he knew would always be on his side—and Grandpa's.

He suspected a long-lost love story was in there somewhere between Jenny and Grandpa, even if just one-sided on Jenny's part. Ashton knew his grandfather had been well and truly hooked on his grandmother for such a long time that Ashton didn't think there was room in there for anybody else.

He walked his horse forward slowly, looking to see just

what was going on with those tire tracks because Crystal was correct. Nobody was allowed to drive through here. This area was dry and prone to problem foliage. So, they generally rode horses through here but kept the vehicles out.

It didn't take Ashton and Crystal long to get close enough to the tracks where they were clearly visible, even though it had been dry for days. Khan, as if he understood the importance, didn't move but watched the two of them.

Ashton hopped down and took several photos. Then he walked up and down the tracks, trying to get an idea where they went, as he stared off into the distance.

Crystal pointed. "That leads to the neighbors."

Ashton nodded. "They still want the land around here?"

She stared at him. "Yes, at least I think so," she sputtered. "Grandpa always said, *No way.* The last thing I heard him say about it was something like, *Over my dead body.*"

He shot her a look and muttered, "Let's hope not." He watched as the color drained from her face.

Crystal stared at him, whispering, "You really know how to make a point, don't you?"

"Not at all. I'm just trying to find our grandfather."

"And you think he could be here?"

"No, I'm not saying he could be here—but I am wondering if he's over there." Then he nodded toward the property on the other side of theirs. Khan stood and walked in that direction, as if understanding something they were only beginning to consider.

"But surely somebody would have said something," Crystal suggested.

"Who? The very people who have always wanted the very land you are living on? There used to be two brothers living over there."

"I think there's only one now," she shared. "The other one? I think, he died of cancer."

"Which one? Max or Oliver?"

"Max died. It's just Oliver now."

"Which is even more concerning."

"Why?" she asked.

Ashton knew why, but he just wasn't sure if she should hear this. But then again, she was in the middle of all this, so she had a right to know. "Because Max would have kept Oliver slightly in control."

"They were both pretty angry at Grandpa for not selling them the land, and they thought it was theirs to begin with. Something about Grandpa stealing from their dad. Max was somewhat reasonable, or he appeared to be."

"And when you get an emotional property dispute like that," Ashton noted, "it can get pretty ugly."

"Yeah, you're not kidding," she murmured, staring in the distance. "You really think they kidnapped him?"

"I don't know, but you can bet I'm going to find out." He struggled to get back on Mirage without the stool he'd used in the barn. When the color drained from her face, he realized she had just seen his prosthetic. "Yeah, looks pretty, doesn't it?" he quipped, his tone curt. He hated to admit it to anyone, but her reaction caused pain inside him, an instinctual pang. He'd seen her face, and the shock, anger, and pity were all so clear. He just had to live with it, but he didn't have to like it. He just wasn't okay with it, not right now.

He moved ahead of her, deliberately trying to stay up front so he didn't have to see her face anymore.

She raced to catch up. "That look wasn't because of what happened to you," she explained, her tone apologetic.

"I knew about it of course. Grandpa told me. However, I'd never seen it. It startled me is all."

"Maybe I should have shown it to you earlier, but you already made your feelings pretty clear here."

"No," she snapped. "That's not fair. I've never seen a prosthetic before, so, if nothing else, it would have been a shock no matter what. The least you could have done was prepared me for it first."

He shrugged, not sure he was ready to believe her or not. It was definitely the kind of reception he had half expected.

"Did Grandma know?" she asked.

"She knew. She even told me not to bother coming home if I wasn't whole. That no cripples were allowed here."

She stared at him in shock. "What?"

"You heard me," he snapped, glancing at her. "If you're thinking there's no love lost between me and Grandma, maybe now you can get a better understanding of why."

She frowned, shaking her head, muttering, "But she's family."

"Yeah, she sure is. Yet she was quite capable of ignoring that fact when it came to my injury."

"What about Grandpa?"

"He told me to get home where I belonged," he replied, with half a laugh. "And, you know, if we hadn't had the big blowup when I was here before, I wouldn't have gone back out on that next mission. And I wouldn't have gotten hurt," he shared. "So, believe me that I have to work my way through an awful lot there."

"I'm sorry, Ashton, for all you had to go through," she muttered. He never replied. She looked around, asking, "Where are we going?"

"Closer to the neighbors," he said, taking the horses farther along the tire tracks. "I want to walk that fence line and see where these tracks go." He pointed to Khan ahead of them, the dog's tongue lolling to the side, waiting for them. "He wants to go there as well."

"I never saw these before," she shared, staring down at the tracks they were following.

"I'm sure they were there days before," he noted, checking the indents. "But the question is, if they were, when were they made?"

She stared, then frowned. "But nobody comes onto this part of the property."

"Well, nobody's *supposed* to come onto this part of the property," he clarified. "That's true. Still doesn't mean that nobody did. Obviously somebody has. So, did they come over with permission? Did Glenn or John ride through this area, knowing that these tracks would be here, wanting to hide them? Or did they not have a clue? Because, well," he laughed and added, "we both know the boys don't have a clue."

She winced. "They're really not the most observant," she noted apologetically.

"I do know." Ashton chuckled. "The question is, were they naïve, or did they really let this slide and not pursue this intentionally?"

"Why would they do that?"

"To hide their own crime."

CHAPTER 10

O NCE AGAIN, ASHTON kept hitting Crystal with truths and possibilities that made her incredibly uncomfortable.

Ashton added, "So, just be aware, if they accuse you of being on the enemy's side, what that could look like."

She just shook her head, wordless, as she followed Ashton and Khan down the tracks. She was trying to work her way through everything he said on her own, without it being something that she was being led toward.

Yet it was hard to question Ashton because she was right here, following these tire tracks, knowing that nobody should be here in a car at all. And the brothers *had* checked out this area.

How did that compute?

For her, it didn't.

It just made her life even more difficult. What was she supposed to do with that?

Right now, there wasn't a whole lot Crystal could say. She was trying to let it all just work its way through her brain and hopefully not give her as much of a headache as it currently was.

Ashton pulled up to a stop at the fence, finding a gate. Obviously, per the tire tracks, this gate had been opened, and a vehicle had driven through and back out again. Ashton dismounted and walked over to the gate, leaned over, quickly unlatched it.

Then, with a maneuver she had never quite managed, Ashton used Mirage to back up, pulling the gate with him. It was an act that she could see they had both done many a time and quite successfully. Khan belly-scooted under the fence instead of waiting for the gate to fully open. She finally murmured, "You made that look way too easy."

He shook his head and shrugged. "Been doing it for a lifetime."

That was another reminder that this had always been his home, despite his military years, even his years away at college.

This was the space where he had been raised his whole life, even longer than she and her stepbrothers had been here. She nodded. "It's easy for all of us to forget that, isn't it?"

"I don't know what it is you're trying to forget," he pointed out, "but I was raised here from birth. My mother was not anybody's favorite though," he noted, with a mocking laugh. "Yet she and my father have been gone for a long time."

"I'm sorry," she said. He just nodded and didn't say anything. "All these wounded people are here," she added. "It's hard."

"It can be, yes," he agreed. "I mean, not everybody has a chance to deal with their wounds in the same way or even with the same degree of success."

"Was Grandma happy when you were born?"

"I have no idea." His tone was casual, calm, and calculated. "I would have been an infant, and I'm not sure that she was ever happy with me. In fact, I'm not sure Grandma was happy anywhere, honestly—which I wouldn't admit to

Grandpa. Regardless, Grandma did *not* like my mother and made no bones about it."

Crystal frowned at that, and he added, "My mother was young, unwed, pregnant, but my father did the right thing and married her. Yet they were so in love, no matter what their marital status. My grandmother didn't have a lot of respect for her. My parents died when I was just a teenager, when I wasn't sure how relationships worked. Yet, knowing Grandma better now, I bet she was so jealous of my mother. After all, my father had a wife, a child too, so the three of us were a family. That didn't include Grandma. She had been relegated to his birth family, not to his chosen family."

Crystal listened intently. "You've never told me this."

Ashton shrugged. "Seems it is the time for sharing. No more secrets, right? Not that these memories were secrets." He had to laugh at that thought.

"I do remember Grandma and my mother having plenty of arguments and fights. Grandma might have been trying to break up that marriage. I wouldn't doubt it now. My mom was tenacious and fought back. Grandpa went to bat for her because she was my mother. He didn't want the family split up. Seems Grandma is all about splitting up the family, now and back then." He shook his head, letting out a deep sigh.

"I bonded with Grandpa over many a year, way more so than Grandma," he admitted. "She was more about appearances. He was more about values. I mean, look at my first profession. I am a financial advisor, just like Grandpa."

Crystal grimaced. "I'm no longer sure I really know Grandma. She used to be a better person, or so I thought. And lately she's gotten really … *mean.*"

He shot her a look and nodded. "That's one of the reasons why I wanted to check with her doctor or an expert because I don't know if her behavior is part of some debilitating condition or if it's really just—"

Crystal waved a hand. "I get it. There's no easy way to say it, but it could just be old age, where supposedly the filter comes off," she pointed out.

"Absolutely. I do understand that is a concern, but a bigger worry is how much she is willing to do, or has already done, getting her life exactly the way she wants it. It seems like she has no idea of the consequences, which is part of the problem. I'm sure she'll make it seem like she's not responsible for anything, but that is a lie.

"Plus, remember that I do have her written agreement from six years ago to pay back what she stole. I watched her sign it, and she was more than ready to get me kicked off the property for good. But Grandpa backed me up, and she hasn't really forgiven either of us for that."

Crystal tried to absorb all this, staring off in the distance as they rode farther through this area. "Wow," she muttered. "I don't think I've ever been on this part of the property before."

"Because it's not ours," he teased. "We are now on Oliver's and Max's property, and we are still following the tire tracks, which *someone* should have realized would have shown up sooner or later." He pointed out Khan. "He's not hesitating at all."

She nodded. "But we also haven't had the rain that was expected either."

"Right, that's true."

"We were supposed to get quite a lot of rain, but then it moved to the south, so we never got that deluge."

"Exactly," he muttered. "So, if the kidnappers chose that time period because the weather would have covered up everything nicely, then that change in weather could explain why the tracks are still here. Still, if you're up to no good, surely you don't leave evidence behind for just anybody to see what you've done, would you?"

"No, of course not," she agreed, as she looked around. "How stupid would that be, because these tracks are definitely coming to Oliver's place or started from here."

"Yeah," Ashton replied, his tone clipped. "I have to follow them to figure out exactly what's going on."

"Will we get a polite reception, you think?"

"Not sure that we will," he admitted, with a note of amusement. "Yet it won't stop me."

She winced. "So, we're likely heading into a confrontation?"

"Possibly. I mean, if you've done something that you're worried about, wouldn't you be confrontational if somebody came to brace you about it?"

She sucked in her breath as she stared at him.

He smiled. "Yeah. But, as far as Oliver knows, we may be coming for a social visit—or to make a deal where he gets to buy the land."

"If he's still trying to buy it, yeah, but that begs a few questions too. Foremost, how many people actually know about Grandma's addiction?"

"Hard to say," Ashton noted. "Yet it won't be long before everyone knows it. I mean, since I've informed the deputies and the sheriff, it's bound to come out. I'm also trying to get the last of that money paid back fairly quickly. So, it depends on how a few things shake out.

"Plus, Roger confirmed that Grandma was poking around, wanting to know about any other accounts that she may not know about. Roger held firm. Thankfully Grandma had no idea and no access to Grandpa's rainy-day emergency account, which Anderson kept a watch over—not even letting me know about it until now.

"However, what really worries me is Grandma's new secret account, where she has seemingly helped herself to a very large chunk of somebody else's money again. Anderson needs that account number—that's the one I asked you and Jenny about earlier."

Crystal frowned, remembering that, now seeing why that info was so very important.

"As soon as I get that account number, that money is going back to the people it belongs to. I just hope she doesn't empty it before I can get to it. And nobody from the sheriff's office has picked her up to question her either."

Crystal winced. "Grandma won't cooperate. So no wonder they are hanging back."

He shook his head. "The sheriff will have to deal with it when Grandpa's clients find out some investment money has been stolen from them by Grandpa's lovely wife. You've got to remember that lots of people around here have their retirement money invested with Grandpa's investment firm. So, I'm just trying to make sure they get their money first and foremost."

She couldn't imagine what that would look like. "It's bad enough to think of anybody doing something like that but to realize it's your own family? ... That's rough."

He nodded. "Exactly my problem. But if I could figure out where Grandpa is, that would be a huge help. I mean, it is possible that the old man walked away and either something got him, which is very unlikely ..."

"Or," she added gingerly, "he collapsed out here on his own and has succumbed to the elements and whatever made him drop."

"I am fully aware that's possible too," he noted, "but I won't consider it as plausible until I have checked out everything else and still find no sign of him."

She sighed. "I really, *really* hope that he's alive and well somewhere, but, if he is, it'll break his heart when you start telling him what's been going on. Yet surely he will already know to a certain extent because he's always known much more about what's going on than most of us. Yet the biggest problem we have had is that he couldn't stop her—or wasn't emotionally in a position to stand up to her."

"But this is a step too far for Grandma."

"Do you really think you'll get that money back from her?"

"From that newest account, not yet, not until I get the corresponding account number. From the other account? Yes, because it's already been frozen, but it might take quite a bit of paperwork with the bank, plus their time involved in due diligence and all that. We do have proof that she took the money from that one specific account, and it's not in her name. Also Grandpa's been missing, and his login was used."

She stared at him and shook her head. "That's a little bit too convenient."

"Yep, but then she is quite insistent that anything that's happened is nobody's business," he reminded her. "At this point, I'm thinking she has an exit strategy, and what I don't know is whether Glenn and John do too."

"When you say, *exit strategy*—"

"I think she's planning on taking the money and running." He shook his head. "Grandpa is out of the picture, in whatever way that is, and she may or may not care. She's already counted me out, and believe me that I'm struggling with that one too. She went after a chunk of money that she knew was in Grandpa's client accounts."

"But, if she had access to his accounts, wouldn't she have taken more than that?" Crystal asked.

"And that is a good question," he muttered, eyeing her. "Maybe she thought that if she took too much it would trigger an investigation, and maybe it did. I was back in town at that time, which also may have triggered her sudden larceny spree."

"Jesus," she muttered. "I can't believe that she stole money from other people's accounts."

"*Again*," he repeated. Then he froze and asked her, "Shit. Does she have access to your account?"

She stared at him in shock. "I sure hope not."

"But you don't know that, do you?"

"No. God, no." She quickly reached for her phone.

"Yeah, I would definitely check that."

"Christ." She swore a few times.

"And, if she doesn't have access, I'm assuming Glenn and John, probably John, might have access to your accounts."

"No way," she cried out. "Why would you assume that? Nobody should have any access at all."

"Well," Ashton explained, "John is the sleazier one out of those two. Still, you should change your password."

Just in case he was right, she quickly tried to log in. Relief filled her expression. "There's been no change."

"Good, now change your password."

With that warning, she did that right away too. Then sighed as she put away her phone. "That's very disconcerting when you personalize it that way."

"Yep, I know it is," he said, with a dry laugh. "Been

dealing with it a little too long myself."

"Christ," she muttered, "I can't, … I can't even imagine. I'm sitting here trying to find a way to justify her actions. And yet …"

"And yet?" he asked, raising one eyebrow.

"It's not so hazy anymore. And you think it's all about gambling?"

"I don't know what else it could be. Yet I do know that her gambling has become the only thing in her life that she cares about. I also know that Grandpa was very close to doing something about it because we'd had enough arguments and other discussions about it. Grandpa finally realized that it couldn't go on and that he couldn't keep covering for her. I don't want to think very far past that."

She let out her breath. "I presume you're avoiding any link to her having something to do with his disappearance."

"Yep, I'm absolutely trying not to, but, when she turns around and takes a big chunk of money out of a client's account, then opens her own account and somehow stole half-a-million dollars to hide there? She is quite possibly looking to skedaddle," he suggested, pulling out his phone. "It's hard to think otherwise."

"What are you doing now?"

"I wonder if she's made any flight plans or other attempts to leave. She hasn't pulled any cash out because hopefully she can't, unless she knows the bank tellers and gets someone to take a risk." He nodded with his phone to his ear. She heard his side of the conversation with his lawyer. When he ended the call, he shared, "Anderson will double-check that she has no flights booked. And he's also brought the deputies in too. He's meeting with them in the next little bit as they try to recover the money she has moved, first to keep it from her, then to get it back into the client accounts."

"And you've been hanging on to all this … for how long?"

"Too long," he muttered, "way too long."

There wasn't so much fatigue as almost resignation in his tone, a grim fatalistic attitude that this was what he had to do. And he never really had another option. Even with everybody else fighting him—left, right, and center—he really had no other option at all. "Does Grandma know that you own as much of it as you do?"

"She's not supposed to." He shook his head. "It depends on whether or not Grandpa lost his cool and told her. If so, that would give her even more incentive to do this, just to screw me over. Because, now that I am back, she would know she's in trouble."

Khan stopped up ahead beside a huge oak tree. His ears up. His tail up. He stilled, those huge eyes staring straight ahead.

And then Ashton pointed. "And there's the house."

He brought his horse slightly behind a tree and looked at the property. She came up beside him and asked, "Is there a reason we're hiding?"

"Yeah, I'm looking for an outbuilding or something close by."

"For what?"

"Someplace where they could stash a hostage."

She shot him a look, but he was serious. As she started to study the area, he was already way ahead of her.

"There's a shed off to the side that looks the part." He shot her a hard look. "You stay here. I'll go over and find out for sure." He slid off Mirage and handed her the reins. "If anything happens or looks ugly, even a whiff of trouble, you get your ass home and call Richard."

She stared at him, swallowed hard, and noted, "This is one hell of a way for you to return to my life."

He smiled at her and nodded. "Yeah, about time though, isn't it?" And, with a wave, he strode toward the property, staying to the tree line the whole way. He called Khan to heel at his side.

Khan moved into position, but, just like Ashton, the casualness was gone. Both were alert. Both were in what she could only describe as hunting mode. It was scary and reassuring.

She wanted to call out something but knew it was already too late. Ashton was already in hunter mode. A strange feeling came over her as she realized just how well he did it.

She moved the horses deeper into the shadows, not wanting anybody to see them because she didn't have any explanation as to why she was here. And just as she thought that maybe Ashton was overstaying his welcome, wherever the hell he was, he slipped out of the one building and moved into another one. She realized this wouldn't be quite so fast or so easy.

Every farm, every ranch, had outbuildings like this all over the place. If he planned to check each and every one, that wouldn't be good. And just when she thought maybe it was all okay, she heard a vehicle approach.

She sent him a text, letting him know, then moved even farther back. With her heart slamming against her chest, she watched as the new arrival parked outside the front of the house and then walked inside, before pausing and staring around the area, as if sensing something. She closed her eyes, trying hard to not even breathe in case he could hear it, which was incredibly foolish because he was a long distance away.

But then he stopped and moved toward the barn that Ashton had gone into. She froze in a panic. Then Oliver's phone rang, he answered it, talking loudly as he turned and headed to the house.

Whew! She let out a sigh of relief.

This time, and maybe only this time, Ashton's luck was reigning. It was enough to know that he was safe, at least for the moment.

WITH THE FIRST building revealing nothing, Ashton moved through the next few buildings, looking for any sign of life. He moved in the shadows, Khan at his side, perfectly in tune, a game they both knew from their own dark histories.

It wouldn't necessarily tell him if Grandpa had been here because, of course, somebody had been. People were moving through these outbuildings all the time. But, on instincts, Ashton kept going. And Khan had turned from a silent companion to an eager animal who raced around, his nose to the ground.

Something was seriously wrong with this particular area, this barn, and Ashton couldn't figure it out. He moved up into the loft, then saw a room segregated off to the side. Khan joined him, then started to scratch and whine, almost howling at the door. It took Ashton a minute to figure out how to get into it.

As soon as he did, he froze. There on a bed, with a gag in his mouth, was Alexander Nelson, his grandfather. And Ashton saw almost no sign of life left in Grandpa.

Khan raced over, shoving his nose into the old man's neck.

Ashton joined him, pulling Khan back so he could check for a pulse, which was thready at best. Then he pulled out his phone and started texting, sending photos, looking for backup.

With Grandpa alive, even hanging on barely, there was still hope. Ashton sat back and considered how he would get Grandpa out of here. Then he remembered that Crystal was outside. If his grandfather was here, someone had brought him here, had kept him here. Was Crystal safe for these few minutes alone? A part of him had been sure his grandfather was here. Yet another part of him really hoped he wasn't because of what that would mean.

He'd seen the earlier text from Crystal and knew that the owner was back on the property too. He would have to confront Oliver, his grandfather's life hanging in the balance while found on Oliver's property.

No matter, this was damning news for all of them. His grandfather didn't wake up, and that was another concern. He was old, had been through way too much already in his life, and, if the prior stress hadn't killed him, this newest nightmare could easily be the end of him.

Ashton hunkered down next to Grandpa, as he waited for backup, turning off the sound on his phone as he watched as the texts rolled in. Everything from shock to mutiny to an ambulance being ordered. Ashton then sent a text to Crystal and waited to hear back from her.

When no answer came, he turned and looked out the barn window, but he couldn't see her. He sent her a message requesting a response. When he didn't get one, he closed his eyes, knowing that somebody probably picked up that he was here, and now things would get ugly. He texted Richard, saying that Crystal was no longer responding to his texts and that he feared the worst.

At that, Richard sent a confirmation, saying three vehicles were on the way, plus an ambulance, and to sit tight.

Ashton had to smile at that. *Sit tight?* Yeah, not likely.

Not if Crystal, who had followed him here willingly, was in trouble. She was his responsibility. He stared down at his grandfather, hating the pale gray look to him, not sure whether it was drug-induced or something else. Torn, he whispered, "You stay here, old man. I've got you now, but I have to make sure Crystal's okay too."

And, with that, hating to leave him, Ashton got up, ready to find Oliver in the main house.

CHAPTER 11

W HEN THE VOICE came up behind her, Crystal wasn't at all surprised, and yet he gave her a start.

Oliver asked her, "What are you doing here?"

She twisted on the horse, backing Mirage up ever-so-slightly and closer to her and her horse. "Hey, we wanted to stop by but weren't sure you were home," she replied in that cheerful, socially awkward tone of hers.

He glared at her. "We aren't friends for you to just *drop by*," he countered. "So, that doesn't wash with me, young lady."

She frowned at him. "I thought you were interested in purchasing some of the property."

His own frown eased somewhat. He almost laughed. "Now? *Now* you want to talk about it, *huh?*"

She was confused. "Hey, we're not here to piss you off."

"Sure, but a phone call would have been normal."

She stared at him. "No, that would not be normal," she argued, tucking back a loose strand of hair. "You and I both know that none of this is normal, … not the way you're handling it. Obviously you don't appreciate the fact that we're here."

"No, I really don't," he admitted, glaring at her.

She shrugged. "Well, when you find Ashton at your house, you can tell him that I'm out here waiting with the horses. He went in to talk to you."

He shook his head. "No, you're coming with me."

"And if I don't want to?" she asked, backing up a little farther.

He gave her a sour smile. "I don't trust any of your family," he began, his expression turning all kinds of nasty. "That grandmother of yours is a piece of work."

She hated the feeling she had inside, wondering just what he knew, because, now that *she* knew, it felt like the whole world still knew even more than she ever did, even after her twenty-three years at Nelson Farm. "And what do you mean by that?" she asked.

"She's a witch through and through." He raised his hands in frustration. "So, I got no truck with any of you, particularly not if you don't understand boundaries."

She shook her head and noted, "I have never known anybody in this area to be so unfriendly. Your behavior right now is a little disconcerting."

"I don't care what it is," he snapped, but his gaze didn't leave hers. "You're trespassing."

"We came for a visit and to say hi," she repeated. "Most people would not consider a friendly visit as trespassing, but obviously we're not welcome here." She barely held back a sniff, but her own sense of injustice was rising, and pretty heavily at that. "I've only ever seen you a couple times in the last decade," she pointed out. "So, I'm not sure how we ended up on such a wrong foot over all this."

"It's called *property* and *property lines*, … that's how."

She stared at him in confusion. "Are you saying that there's a discrepancy regarding the property lines?"

He snorted, then howled with laughter. When his laughter died down a bit, he declared, "Hell yes, there is."

She shook her head. "I heard you wanted to buy property, but that's the first I've heard about any discrepancy."

"Because your great-granddaddy paid way too little for it, knowing it was worth a lot more."

She stared at him, not really getting all this hostility. "Okay, so now I'm confused. The Nelsons have owned that land for a very long time."

"Yeah, they sure did. Wouldn't let me buy back any of my pieces, the pieces I wanted."

"So, you used to own it?" she asked.

"Yeah, I sure did along with my brother after my father passed on." He stared at her with amusement. "You really didn't hear the story?"

"No, I didn't." She wasn't sure what to say about that. His penetrating gaze made her uncomfortable.

Oliver continued. "You really seem to think I'm making something out of nothing."

"No, I'm not saying that at all," she countered, hard-pressed to get out of this conversation. "I have recently learned that not everything is the way I thought it was."

"No, it sure isn't," he spat, "but your great grandpa bought the land off my father when prices were down."

"And your dad didn't need the money?" she asked.

"Sure, he needed the money, but the greedy bastard could have let him buy it back again when things were better, but the old weasel wouldn't let him."

"Okay, so it's not so much that you didn't agree with the original deal, just that you wanted it to be reversed when things got better. Is that it?" she asked.

He nodded. "That was also their agreement, but your great grandpa didn't go for that. That's where the problem comes in," he shared, with a shrug. "So, I don't really care what he does at the moment, since I'll be taking it all over."

"An awful lot of people seem to think they have owner-ship rights to the Nelson land right now."

He pointed a finger at her. "I'm buying it fair and square, so I don't know what you're talking about." She sat back, and he called out forcefully, "Now we're going inside. I don't know what's going on here, but I don't like this. Your whole family is a big bunch of screwups, and I don't trust any of them."

She shrugged. "Maybe that's wise, depending on who you've been dealing with."

He stopped in his tracks, then turned back to her.

She knew right away that she had said the wrong thing. "Look, Oliver. I don't know what's going on, but I can tell you that things are a little bit messy right now."

"Just a little bit?" he quipped, with a snort. "You should be a comedian with that statement."

"Did you have anything to do with Grandpa's disap-pearance?" she asked.

He seemed surprised by the question, but then a smile came on his face. "Hell no. I don't have nothing to do with that kind of crap. The old man probably just wandered off. I heard he was missing." He frowned at that. "Good thing it don't matter to get his signature anymore."

She stared at him, something clicking in the back of her mind. "Whose signature did you get?"

"Your grandmother's," he declared quite proudly. Then he turned to her, frowning. "Why? She's the one who owns it, ... doesn't she?"

"Does she really?" she asked him.

He gaze narrowed. "Are you telling me that she isn't the owner?"

"I am telling you that is definitely in question."

"No, no, no," he roared, his face turning pale. "That's not happening. I've already paid her a big chunk of change."

She closed her eyes and whispered, "Jesus."

He stepped closer to her. "Hang on here a minute, young lady. You're serious, aren't you?"

She nodded. "I'm very serious."

"We need to get into the house. I've got," he grumbled, "I've got paperwork. That house, … the whole property, … it's all mine now, and I've got the paperwork to prove it."

She didn't say anything as she and the two horses followed Oliver on his determined trek back to the house. She felt everything around her collapsing as she realized just what a nightmare this had become. She didn't know whether Grandma could be held liable for all this or not, but the pain that she was causing everyone was unimaginable. And Crystal couldn't begin to figure out what was going on in terms of how this would affect Ashton and the Nelson homestead and his grandfather.

She slid down off Bessie. "I need to see that paperwork."

"Well, I've got it." But now he was looking uncertain and blustery. "I paid a lot of money to her over this deed. She better not be screwing me over."

"I hope not," she replied, "but I've got to tell you, you're not the first person she has conned." He stopped, frowned at her, and then raced ahead, as if terrified at what she said.

Trouble was, she wasn't lying. Yet, for Oliver, as far as he was concerned, this was a done deal. She tied up the horses to the railing outside, vaguely wondering where Khan had gotten off to, then walked toward the front porch of Oliver's house.

He headed off inside and returned almost immediately

with some paperwork. She wasn't a lawyer, but, from her perspective, it looked legit. And that just made her even sadder. She looked over at Oliver and asked him, "And you have no idea what's going on with Grandpa?"

"No idea what's going on with him. I gave up trying to deal with him years ago, the stubborn old ass. But finally I got what I wanted. Maybe we should have been dealing with Johanna all along," he stated, staring at her. "What's with all the questions? What are you up to?"

She sighed and replied, "Because things are about to blow wide open, and I gather you don't know anything about it." He just blinked. In that moment, she realized how somebody else had been used and had been taken advantage of by Grandma. She held up the pictures Ashton had sent her. "Do you recognize this place?" she asked.

He looked at it, frowned, and shook his head. "I don't think so." And then he frowned again. "That's Alexander."

"Yeah, it's Grandpa," she confirmed. "He's being held captive, here on your place."

He looked at her, his face ashen, then shook his head vehemently. "No, no, no, no way," he bellowed. "We don't do that kind of shit. We got a problem, we bring it out in the open."

"Well, I tried to visit you today to see what the hell was going on, but you weren't open to that either."

He again just blinked at her.

She continued. "So the deputies and maybe even the sheriff will be here soon, and I don't want you getting even more irate than you already are because it appears somebody may be setting you up as the fall guy here."

He stared at her in shock. "I didn't have anything to do with this," he yelled.

"Are you sure about that?" Ashton asked, as he stepped into the living room.

She looked over at Ashton, glaring at Oliver, but Ashton's hand was holding back a very agitated Khan. "I only ask because my grandpa is up in your barn loft—in the secret room that you've got built in there."

He shook his head, his face flushed. "You must be out of your mind, young man. What are you talking about? What secret room?"

"Why don't you come with me? The deputies are already on their way. And, if you didn't do this," he added, "we still need to know who the hell has access to your place and who's behind this. Because my grandpa needs to get to the hospital quickly, and I don't even know if he'll survive."

"That's—" Oliver stuttered.

"We'll settle this like gentlemen, and, if you aren't involved, that's one thing," Ashton explained. "However, if you are involved and if Grandpa dies, you'll go down for murder."

ASHTON HAD LISTENED in on part of the conversation before making his presence known, surprised and disturbed to hear just what was going on. Pulling out a leash, he hooked it onto Khan's collar, keeping him at his side, as he'd stayed in the shadows, still trying to understand the motive here. He also knew a rescue mission would soon hit the property, and he didn't want Khan getting on the wrong side of the chaos.

From the sound of it, somebody had taken Oliver for a ride. Ashton still had to get to the bottom of it all.

Oliver slowly turned to Ashton and asked, "Are you serious? He's up there in my barn?"

"He is, indeed." Ashton glanced at his watch, "Deputies and an ambulance will be here any minute. We need to get back up there to Grandpa."

"I'm coming with you," Oliver declared, "because I didn't have anything to do with this."

"Then you need to explain how he's on your property." Ashton took off for the barn.

A wild look came into Oliver's gaze, as he shook his head. "I can't explain it because I didn't do this, and why would I? Especially now." He looked from one to the other and yelled, "What the hell is going on?"

She called out to Ashton, "Oliver's got signed documents that he's purchased the entire Nelson farm, Ashton. The house, the property, … all of it."

He stopped in his tracks, then turned and looked from one to the other. Because surely there was more than she was saying; he could almost see it.

"And he has given Grandma a big chunk of money as a deposit."

He closed his eyes at that; exactly what he had expected. "Fuck," he swore, despite being prepared for supposedly all contingencies. "Yeah, first things first," he announced, "we've got to get Grandpa some help."

By the time they made it up to where Grandpa had been kept, Crystal cried out and collapsed at his side because he did not look good at all. There was a gray cast to his face.

When Oliver first got sight of Grandpa, a horrified expression took over Oliver's face. He shook his head, pointing. "No way," he muttered. "I didn't do this," he declared, his tone sharp, his voice getting louder. "I didn't put him up here."

Ashton asked, "So, who could possibly have come here and done this?"

"I don't know," he yelled in shock, looking from one to the other. "I didn't do this."

They all heard the sirens in the distance.

Oliver grabbed Ashton's arm. "Young man, Alexander and I might have had some issues, but I didn't do this. And she's right. I just paid a shitload of money to your grandmother to buy his whole place."

"When?" Ashton asked.

"Just a few days ago, I made a deposit. I have to pay off the rest this year, then it's all mine."

Ashton just looked at him and groaned. "And you have no idea, … do you?"

"About what?" Oliver bellowed.

Khan growled at Ashton's side, definitely taking offense to Oliver's raised voice. Ashton calmed him down. "The farm … wasn't hers to sell."

"What do you mean, it's not hers to sell?" He cried out, "Then whose is it?"

Ashton looked at him with a sense of finality because the man needed to know where he stood. "It's all mine— assuming anything is left after all her stealing, cheating, gambling, and back-ended deals come to light," he explained, as Oliver turned white and groaned. "You're now another victim of her schemes."

The old man looked at him in shock, muttering, "Johanna had her own Realtor close the deal, and he did strike me as …"

"Shady?" Ashton asked.

Oliver frowned, shaking his head. "Yeah."

Ashton suggested, "Like a bookie maybe?"

"Damn that Johanna," Oliver snapped, now realizing just the tip of the iceberg here.

"Bet no title search was done before closing either," Ashton noted. "We'll get to the bottom of this. When did you finalize the deal?"

"Not very long ago, … just last week."

"So, right around the time that Grandpa went missing," he stated, frowning at Oliver.

"I didn't do this though," he repeated, then his expression changed to one of horror. "Oh my God. Will the sheriff say I kidnapped Alexander just to get the property?"

"I don't know," Ashton admitted, "but obviously there's no shortage of bullshit going on around here. And this is just another aspect. Better go meet the deputies and bring them up here."

"But they may shoot me on sight," Oliver noted, his eyes wide open. "If you've already told the sheriff that Alexander's here and been a hostage on my place—"

Ashton thought about it and then nodded. "Good point. I'll go get them. Do not move."

"I'm not going anywhere," Oliver stated. "I'm sitting here right beside Alexander because I didn't do this, none of this."

Ashton handed Khan's leash to Crystal, not only to keep Khan safe from the upcoming chaos but in case Oliver tried anything. Khan would keep Crystal safe. And, with that, Ashton bolted down the stairs, met the deputies and the medical personnel in the driveway, and pointed them all to the barn loft.

He turned to Richard and the deputies. "So, we have another new twist to add to this mess now."

Richard groaned. "What did she do now?"

"According to Oliver, who is up there with Grandpa and Crystal, he had nothing to do with this. And he seems truly shocked that we found Grandpa in his barn. There's a separate and kind of hidden room up there, and that's where Grandpa has been kept. Now, I don't know who's behind all this, but Oliver lacks motive because, as far as he's concerned, he's already purchased Nelson farm, has recently paid a very hefty deposit on my land, and, yeah, without my approval."

Richard just stared at him for a long moment. "*What?*"

"Yeah. According to Oliver, he paid my *grandmother* a large chunk of money against the sale of the whole place, with the balance due by the end of this year, at which time we all would vacate, and he would totally own it. He had no idea that I own the land and that Grandma had no rights to sell it—well, he knows now, but that's another huge issue. He also says that she got his down payment money recently."

Richard stopped, pushed his hat back, and asked, "What do you think is going on?"

"I think my grandmother is planning to escape and needed a large amount of money before leaving. So, she fraudulently sold off the property. I don't know how or why, and I highly doubt she hired a real lawyer or a true closing agent for this supposed sale. It's just another con. I think the plan was to get Oliver's down payment money, which is one-half-million dollars. Now, whether to supposedly pay off her bookie to release Alexander or to just selfishly supply her own needs, I don't know. But, Richard, Grandma already snagged that extra chunk of change in the amount of one-quarter million from one of Grandpa's client accounts. So, with about $750,000 total *that we know of*—and no place to live, plus I had already sicced you, as the sheriff, on her—Grandma's got to be planning to leave as quickly as she can."

"Well," Richard began, hesitating, "we are struggling to find her right now."

"What the—"

"No need to panic, Ashton. We have frozen the accounts. She can't get at the money, but she has pulled yet another bunko."

"Of course she has." Ashton just stared at him. "So, do you need any more proof about what the hell this woman is up to?"

Richard groaned. "We've just never seen anybody do this before."

"You mean, steal, cheat, and lie to get everything they want? Of course you have," he declared, staring at him. "It happens all the damn time."

"It just doesn't happen in our neck of the woods. And there was no reason for her to get that money when she already owned the place."

"Except," Ashton stated, with a snort, "she doesn't own anything."

"Right," Richard muttered. "Do you have legal documents proving your claim?"

"Sure I do. Everything is registered in my name. You can contact my lawyer." Then he gave him the name and address of Anderson Moore.

"Well, at least a reputable lawyer is involved on your end," Richard noted, with a sharp look. "Although lawyers aren't my favorite people to deal with, but that may at least give us some idea of what's going on."

"Well, it looks pretty clear-cut from where I'm standing. Still, I've got to tell you, I don't think Oliver had anything to do with any of this, but you'll have to do your own investigation into that."

"Oh, thank you," Richard replied skeptically. "You're letting us do our own investigation."

He glared at him. "I personally don't think any of this is very funny, and I am worried that my grandpa won't make it. And, if he doesn't, this will go from kidnapping and confinement and elder abuse and whatever else to some kind of homicide charge. A whole different kind of headache. Plus, nobody has found Sean Keaton yet, right?"

Richard glumly shook his head. "Christ," Richard muttered as he turned around, Oliver walking toward them.

Oliver told Ashton, "Alexander's still not conscious, but he's still alive, and the EMTs are loading him up now."

He nodded. "Thank you for that."

Oliver looked over at Richard and announced, "I didn't do this."

Richard nodded. "I'll need to get your statement."

"I ain't got a statement. There ain't nothing to say. And apparently his goddamn grandmother screwed me out of a ton of money."

"How much money?" he asked, double-checking.

"Half-a-million dollars."

"Yeah, that would be her," Ashton noted.

"The only good thing is, if it was a recent transaction, we might get it before she does. If it's not recent ..." Richard left it with a shrug. "Yeah, I don't know what to tell you."

Shaking with rage, Oliver yelled, "I'll sue that whole goddamn family. Bunch of liars and thieves."

"You can try," Ashton replied, "but, before you spend a bunch of money on lawyers, you should know that I may not have anything left when this is all over with."

"What do you mean?" he asked, staring at him in shock. "That place is worth millions."

"Well, it was until she started stealing money from not only the household accounts but also the client accounts in my grandfather's business."

Oliver just stared at them, stunned.

"Yeah," Ashton confirmed. "We've put a freeze on that transaction because she took one-quarter million out of one client account alone, about the same time as I hit town," he shared. "Grandma shouldn't have had access to any of those accounts for the last six years. We're still working on how she did that, so lawyers are involved, deputies, Sheriff Richard here, and God-only-knows who else. There is no end to the hell in my world right now."

Oliver shook his head. "I thought having my family and losing all of them was shitty," Oliver began, "but you would have been better off if you lost your grandma. You've lost so many family members already, at least you could have lost the one causing you all the trouble. Wouldn't that be nice?"

Ashton muttered, "I would rather have the earlier version of Grandma back. Regardless, life doesn't seem to be quite so accommodating in giving us choices."

Oliver snorted. "No, it sure as hell isn't. It ain't been the same for me since my brother died. And I was trying to buy the place for him because he's the one who was all bent over backward about the whole thing. But I sure didn't expect this to happen."

Ashton asked, "How did you pay her?"

"Via a wire. She wanted the money wired to her."

Bingo. "I need that wire info," Ashton declared. "Now."

Oliver frowned but headed to the house, was soon back outside with one single sheet of paper that he handed over to Ashton.

He quickly took a photo of it and texted it to Anderson. **Freeze this account.**

Oliver shook his head. "I feel like an absolute idiot, letting that old gal con me out of that kind of money."

"I wouldn't worry about that because she's conned plenty of others. So, this isn't on you, but I've got my attorney freezing those funds, before Grandma takes off with them."

CHAPTER 12

IN THE HOSPITAL, Crystal sat beside her grandpa, the covers pulled up under his neck. The doctors had been in to check on him again. Khan was at home with her dogs. The three seemed to be thoroughly enjoying themselves together.

Grandpa had apparently been given a hefty dose of ketamine, and they were hoping he could just sleep it off. But given his age and his current condition, they weren't exactly sure if or when that would happen. The ketamine had supposedly already been processed through his system.

So, *wait and see* was the only course of action they had, which didn't feel like action at all. Grandpa had been given fluids and drugs to counter the effects of the ketamine. She sat here with tears in her eyes, staring down at this man who had been the kindest, most caring person she'd ever known. He had been the one who insisted she stay with the family, after they lost their son and then, not long afterward, their daughter.

And Grandpa was the one who had been there for Crystal this whole time. He'd been the one who had gone to her graduation and had been to all her milestone markers at school. He'd just been the best grandpa anybody could have.

And to see him in this situation right now, brought on by God-only-knows what kind of craziness in this world, was just heartbreaking. When she heard something behind her, she turned to see Ashton smiling as he came over and looked down at their grandpa.

She could see the toll all this had taken on him. She smiled at him, asking, "Did you ever think that maybe you came home just in the nick of time? Plus, you'll probably go crazy worrying about *what if you hadn't come home right now.*"

He nodded. "Yeah. I probably won't sleep for a very long time, and I'll end up with PTSD over being too late on this one. Absolutely nothing is worse than knowing you should have come home a little bit earlier but didn't."

She reached up a hand and squeezed his. "I'm so sorry. This isn't exactly what you were hoping for as a homecoming."

"No, it sure wasn't," he admitted, looking down at her, "but we found him, and that's the main thing. For the rest, I don't know. That's in the hands of the lawyers and the sheriff and his idiot deputies. They are still looking for Grandma right now."

"Isn't she like eighty?" Crystal asked, turning to look at him, "Where does an eighty-year-old go? And how does an eighty-year-old even know what to do in this situation?"

"Those are really good questions," he noted, "and I am not sure because I don't know if she's done this on her own or if she has a partner in crime or if a completely different scenario is at work here."

"Like what?"

"Like the fact that she has gambling debts."

"Maybe she really was trying to get enough money to get Grandpa back."

"Except," Ashton pointed out, "I don't know why anybody in the gambling debt world would keep Grandpa over at Oliver's place."

"Maybe because it's the least likely of all places we would look. Having found him now, of course, everybody's looking at Oliver as being the guilty party. So, in a way, it was a very smart plan."

He nodded and added, "I did consider that, but also it brings it very close to home—*our* home—because how many people would know about the feud and the unneighborly relationship between us and Oliver and Max in the first place? Plus, who else has easy access to his place from our place? Those tire tracks on our property lead right to his."

She frowned at that and nodded. "I wasn't really thinking along that line, but you're right. Somebody had to get in the barn to check up on him."

"Or maybe they didn't and just decided he would live or die, and that surely is the way it looks to me."

She felt the weight of his words pulling on her heart as she thought about Alexander lying there in that barn for days. "Do you think he was conscious at all during this? Would he have known what happened?"

"I don't know." Ashton sighed. "We would hope not, but that hope won't save anybody when it comes down to the fact that we have something truly nasty going on here. I would say we have a very limited scope of bad guys to look at."

She nodded. "I can't even imagine the scope of what we have," she muttered. "It just seems so unbelievable to do something like that to such a nice old man. Then to even think of your grandmother having the know-how to do this is a stretch too. That's another part that bothers me. I'm not saying she has *not* got the know-how because she's always been pretty tricky, as we have repeatedly been shown."

Ashton agreed. "Gamblers will do all kinds of things to keep feeding their habit, their addiction. What I don't know is whether all the money she's collected was to pay back a gambling debt or just to escape being caught. But I'm sure she's thinking, *Who cares?* After all, I would end up paying any ransom to buy Grandpa back anyway."

Crystal frowned. "Or she was getting the money to run with, knowing she has nothing left here, what with everyone soon finding out about all the bad things she has done. Particularly if she figured that Grandpa didn't survive all this time. And where will she run to anyway?" she asked, looking at him. "I mean, how is it even possible for her to run? She's not a spring chicken."

"No, but she still drives on her own, and she's still got her cognitive abilities, at least according to the doctors. My lawyer confirmed that she had a full checkup recently, and everything was fine."

"Unless she bribed them to say that," Crystal suggested.

"*Unless she bribed them to say that.*" He nodded. "Totally possible, I don't even know what to say at this point. … My first priority is getting Grandpa back on his feet, hopefully alive and well."

"Yes," she whispered. "I agree with that one."

"And God help anybody else who's decided that they should steal anything from our family, which then brings us to the brothers. Do you think they had anything to do with this?"

She knew exactly who he was talking about. She thought about it and admitted, "I guess I wouldn't be shocked if they did, but, in a way, it's too easy of an answer."

"Whether they had anything to do with Grandpa going

missing or with Grandma's newest cons is just one aspect, but whether they knew what they were getting into is another thing."

She groaned. "Meaning that Grandma may have set them up for this too?"

"Knowing how lazy the twins are, they may have thought that whatever they were doing to help Grandma would get them a pile of money because she obviously knew what she was doing."

"Are they that stupid?" she asked.

"What do you think?" he quipped, rolling his eyes.

"I hate to say it, but they're as uneducated as anybody that age can be. I mean, they both read and write, but they didn't finish school. They barely have any cognizant understanding of what's going on in the real world. They don't have girlfriends, which would, if nothing else, maybe keep their brains focusing on other things to some degree. As it is, their friends are basically like them. I mean ..." She broke off and just nodded. "They are bullies."

"I hear what you're saying. It just confirms how stupid and useless they are."

She chuckled. "It sounds absolutely ridiculous that this is where we're at."

"That may be, but the fact remains, if the brothers were paid to put Grandpa up there and got a big chunk of money—or the promise of a chunk of money—they might've done it."

"Could be, but again there are other possibilities."

"Like?" Ashton asked.

"They were doing it as a favor, thinking it was a lark, and they might've done it. If they were doing it for Grandma, who had a reason they could actually understand, they might've done it," she shared, "but all those are just ideas, so we really still have more questions than answers."

"Well, Glenn and John have been picked up for questioning," he shared, "so hopefully, by the end of the day, somebody will tell us something."

"Theories aside, it's almost always something simple in the end though, isn't it?"

"It is," he agreed. "It almost always comes down to greed. And, so far, considering the amount of money Grandma has been stealing from everybody, including Oliver, greed appears to be the bottom line. What I don't know is if it's that simple."

Just then Grandpa groaned, shifted uneasily on his bed, a half murmur coming from his lips.

Crystal leaned forward and spoke softly to him. "Grandpa, hey, I'm here. It's okay. It's Crystal. Take it easy. You're just waking up."

He shifted again, and another whimper escaped, and she hated it. She hated everything about seeing him in pain. She told Ashton, "Get the nurses in here. Maybe we can get him something for pain."

"I'll go get them right now," he said, heading for the door. "They'll want to know he's awake anyway." And he quickly disappeared, only to return a few minutes later with one of the nurses.

The nurse looked down at Grandpa and smiled. "Good, he's starting to come out of it," she said, checking him over. "It'll still take him a bit. So, let's just give him a chance to wake up on his own. It will help him get oriented if he does it on his own."

And, sure enough, Grandpa opened his eyes not too many minutes later and stared from one to the other. He frowned when his gaze landed on Crystal, but then his gaze cleared when it landed on Ashton. He whispered, "Thank God, Ashton. You're home."

"Yeah, I'm home," he said, "but you should have called me a lot earlier."

He shifted in his hospital bed. "I know. … Johanna's gone nuts." He took a deep, labored breath. "It's bad, Ashton."

"I know, Grandpa. It's way worse than you even know," he added, "but I'm home now. So, we can get to the bottom of it."

"I hope so," he whispered, "because I don't think I can handle this anymore. Honest to God, in a way I'm sad that I'm even awake right now." He glanced around the hospital and noted, "It must have been bad for me to have gotten here."

Ashton nodded. "It absolutely was."

Then Grandpa reached out both hands. Crystal and Ashton each grabbed one. Grandpa added, "I guess I can't leave yet, not while everything's in chaos."

ASHTON STOOD OUTSIDE the hospital and stared up at the sky. This was a good ending, yet it wasn't any kind of ending at all.

They had so many more things unsettled and yet to be discovered, and he knew the answers to come could be even more painful than even he suspected. When a hand slipped into his, he looked down, squeezing it gently, and muttered, "Hey."

"Hey," Crystal muttered back.

"How's he doing now?"

"Well, he's asleep now," she admitted.

"That's a good thing."

"The doctors wanted him to get some rest and suggested that I leave."

He nodded. "Better for both of us in many ways. Let's just give Grandpa his time and space and hope that he can recover from this."

Crystal noted, "It's also a little frustrating that he wasn't quite all there and couldn't really tell us anything yet."

"Well, what he could tell us wasn't helpful either," he pointed out. "So, as much as we might think that we now could have answers, we don't. He couldn't even tell us who put him in that barn or how he ended up there."

"He had been drugged, so he's still fighting the effects of that. Plus, we don't know how quickly he was drugged. So, if somebody came up behind him, it's possible he never saw them anyway." Crystal wiped the tears from her eyes.

Ashton let go of her hand to pull her close into a hug. He whispered to her, "We found him. He's alive and recuperating in the hospital. That's all that matters for now."

She looked up at him and clarified, "You found him. I had no idea."

Ashton shrugged. "We all expected that he had met a foul end at the hands of Mother Nature."

"Not one of us thought it was foul play," she stated, then turned to him. "Except you, you had some idea."

He nodded but didn't say anything, unsure of what he could say to make her feel better. He was still angry and hurt, feeling guilty for not being here sooner.

"The fact that you even thought of foul play made all of us look at you in shock, horror, and disbelief," she admitted, with a wave of her hand. "And yet you held steadfast. I don't understand. How did you know?"

"Partly instincts," he replied. "Partly because there was absolutely no need for this to happen to him. This is his property. He knows the ins and outs of it better than anyone," he shared. "And, although he could have had a heart attack and collapsed, he would have been found with all the people out and about on the property. But the fact that he was nowhere, that made me the most suspicious."

She sighed, rubbing her head against his chest.

He just tucked her up closer as they stood here, watching the rest of the world go about their business all around them.

Crystal sighed. "It's rough to even imagine that he was stuck there. And for how long?"

"We know he's been missing for four or five days," Ashton replied. "Maybe his kidnapper didn't expect the ketamine to affect him like that."

"Perhaps they thought it would just knock him out temporarily."

"But even then"—he nodded, his chin brushing her head—"what were they planning? They had an eighty-year-old man tied up in a barn. What did they hope to gain?" he whispered.

She stiffened ever-so-slightly and then relaxed.

Finally he said, "I need to go back home and take care of a few things."

"Like what?" she asked.

"I still have a packed day and then some. I still have people I need to contact. And we still need to see that the deputies do their damn job."

"What about Oliver?" she asked, turning to him. "Doesn't sound like he'll have an easy time of it either."

"If he had nothing to do with Grandpa's kidnapping, then at some point the sheriff will let him go," Ashton pointed out, "but it might not be fast or easy."

"And, if he had nothing to do with it, that's so not fair," she muttered.

"How do you feel about Oliver now?"

"I think he's innocent," she stated. "I think he's just another victim. A victim of my, I mean, *our* grandmother," she added, turning to him.

He nodded, albeit a little grimly. "Yeah, and don't you see that it's all coming down to a pattern?"

"But surely not Grandpa's disappearance, surely not out of something so base as greed or spite."

"I don't know yet," he admitted. "I haven't figured that one out. What I do know is that the sheriff hasn't been able to find her. And now I don't know whether that is also a part of this kidnapping mess, part of her gambling mess, or something else entirely."

"Oh my gosh," she muttered, "I didn't even think of that."

"Right," he replied, "so now we essentially have yet another missing person, our grandmother."

"And yet, as far as most of us are concerned, she's probably just booked it in order to save her own butt." She pulled back slightly and added, "She has gotten a little weird over the last while."

"More than what you've already told me?"

"When I say a little, I mean a lot. But I wouldn't have thought that she would have done something like this to Grandpa."

Ashton didn't say anything but stared off in the distance. "Let's head home, and I can carry on with the things that I need to get done there and in town, if needed."

"Agreed. I also have the horses to feed."

"Yeah." He nodded, with a grimace. "We did get them back to the barn, but they do need to be taken care of." And, with that, he led her back to the truck, and he drove home, his mind preoccupied with everything that had just happened.

After parking, they walked into the main house together to see Jenny standing there. The three dogs came racing in the front door to greet them. After several moments of chaotic greetings by the dogs, Jenny waited for them, a stillness that showed how much the news meant to her.

He smiled at her. "Alexander's awake. He's alive, and he's awake." The look of relief on her face said so much. He nodded. "I know it's been a pretty rough few days, but he is alive."

The tears welled up in her eyes.

He walked over and gave her a gentle hug. "Thank you for holding down the fort and keeping the faith that he was okay."

She sniffled and nodded slightly. "It's a good thing you came home."

He winced at that and then realized that she meant it sincerely. "I don't know how much of it anybody will be grateful for at the end of the day," he clarified, "but I'm here, and I'm here to stay."

She stepped back, looked up at him, and smiled. "And that's the way it should be. It's your place. It's the passing of the line, the right and proper thing."

He nodded. "If you will put on some coffee, I'll go to the office and try to pick up the lines that still need help right now. We have a lot of unanswered questions."

Crystal stepped back. "I need to go home and get chores done. I'll take Khan with me and my dogs." She smiled at both of them, then turned and walked out, the animals with her.

Ashton turned to go to the office, but Jenny called out, "Was it really Oliver?"

"No," he replied, turning to look at her. "Who told you that it was Oliver?"

She frowned and asked, "I thought Alexander was found at Oliver's place."

"He was, but Oliver didn't know anything about it."

Her eyes widened. She stared at him for a long moment.

He hesitated and asked, "Have you seen Oliver over here? With Grandma?"

"I did see him with Johanna a couple times." She frowned. "It was more casual than anything else. I did worry that there might be some shenanigans going on between them, but I don't think he necessarily saw your grandmother in that light."

He stared at her, his mind balking at the idea of his grandmother even having a beau while her husband was missing somewhere, possibly dying.

Jenny frowned at him, questions in her gaze. "I don't think that's what it was about, … but, anytime I asked her, she got very defensive."

"Of course she did." He thought about it and then began, "I guess we might as well just put the truth out there. Trying to protect Grandma's secrets has been part of the problem as it is. So you should know that Grandma sold this property to Oliver and accepted a half-million-dollar deposit."

Jenny just stared at him, her jaw dropping. "But it's not hers."

"Yeah, and Oliver didn't know that. She gave him the impression that it was hers and that she wanted to sell it. So, he paid her the deposit and became yet another victim, at least for the moment," he said. "And that'll be another huge problem for me to resolve."

"Oh my gosh." She stared at him in outrage and shock. "But that is so wrong."

"It absolutely is so wrong," he confirmed. "And, of course, now she's nowhere to be found. You haven't seen her, have you?"

"No, no, not at all," she muttered, staring at him before glancing around.

Jenny's shock and dismay echoed his own feelings all over again. "So, no idea where she would have gone?"

She shook her head. "No, she always comes home. She's always been the lady of the manor, and, in order to be the lady of the manor," she noted, "you have to be in residence."

He smiled at that. "Agreed, and that makes sense. It also says an awful lot about how she looked at this property as being hers and her source of income, regardless of the damage she did to it and to us."

"I've never …" Then she stopped.

He looked at her, questioning. She frowned, and he knew she was thinking something over. "It's really not the time to hold back anything." She stared at him, but there was a stiffness in her gaze. He added, "I understand that you're worried about what's going to happen to you in the future." She winced at that, and he nodded. "Because you were promised a place here until the end of your days, weren't you?"

"Yes," she replied, "although Johanna hasn't mentioned it lately."

"That's because she sold it," he snapped. "And, no, you and me and Crystal and Grandpa didn't come into that equation."

Jenny's gaze hardened, and she nodded. "Right, so just because Alexander made that promise, and Johanna was right there with him, doesn't mean she'll honor it. And, if he passes on, she doesn't have to."

Ashton added, "But I do."

"Yes, but you didn't make that original promise," she pointed out, her gaze searching.

He smiled because he knew this fierce-eyed lady so well. "No, but, as long as I keep this place, you have a home here," he told her, with a smile, "which will be a challenge because of everything that's happened. I can't guarantee you that I'll hang on to the property. That's obviously the next issue. If we get sued for all the crap that Grandma has done, and she can't pay Oliver back, then it's pretty well a slam dunk that everything we have put into this property is gone," he explained. "So, as much as I would like to say you absolutely have a home here, I cannot because I may not have a home here either."

She stared at him hard, her jaw slacking. "Good God," she whispered, "the tangled web we weave."

"Well, some of us," he muttered. "Some of us apparently thought this was just a big joke, an endless bank account to pull money from. And that is the issue for all of us now because Grandma wasn't thinking of anybody else but herself, just her and her gambling issues."

"And is it even gambling at this point?" Jenny asked.

He frowned at her and asked, "What else could it be?"

"Well, if she sold the place, she'll need running money and a new place. So, I'm not sure how much of it's even about gambling anymore as much as it's the need to have something to leave with and to live on. I don't know how far she thinks half-a-million dollars would get her or how far she thinks she can run with that. But most people would recognize that it's not really enough to do a whole lot with, not in this day and age."

"It also says," he pointed out, "that she has no idea how much money it takes to look after a property like this."

Jenny nodded. "It's been one of the constant arguments between Johanna and Alexander. The fact that he always put the money into the property and not into her pocket, which has been one of their biggest issues throughout all the time I've been here," she shared. "If there's been an argument I have listened to a thousand times, it's that one."

He nodded, then asked, "What about the twins? What have they been up to?"

She looked at him and frowned. "Honestly, I'm not sure. … They come in, they eat, and then they leave, but I don't know that they necessarily do anything. They consider themselves gamers."

"It figures," he muttered. "Are they gaming for entertainment, stress relief, or what?"

"I don't know, but it's all they talk about."

"Let me put it this way. Gaming is a lifestyle for those who make huge money, as some gamers do. Gaming to avoid having to get a job and to do other responsible things in life is not cool."

She smiled. "I think that was your grandfather's point of view as well. He was also very much of the thinking that they needed to find a way to support themselves. I know that was a discussion they had recently, but it didn't go all that well, and your grandpa was left kind of upset about it."

He looked at her and asked, "And when you say, *kind of upset* ..." She winced, and he stressed again, "Come on, Jenny. I know you don't want to say anything bad. However, we are way past that point now."

She sighed. "It feels like, no matter what I say, it'll sound like I'm turning on them. I'm not. I don't think they're criminal, just lazy. The twins have never educated themselves as to the world around them, and Alexander and Johanna let that happen. The twins had all these plans, which Alexander tried to help fund for a time, until he gave up on that too."

"I don't think I heard about any of that," Ashton said, turning to her.

"They had all kinds of ideas. They wanted to set up a bunch of online stores, you know, things that could be run from home without them having to put out too much work."

"So, they did have some intention somewhere along the line?"

She nodded. "I think so."

He walked over to the coffeepot, poured himself a cup, and headed into the office. With his grandfather alive and safely out of harm's way, recuperating in the hospital, he needed to connect with the lawyer and the bank to see what the next steps should be. Not to mention the sheriff.

Richard already knew, even if his worthless deputies didn't. As soon as Ashton sat down in the home office, he picked up the phone to call his lawyer. Ashton felt everything moved in slow motion, while he went into heavy damage control as he informed everybody about his grandfather being found and alive.

Anderson was not only shocked, he was stunned. "He's alive?"

"Yes, but he's in the hospital now. We are cautiously optimistic at this point, but it's a bit early to tell. I'm really hoping that he'll pull out of this, and we'll get a lot more years," he added. "But he also doesn't know the ins and outs of what has happened to him. And so he must recover from that as well."

"Jesus Christ," Anderson murmured.

"What's happening on your end?"

"So, the freeze is on your grandmother's newest account. And another account has been accessed, and we aren't exactly sure by whom."

"And?" Ashton was afraid to hear the answer.

"Another chunk of money missing."

He sat back and closed his eyes. "What the hell?"

"Yeah, that appears to be the common thing at the moment," Anderson noted. "So, I don't know that your grandmother did this one, but, of course, that's what we're assuming."

Just the way Anderson put that had Ashton opening his eyes and staring around the office. "When you say that, what does that mean?"

"While we don't think anybody else is involved, we have to consider that somebody else could be."

"I don't even want to think about any more involvement by others. We still have to figure out who kidnapped my grandfather."

"And you don't think it was the neighbor?"

"No, I don't think it was Oliver. I think Grandma saw him for easy cash, but somebody was trying to set him up to take the fall for holding Grandpa. But what do I know?" He groaned. "It appears something is still messed up, and we need to sort that out," he admitted. "Unfortunately, until my grandfather is fully awake, we won't get an update from him on any of this. I haven't had a chance to talk to him beyond letting him know that he was alive and that we were looking after him," he added.

"So, talking to my grandfather would be paramount, yet he was drugged, probably snuck up on from behind. He may have absolutely no information for us. Now the deputies did take Oliver in for questioning, but I really don't feel that he had anything to do with it, though it's pretty amazing that somebody could have gotten to his property and could have done this without Oliver knowing."

"Yeah, that does sound a little sketchy," Anderson agreed.

"I know, and I think that's why the deputies aren't sure they're buying Oliver's story. At the same time, I think he's quite panicked because he obviously knows they aren't taking his words seriously." Ashton sighed. "So that's another entirely different challenge we're facing. The sheriff is keeping Oliver at the moment while they try to sort it all out, but I don't know what that will entail." Ashton added, "He also has animals on his place, and I don't know if he has anybody to look after them."

Anderson snorted. "So you'll go over there and take care of them?"

"The animals aren't responsible for any of this," Ashton stated. "And that's not how we do things here."

There was silence, and then Anderson replied, "I know you haven't been here for a long time. Do you think the neighborhood is still the same? Because it seems to me that whatever the hell is going on in your world here now, something uglier has moved in."

"I don't know whether something uglier has moved in,

or it's always been here, and I just didn't see it. And, yes, I am fully aware that's a possibility."

Anderson laughed. "You and the rest of us," he muttered. "Let's find out what we need to know, and then we can start cleaning this up. Meanwhile, we do need to get some of this money sorted. We can't keep a lid on it for long."

"No, and we need that money back ASAP. We do have insurance, but I don't know that they'll cover all these losses."

"No, I'm not sure they will," Anderson agreed. "Somewhere along the line, somebody felt they would lose out."

"You mean, outside of my grandmother?" he asked, with a groan. "Because she definitely falls into that category."

"I always think of grandmothers as these tiny little ladies baking apple pies," his lawyer shared. "But yours seems to have blown that image completely out of the water."

"Because she is an anomaly in many ways," he noted. "And we've certainly seen her in both good times and bad, but, man, it's really bad times right now. That's also something I'll have to deal with when my grandpa is cognizant again. Right now though I'll phone Oliver and see if he can talk."

"What if he can't?"

"If he can't, I'll call Richard and see if I can set up a phone call with Oliver. Then I need to figure out what needs to be done at Oliver's place until he can get back home and can look after his own damn animals." And, with that, he disconnected and tried calling Oliver.

When Ashton got no answer, he called Richard.

When the sheriff came on the line, the man sounded exhausted. "He's still here and hasn't changed his story at all," Richard shared. "We haven't decided if we're keeping him."

"Well, you may not have decided if you're keeping him, but he has animals, and I need to know what chores I need to do."

"You're going to do them?" Richard asked.

Ashton replied in a resigned tone, "Look. I don't know what's going on here, but I've never had a problem with Oliver before. And, yes, there's a possibility that he might be behind this, but his animals don't need to suffer because of it. That's not the way we do things. Not to mention that my grandma ripped him off for half a mil."

There was a quiet sigh on the other end. "Well, there's that too. Hang on a second." Apparently he walked into a different room. And then he called out, "Oliver, I have Ashton on the phone here. He wants to know what animals need to be looked after at your place, since we haven't decided whether we're releasing you or not."

Ashton could barely hear the other side of the discussion going on.

Then Richard came back online strong. "Ashton, I'm putting you on Speakerphone."

Ashton began, "Oliver, I don't know what's going on. I don't know how long they're keeping you, but do you have animals that need to be fed and watered tonight?"

"Yes," Oliver replied. They discussed which animals and what they needed.

Ashton confirmed, "Okay, I'll head over there now."

There was a pause, and then Oliver, his voice awkward, said, "Thank you."

"Look. I don't think you had anything to do with my grandfather's kidnapping and incarceration, and I don't even know what the hell to say about my grandma at this point. But, all of that aside, your animals didn't have anything to do with anything. So let me go see that they're doing okay, alright."

And, with that, the call ended. Ashton headed out, determined to make sure that his neighbor's animals were at least doing okay, even if the rest of his family was falling apart.

CHAPTER 13

CRYSTAL HAD TO admit she was keeping an eye out in case Ashton came outside again. He'd looked world-weary and tired when he had dropped her off at the barn. As soon as she saw him step out and head toward her, she walked over and said, "Hey, you look like hell."

Khan bounced forward, giving Ashton a huge greeting.

He smiled at the dog's antics, as he cuddled Khan. "Thanks *so much*, Crystal."

She chuckled at the way he said it. "Well, I didn't really mean that as bad as it sounded."

"No, you meant it exactly the way it was. And that's okay."

"What are you up to now?" she asked, as he stopped halfway between the barn and the house.

He shook his head. "I was going to ride over, but I guess I'll just take the truck."

"Take the truck where?" she asked.

He started to walk, as she raced up beside him. "I have to go take care of Oliver's horses, and he has dogs, and we don't know if he'll be kept overnight at the jail," he shared. "So, I'll go fork them some hay, check on their water, and give the dogs some dry food. Oliver's not sure they'll eat and probably won't be very happy because they've been locked out because of all the first responders' presence. I want to take Khan with me." He whistled, and Khan came running and jumped into the back of the truck.

"Is Oliver okay with you being over there?" she asked.

"I talked to him and have an okay from him and the sheriff to do chores."

She nodded. "I'll come with you but will bring my dogs with us this time."

"You don't have to," he said, shooting her a sideways glance.

She opened the passenger door. "No, I don't. And, given the circumstances right now, you're right. I mean, his animals need to be looked after. And Piper and Joe have been left alone enough these last few days. They can sense the unrest, just like the rest of the animals. This will be good for them and Oliver's dogs too. Besides, Khan shouldn't get all the fun."

"I also don't think Oliver had anything to do with this," he added.

"I was thinking the same thing, but that leaves very little in the way of options as to who did have something to do with it."

"I know," he agreed. "I was hoping I could go back in and take another look at where Grandpa was being held and see if I might have missed something."

She didn't say anything but settled into the passenger side of the truck. When they got over there, she looked around and suggested, "Horse barn first?" They walked into the barn, dogs barking in a pasture to the side, several of the horses nickering. Oddly enough, Khan was also wandering nearby the main house, as if searching for something.

They both patted him, gave him some treats, and he walked around the barn, staying close but seriously interested in the house. Not the stables. Not farther back where the equipment was parked.

Ashton kept an eye on Khan while checking the horses' water, then grabbed the grain. Crystal's dogs, instead of following Khan around, stuck closer to her.

As Crystal grabbed a hay fork, she shared, "We're doing the right thing, and, with any luck, at least the animals will feel that life is continuing as normal, as it should."

He looked at her and asked, "How long ago did Max die?"

"Oh gosh. Last year, I think? Not all that long ago."

"Do you know what he died from?"

"Cancer," she said, "at least that's what the rumor was."

"Cancer?"

Something odd was in his tone that she was not getting. "Ask Oliver about it." She stared at him, and he was lost in his thoughts. "You don't think he had something to do with his brother's death, do you?"

He turned to her and shook his head. "No, I don't. I mean, unless somebody tells me that Max was murdered, then that would be something else entirely."

The rest of the time, they both worked in silence, taking care of the horses, putting water in the pens. Khan stuck around, watching them but staying close to the main house. Finishing off the chores, they both stepped out into the yard.

"So, the other issue," he began. "We know what happened with the Wilfords—that Sean was knocked down and they took the War Dog."

"Yes, and your point is?" Crystal asked.

"We got Khan back. We got Grandpa back. What we didn't find," he said, turning to frown at her, "was Sean."

She stopped in her tracks. "Surely that's not connected."

"I don't know," he replied, frowning at her. "Obviously we found Grandpa, and I'm delighted for that. But where the hell is Sean?"

She groaned. "And you feel responsible for that too, don't you?"

"No, I don't feel responsible," he corrected, as he walked closer, reached out, and cupped her face. "Yet I came here for the War Dog. I came here for Grandpa. I've got the dog. I've got Grandpa. We still have a big mystery as to where Grandma is hiding—or off doing whatever she's doing. And we still have to find Sean."

"Shouldn't the sheriff be doing that—finding Grandma and Sean? Don't you have enough problems to deal with already?"

"I don't like things that are not tied up in neat bows."

She smiled, leaned in, and whispered, "I'm really glad you're back. I mean, things were *so boring* before you got here."

He burst out laughing, dropped a kiss on her forehead, and muttered, "You knew I was coming back."

"Yeah, I knew you were coming back," she quipped, "but not when, and I sure as hell was getting damn tired of waiting."

He shot her a look and shrugged. "I did say five to six years."

"Yeah, and it feels like I've been counting every day since five years came and went," she muttered, half under her breath.

He nodded. "Me too, but the recovery was a whole lot worse than anticipated. And, I have to admit, I was a little worried about how you would handle it."

She shot him a look.

"And I know Grandpa told you about it, so that's obviously not an issue."

She snorted. "Maybe not an issue," she began, "yet I didn't know that much. I mean, in terms of details. He told me that you'd been injured, that you were in rehab, and that you apparently didn't want any of us to show up."

"It's not that I didn't want any of you to show up," he corrected. "I just needed to get into a better state first."

"That makes sense too, knowing how hardheaded you are," she snapped, "but it was pretty damn hard on us. I kept getting every detail from Grandpa, but it was always secondhand."

"And yet you sent me birthday cards, Christmas notes," he teased, "all very impersonal."

"Sure, it was always like that. We shared a kiss and nothing else. Everything you did was impersonal," she pointed out.

"Except for the last time," he noted, with a twinkle in his eye.

"Yeah, except for our last *reunion*, six years ago. And you saying you would be back for me, but then you didn't come back, so what the hell was I supposed to do with that?"

"You were supposed to move on with your life. And have a chance to find somebody to move on *with* in your life," he explained. "I was trying to give you time and space. After the accident, Grandpa told me that you weren't dating anybody. So, I worked harder than I even thought possible to try and get myself whole again, just so maybe I could be here before you found somebody else."

"What else did he tell you?" she asked playfully.

"He told me about your stepbrother asking to marry you."

"Yeah," she grumbled, "that was a shock and a half. And I still don't quite understand what was going on in his mind."

"I suspect what was in his mind was the thought that you might end up with part of the property," he suggested. "John's always thinking ahead if it suits him."

She stopped to consider that. "Jesus, does anybody do anything for the right reasons?"

"Sometimes," he replied, with a cheerful grin in her direction. Just then came a sharp bark from Khan.

He turned to Khan, staring at the dog.

Khan barked again, spinning to stare at the house. Piper raced over to stand beside Khan whereas Joe stood at Crystal's side.

Something bothered the dog, and, even as Ashton stared closer, the hackles on the back of Khan's shoulders slowly rose. The growl in his throat deepened.

He stepped forward, placed an arm around her.

She muttered, "Okay, I don't like the sound of that."

"Neither do I," he confirmed.

"Oliver's dogs are in the back pasture," she noted.

Sure enough, Ashton heard dogs howling in the back. "So, they sure don't like something either." He nodded. "Okay, we're done with the horses." He called Khan over, and he came but reluctantly. Ashton snapped a lead onto Khan's collar and announced, "We need to go check this out."

"Are you sure?" she asked in a quiet tone. "For all you know, whoever is involved in Grandpa's kidnapping is there too."

"And maybe Sean is there."

"Given his reaction," she said, pointing to Khan, "we

don't know what's going on."

He turned to her. "You're right. I want you to go back to the truck and stay there."

"Yeah, *no*. Last time you left me with the horses, Oliver came up behind me and scared the bejesus out of me," she shared. "No more spooky stuff like that. I'm coming with you."

He frowned, obviously not liking it.

She shook her head. "Too bad. Let's go." With that, she strode off, with much less confidence than she hoped she was showing, as she headed toward the front door of Oliver's house. They stepped inside and were met with an odd and eerie silence.

She looked at him and asked, "Weren't you in here before?"

"Sure. Same time you were. And then we came out when the deputies got here."

"Right. So, we were in the living room, but we weren't anywhere else."

"No, we weren't." He walked around the main floor and called out, "Everything looks okay here. Nothing out of place."

"Let's go check on the dogs out back. Maybe that's the whole purpose of Khan's disgruntlement."

Khan's nose was on the ground, focused, sniffing around.

She watched him and asked, "Is he a search and rescue dog?"

"No, but all dogs have an innate ability to do so much more than we do. Believe me that I'm keeping an eye on Khan." As he went farther through the house and into the kitchen, he stopped and looked at her.

Checking out the whole mess, she nodded. "Looks like somebody was in here, making food."

He glanced around and replied, "Or it's leftover from yesterday."

She shook her head. "That teakettle," she noted, walking over and placing a hand gently on the side, "it's still warm." She heard the stillness come over him as he nodded.

"Now that changes things." He walked over, checked the teakettle for himself, and then asked, "The dogs, were they out there before? I haven't been around here much, so you would know more than I do."

"No," she replied, shaking her head. "They were locked in the yard, and now they appear to be out in a pasture set back from the yard, and they are still barking."

Whether it was at them or at something else, she couldn't tell. Now, as far as he was concerned, with all the animals upset, definitely something was going on.

He looked down at Khan, still glaring at the world around him, as if liking nothing here. He'd stopped growling, but it was obvious he was still not happy. As he studied the dog's actions, she walked over and checked on the dogs out the window.

"They're racing back and forth at the gate, but I'm not sure what's got them disturbed." Then again her own were not happy either, racing around the two of them as if also unsure of what was happening.

"With Oliver taken from here and all the activity with the deputies and the ambulance," he explained, "any and all of that could have had a huge effect on the dogs. It doesn't look like they're starving, but it also doesn't look like they have access to their regular food." He frowned. "Oliver told me to just put out food on the back deck for them."

"Which means, as far as Oliver's concerned, the dogs should be out back," she declared, turning to him. "And that, along with the hot teakettle, implies that somebody else has been here." She looked at him and asked, "You don't think the deputies would have made themselves at home or would have moved the animals?"

"No. They may have moved the animals, but they were already outside. So short of their having to go into the backyard, it's not likely they moved the animals at all. And they wouldn't have made a cup of tea. … Plus, I'm pretty sure they've been gone for a while, and there's no sign of any vehicles around here."

"So, whoever is here didn't bring a vehicle," she began, "or didn't park it where we could see it." He nodded, and she could tell that, whatever this was, Ashton didn't like it at all.

"Stay here."

"No," she snapped. He frowned at her, and she shook her head. "Not happening. This time, you need to make sure that I stay with you. I don't like anything about this."

"Neither do I," he agreed, "but I want to check if a vehicle is outside because that would tell us if anybody is here."

"Not if they walked," she pointed out. "I know we can ride over here, but it's not that far of a walk either, particularly if they go kitty-corner and don't follow the truck tracks that we followed earlier. That's what took us a little bit longer."

"You're right," he agreed, as he studied the area.

"So, what we don't know is whether we have somebody else here or not."

"Well, we do know that we've surprised somebody," he pointed out, "and that is a concern."

Just then someone spoke behind them, and he stiffened, recognizing the voice. He turned slowly to see Jenny standing there, with a long-ass rifle in her hands.

ASHTON STARED AT Jenny and saw what he'd been missing all this time. He felt the pain and shock coming from Crystal right beside him. Khan growled low and deep in the back of his throat. Piper walked over casually to Jenny, of course they were long time family so Piper and Joe might not understand who really the viper was here.

Jenny turned the rifle in his direction.

Ashton placed a hand on Khan's shoulders, the movement telling him to wait. Ashton's gaze remained locked on Jenny. "Did you really do that to Grandpa?" he asked, calm and cool. After what happened to Grandpa and his grandmother wreaking havoc on his life, nothing surprised him much. But, even after all that, this betrayal cut deep.

Jenny shrugged. "I didn't have much choice. I am glad you found him though. I wasn't sure what to do when the ketamine caused him such a problem."

"What did you expect it to do?"

"I wanted to talk with him and make him see sense."

"What kind of sense?"

She hesitated, then shared, "He had already told me that the property was broke and that there was no money for me anymore. He went on to say that I wouldn't get a pension and that I wouldn't get a home to stay in. He told me that I could blame his wife for that, but, honest to God, I thought he was just lying."

Ashton snorted. "He wasn't."

"Oh, I know that now, but only after you told me the truth did I realize how wrong I was," she shared, her hands trembling slightly. There was a hitch in her voice as she realized just how drastic her own actions had become.

He stared at her and sighed. "So, you kidnapped him and got him upstairs in that loft room, all on your own, without any help?"

"I didn't say that," she stated. "I didn't say that at all, but I didn't have much help."

Ashton shook his head. "The boys helped you, didn't they?" When she remained silent, Ashton continued. "You bribed them too with owning this land, didn't you?"

Jenny snapped, "I was promised a home here forever. I was looking after my own retirement. I took a lesson from Johanna on that."

Ashton was so disappointed, didn't want to know the worst about his family. Yet it had to be faced head-on. "And what about Oliver?"

"Oliver doesn't know a thing," she muttered, with a headshake. "And I don't know where all this goes right now," she added, "but I can tell you that he doesn't know anything about it."

"So you drugged Grandpa, then had the twins put him in a truck and drive him over to Oliver's place?"

Jenny stared at him and smiled. "I may be old, but I'm not weak. I may be poor, but I am resilient. Oliver had come over to the Nelson home and had quite a fight with Alexander about buying the property in dispute again. So Oliver stomped off back home but called me almost immediately, asked me over, wanted to chat because he was having a hard time."

Ashton asked, "Why? About his brother passing, about

Alexander, about the property?"

"Oliver's got heart trouble," she said, "takes certain medications, was worried about all this fighting and what it would do to his heart. He knew I used to be a nurse, so I guess he just wanted some reassurance that he would be okay. I made him some tea, settled him down. Oliver mentioned he still had some ketamine from his brother's illness. He didn't know what to do with it, so I told him that I could dispose of it for him."

"And?" Ashton asked, frowning at her.

"I returned home and found Alexander half collapsed on the floor. I thought about moving him into the downstairs bedroom and but then realized I had a golden opportunity. I now had Max's leftover ketamine. So I gave Alexander a dose, according to his weight. After all, that was part of my repertoire when I worked as a nurse."

"Along with kidnapping?" Ashton asked.

"I didn't have to kidnap Alexander. I just had to move him," she snapped, her tone sharp. "I did enlist the twins to load him into their truck and drive him over to Oliver's barn, but John refused to climb the ladder into the loft. Idiot. Did you know that John is scared of heights?" She harrumphed. "So Glenn got Alexander up the ladder and into that back room up there."

"And how did you know about the hidden room?" Ashton asked, as he stared at the woman who he didn't even know anymore. His home had become one giant petri dish of betrayal.

She smiled. "Because Max and I were lovers for a very long time." He stared at her, and she nodded. "I know, he's a lot younger than I am, ... *was* younger than I am." Her voice broke at that. "But he was a good man. Only a few people knew about us, thought the two of us were oddities, and maybe we were. We preferred to be alone more than anything. Kind of like the twins," she stated, with a nod toward Crystal.

"Max and I were going to move in together. He wanted to buy a big chunk of your grandpa's place years ago, just for us, but Alexander backed out of it again and again. At one point Johanna was willing to sell it to him, and we all knew about her gambling. Max talked her into selling it to him so she could clear her debts, but Alexander blocked it once more." Jenny sighed. "Johanna didn't know that I had anything to do with Alexander going missing. She just knew that he was missing."

"So you were exacting revenge on both of them?" Crystal asked.

"Maybe I was."

"But Ashton was taking care of it," Crystal told her, frowning. Piper nudged her hand with her nose, the tone of voice upsetting her. Crystal instinctively dropped her hand to caress the top of her head, wanting to give reassurance but needing the contact with her dogs herself.

Jenny gave a one-arm shrug and sighed. "Oliver doesn't know anything about my doing this," she admitted, with a shrug, "but it was certainly convenient for Johanna to sell him the land."

"You didn't tell Oliver it wasn't hers to sell?" Ashton asked, frowning.

"I wasn't thinking of anything at that point, except looking for a way out myself."

"So, you knew before I even told you that the place was mine?"

"Yes, I knew. Alexander told me all about Johanna's

misadventures and how you were going broke yourself, trying to hold it all together for them."

"*Great.* So, he cared enough about you to share the truth, yet you put him in a loft to die?"

"He let this whole thing happen," Jenny shouted, tears running down her face now. "I'd gotten into a bit of a fix when I locked him up. I figured, if I just left him there, he would expire naturally," she noted with a sigh, resignation in her tone, not looking at either of them. "His body would have been found somewhere along the line—in twenty-odd years when the place either burnt to the ground or when someone found the little love nest that Max and I had together."

Then she stood taller and declared, "At some point in time, you make a choice, and that choice commits you to something that you never thought you would ever do. After Max died, I began to realize that I had nothing.

"Then your grandfather told me how I wouldn't get the pension or the home he had promised me all these years, and everything disintegrated inside. Nothing like realizing you have worked an entire lifetime for one family, only to have that family go broke because of a selfish bitch who stole from a good man, leaving the rest of us with absolutely nothing," she explained, staring at Ashton. "Can you imagine that?" she asked, pain filling her words.

Ashton nodded, realizing the extent of it. "And you made that life-changing decision when Grandpa told you, didn't you?"

"I don't know that I made the decision right then," she hedged, waving the gun, "but the opportunity presented itself, after Oliver took off and needed calming down, and then I found Alexander, out cold on the floor, when I returned home."

Ashton asked her, "So, you were here earlier, inside Oliver's home, even with the deputies out and about?"

"I often come over here on my own," she muttered, "just needing space. I would sit in that room where I spent so much time with Max. It was my safe space, just a quiet spot where I could feel love and could be loved and could remember what it was like when he was alive. His death caused me so much pain," she whispered.

"And nobody knew about these visits?"

"Exactly. I don't even know that Oliver knew about our love affair. I mean, there's been times when he may have thought so, but I know Max never told him, so I didn't really know how much he understood."

"Maybe he didn't have to be told. Maybe he figured it out for himself," Crystal suggested.

"Maybe." Jenny smiled, a pained look on her face. "If Oliver did know about us, I would want to know. We could remember Max together. Losing him was so hard, so very painful, and I didn't have any way to grieve. It was not just the loss of Max. It was the loss of that future we had together, a home, a space of our own, a place to retire, just the two of us. If Max were alive today, we would have been happy."

"Would he have wanted this?" Ashton asked.

"No, he would not, but he can't do anything about it now. He's gone and I'm here. Nothing to my name, left holding the bag. An empty bag. As much as we were together, there was a hole in him too. Max was all about getting the property back together, and, at the time, Oliver was the one looking for a chance to get away and to have a different life, a separate life. It's funny in a certain way."

"Why is that?" he asked.

"After Max died, Oliver basically picked up his brother's dream and wanted to have the property back together again. Yet your grandpa refused to consider it and was being difficult, while everything just blew up all at the same time in my life," she pointed out. "I'm not proud of the part I played in it, which is also why I'm thrilled Alexander survived."

"No thanks to you," Ashton stated.

"So, what's with the rifle?" Crystal asked, taking a step closer to Ashton. "Why are you doing this now?"

"Because I need to leave," she snapped, her tone sharp. "I mean, the kidnapping alone will cause me trouble, but then there's the rest of it."

Ashton stared at her, and suddenly it all clicked. "You're the one stealing from the company, aren't you?"

She smiled at him. "Well, it certainly wasn't my idea originally. Yet I realized Johanna was doing that and how you were struggling to save it all. Johanna was the reason I wouldn't have a home, and then you told me about all you were doing to save it. And, of course, I *would* have a home if you could do something, but I'd already taken a big chunk of money, and you could do nothing about that."

Jenny sighed. "By then I also knew that there was no way to recover from what I'd already done to Alexander and no way to go back to that nice planned retirement that I deserved after so many years here, especially not with your grandmother being such a crazy old coot," she explained, shaking her head. "I didn't have a choice. I had already gone too far," she admitted.

She cocked the gun, looked at them both, and stated, "I really don't have any choice now."

CHAPTER 14

"AND GRANDMA? WHERE is she?" Crystal asked.

Jenny frowned at Crystal, then shrugged. "You should be worried about yourself."

"Where is she?" Ashton asked, his tone angrier than ever.

"I don't know," Jenny snapped. "I told her to run as far and as fast as she could, but she's not very ..." Jenny shrugged. "No offense, but she's not very smart. She's not very cognizant of the larger picture. And she's been running a con for so long that she doesn't know what's going on in her life anymore."

Ashton snorted. "But you know, don't you?"

"Maybe I do."

"Care to share where Grandma is?" Ashton asked.

"Well, I think she's probably holed up in a hotel, trying to figure out what happened to her life. She's alternating between grief and ranting and raving about her circumstances," she added, with a shrug. "I've been watching her take advantage of that old man for years, then him coming up with excuses for her behavior, while this place was going to pieces around me. I started to doubt that I would ever get the opportunity to enjoy that peaceful retirement they promised me," she shared.

"After Max passed away," she added, as tears choked the back of her throat, "I realized that, if I didn't do something to save myself, I would lose everything."

Ashton just sighed and shook his head at her. "You do know that you're losing everything now anyway, right?"

She gave him a bitter smile. "You aren't in control anymore."

"At least, according to you, I'm not."

"I have the gun, so I have the control now," she snapped. "Your grandfather used to always say that whoever holds the weapons in life are the ones who make the decisions for everybody else. He certainly proved that time and time again."

"Did you really hate him so much?" Crystal asked, staring at her. "Was he really so awful that you had to do that to him and just leave him to die?"

"I really hated doing that," she said. "And I didn't *plan* any of that. It just seemed like an opportunity that came up in the moment." She sighed, looking at Crystal. "You're young and naïve, but you'll learn. Sometimes opportunities come, and you just make the best of them in the moment. I get that, for you, everything is all about having the life you want. You were planning on moving out, weren't you?"

"I was because I was giving up on this guy ever coming back," she admitted, as Jenny's gaze went from Crystal to Ashton and back again.

Jenny laughed. "Well, hell, I didn't see that coming."

Ashton shrugged. "We connected before I left, six years ago, but then I had my accident, and life was not very kind to me from that point onward. I didn't want her waiting on me, when I could potentially not end up in very good shape."

"That wasn't your decision to make though," Jenny snapped, frowning at him.

"As Crystal has also told me," he noted, with a happy smile. "So we very much want to have the life that we had planned." He eyed Jenny. "That you're holding a gun on us, plus the fact that our grandmother is lost and confused, not even sure what she's supposed to be doing, is another big issue."

Jenny shrugged. "Well, Johanna's a user and an abuser, so I don't have any sympathy for her."

"Maybe not," Crystal noted, "but are you really prepared to take us out, to murder us in cold blood, when we've done nothing to you?"

Jenny stared at her, then shook her head. "But, if I don't, there's no freedom for me either." She tilted her head as she studied them. "It's a good idea, the two of you together. It never even occurred to me. Not even once. Did your grandpa know?"

"To a certain extent, yes," Crystal replied. "He was the one who kept telling me to stick around. Ashton was just more stubborn than any of them."

Ashton smiled. "Meanwhile Grandpa was busy telling me that I needed to get back on my feet. That Crystal wasn't finding any good men, so she was still waiting for me."

Jenny shook her head. "Of course he was. And, from his perspective, I can see that was probably something he really, really wanted."

Ashton didn't say anything.

Crystal watched as he studied every move Jenny made, knowing that the upset old woman, rifle and all, was no match for all that Ashton had been through. Crystal just hoped to God that nobody would get hurt. Crystal sighed. "You know, Jenny, no good endings, no happy endings can come out of this, right?"

"I know," Jenny conceded. "So, I'm looking to see what the biggest, happiest ending could possibly be for me," she shared, staring at them. "And the only thing I can think of is that I need to leave."

"With the money that you stole from Grandpa's accounts?" Ashton asked.

Jenny flashed an angry look at Ashton. "Like the promise of a home that he stole from me? What do you expect me to do, Ashton? I am way past the age of working full-time, way past the age of everybody ordering me around. And I've changed, I admit it."

She was getting hoarse from all the talking. "I changed after I lost Max," she stated, "and, for a little bit, I wondered about connecting with Oliver, but he wasn't the same. He wasn't my Max. They were similar. God, they were similar," she muttered. "Yet it wasn't the same. And he couldn't love me like Max did. And that was, … that's the thing I miss the most."

"Of course," Ashton agreed. "And there is nothing quite like that loss."

She sniffled and nodded. Then she glared at him. "And yet everybody was happy to take that away from us."

"No," Ashton whispered, "nobody took it away from you. However, life is not easy, and, when you lose the love of your life to cancer, nobody is to blame. I also don't believe that this world is out to make us suffer either. Yet it's still hard to recover from lost loves, losing a limb, financial hardships. I get it. I get it all."

"Yeah," she muttered, "you get it. But it doesn't matter now. I still did what I did. And there's no happy ending for me."

"You have to tell us where Grandma is," Crystal repeated.

Ashton added, "And I've got another question for you. Do you know where Sean is?"

She winced and glared at Ashton. "He's here."

"And what were you going to do with him?"

"I don't know," she admitted. "I didn't think that far ahead. Grabbing Alexander was something I didn't expect to do either," she noted. "And then, when I did, I didn't know how to make peace with any of it."

Crystal cried out, "Stop with the victim card. Where is Sean? Is he okay? Why is he here? What does he have to do with any of this?"

"I don't think he looks very good," Jenny muttered. "I should have stuck it out longer, Ashton, knowing you were coming back. But Alexander told me that Johanna had taken everything and that there was just no money anymore."

"And he was right, she did," Ashton confirmed. "As you know, I've been trying rather hard to make things right. Given enough time, I could have paid back all of Grandma's theft."

Jenny nodded slowly. "But I didn't give you time, did I?"

"No, you didn't," he said.

"And, for that, I'm very sorry because the outcome now is something that I don't know how to deal with." Jenny frowned at him, her shoulders slumping.

He sighed. "You know this can't go on."

"I know," she admitted. As she moved back a step, toward the door, he lunged suddenly, ripping the shotgun from her hands.

She glared at him, then stared down at the floor, resignation on her face. "Why don't you just shoot me?" she whispered. "It would be the easiest all around."

"I can't do that," he stated firmly. "No easy outs for you."

"No," she muttered, "instead I'm going to jail for however long because of this."

"Well, first, we need a few more answers," he said, holding the shotgun against his leg.

"Like what?"

"Like why the hell did you go after Sean?"

She frowned at him, grimacing. "Your grandmother and I were sitting in the park, near the coffee shop in town, making plans for her to escape," she began. "Sean came out of the wooded area nearby, on his walking sticks, with his dog. I thought surely he didn't hear us. Even if he did, surely he didn't really understand what was going on, but when I stood up to leave, he crossed my path, muttering something to me about creating problems, about starting things I had no business getting into. I just looked at him, and I knew. I just knew that he understood what I'd done, what I'd set in motion." She shook her head.

"I didn't know what to do about it. I tried to talk to him, and he did listen. Then he told me how he'd spent a long time understanding people, and the ones he didn't see coming were the most dangerous. He made a couple other comments, and that was enough for me to realize that, if he stuck around, he would be another big issue."

"Where is he?" Ashton asked.

Jenny stared at him, her jaw clenching.

"If you killed him," Ashton noted, trying hard to not say anything he would regret, "there are no options going forward. *That* I can tell you."

"He's alive … maybe." Jenny sighed. "He's alive," she

repeated, her voice cracking, "not necessarily because of me, but more because I didn't know what else to do with him."

"He's been missing for several days," Crystal pointed out. "We need to find him soon."

Jenny shrugged, turning to Ashton. "When you came after the dog, I just … I didn't even know what to say." She stared down at Khan, with both Piper and Joe flanking him now. An odd stillness in their postures as if understanding something serious was going on but unsure what to do about it. "Sean doesn't even know that I'm the one responsible."

Crystal asked her, "Is that what you're looking for? Confession? Some way to pay for all the pain you've caused? All the heartache?"

"I didn't mean it, … not any of it," Jenny muttered.

Crystal sighed. "No, you didn't mean it, but you did it. You put a lot of people through an awful lot of heartache. Now, where the hell is Sean?" Crystal asked.

Jenny groaned. "He's somewhere close."

Ashton waved a hand about. "You better take us to him. That's the only way that I can see anything positive for you coming out of this," Ashton shared. "Full cooperation is the only card you've got left to play. I don't know if that will save your ass, but telling us everything is the only chance you've got. If we get everybody back where they belong, we can start dealing with the consequences of their actions. For example, my grandmother does not get off scot-free in this."

"She will though. You know that. Alexander will see to it."

"Yeah, well, my grandfather is no longer in control," Ashton announced. "And that must be considered."

Jenny shrugged, her tone fatalistic. "It won't matter. Nothing ever matters. Everybody makes their own decisions, leaving people like me behind in the dirt. Oliver, Max, Glenn, John."

"Do you think Max left you behind?" Crystal asked. "Do you think he chose to die of cancer? I bet he didn't want that either." She stared at Jenny. "Do you think he really wanted to see you like this?"

"I know he didn't, but neither did he leave anything to help me get out of this."

"Is that why you're angry?" Crystal asked, frowning at her. "Because he didn't leave you anything in his will? Did you expect him to?"

"I don't know. I didn't necessarily expect him to, but I hadn't expected our relationship to end so soon, to come crashing down," she muttered. "When it did, I didn't know how to handle it. I lost him, and that alone was just horrific. I don't know if anybody can even understand that."

Ashton added, "Just as his death was fast for you, maybe it was fast for Max. Some people think they have more time before they deal with the harsh realities of getting wills in place, powers of attorney, medical directives, and such."

Jenny shook her head. "Max knew he had cancer. He should have acted already to set aside something for me in the future."

"We can all understand that, yet we don't know when we are gonna die," Crystal interjected, walking over to Jenny. "However, the choices you made afterward are not what anybody will understand."

Jenny nodded, then looked over at Ashton. "Why don't you just shoot me? It'll save so much in so many ways."

"I cannot do that. Not for no reason, not when I have the situation under control," he replied. "You lost that opportunity when I took the weapon away from you."

"Well, give it back then," she snapped, glaring at him. "Let me die in peace. Let me go to Max. That would be a kindness."

"And yet what kindness did you give to anybody else?" he asked Jenny. "What kindness did you give my grandfather, who spent five days tied up and drugged? Did he wake up at all?"

She nodded. "He did, but he was pretty out of it for a long time," she whispered. "And then he woke up again."

"And?" Ashton prodded her.

"I just … I just kept feeding him drugs because I didn't know what else to do."

Ashton muttered, "If he dies …"

She looked at him and nodded. "Yeah, I know. If he dies, it's murder."

"Absolutely." Ashton looked over at Crystal.

Crystal nodded. "Call the authorities. We must find Sean and figure out where Grandma is."

Ashton turned to Jenny. "Take us to Sean."

She frowned, and they could see that stubbornness rising again in Jenny. He shook his head and yelled, "Enough! Show us where you left Sean so we don't have to start tearing apart Max's place. Then we can at least tell the sheriff that you cooperated. And, if everybody lives through this," he added, "maybe you get an easier ending."

"My ending won't be easy," Jenny argued, staring at him. "Everybody will hate me. It's not as if I have any life left."

"You made the decision to do all this," he pointed out, focusing on her. "Sometimes those decisions are beyond what people can live with. I don't know what kind of reception you expected, but this isn't something most people will understand." When her bottom lip trembled, he nodded. "And you and I both know it."

She glared at him, then her shoulders slumped. "Yeah, … you're right. Fine."

"What did you do to Sean?"

"Nothing he didn't deserve. He was being a mouthy jerk the whole time he was preaching to me." When he looked at her, she shrugged. "Okay, I don't have what it takes to look after him, and I sure as hell hope you take him away because all I can say is he's been caterwauling constantly."

And, with that, she turned and headed back outside to the smaller barn, the equipment barn. When she got to the far side of it, she led the way to the back corner, where a ladder was.

They followed her there, moving cautiously, now hearing somebody yelling for help.

Jenny glared in that direction. "See? I told you. He's up at the top of the loft."

Ashton balked. "The twins helped you with Sean too?"

She refused to answer his question and added, "You can go get him."

He hesitated and then shook his head. "I think you need to show me." She glared at him, and he shook his head. "I still don't quite understand what's going on here, and I'm not prepared to let you walk away from here. You need to show us exactly where Sean is."

"You can hear him," she said in a mocking tone, pointing up to the loft.

Something about her mannerisms bothered him. "Yeah, I hear him," he agreed, not moving.

She hesitated, then relented. "Fine." She climbed the ladder into the loft. Then walked toward the room where the screams and hollers were coming from, but she stopped abruptly, glanced back, and shrugged. "Sorry, Ashton. I can't do it."

Then she bolted off to the left and threw herself from the top of the loft, hitting the cement floor below.

ASHTON SWORE AS he looked over the edge, and it was easy to see it was too late, from her broken body and from the pool of blood slowly seeping outward.

Crystal closed her eyes, her bottom lip trembling, then determinedly headed to where the yells were coming from. Ashton quickly caught up with her. When they got to the small room, they saw a padlock on the outside, the lock on the top part of the doorframe. Yet it wasn't closed. No combination nor key needed.

Khan started barking, jumping up against the wooden door, pawing at it, whining now.

Ashton reached up, twisted off the lock, and opened the door.

As he stepped inside, Khan bolted forward and jumped all over the man lying on the makeshift bed, which appeared to be a set of reeds on the floor with a couple old mattresses on top. The man on the bed started to sob, as Khan licked his face, clearly overjoyed.

Working around the wiggly Khan, they finally managed to untie Sean, and, when they helped him to sit up, he groaned and fell back in pain. Crystal bent and started rubbing his hands and legs to get the circulation moving again. Ashton squatted in front of him, gently pulling back Khan. Ashton smiled at him and said, "Hey, you must be

Sean."

The other man gave him a heartfelt look. "Yes, dear God, yes." He looked down at Khan and muttered, "I can't believe he found me."

"Well, it wasn't for lack of trying," Ashton replied. "A whole set of circumstances haven't been right for too long."

The old man looked at him and nodded. "None of it's been right. I don't know what the hell happened with that woman, but she's off her rocker."

"Well, right now," he said, "Jenny's dead."

He looked at him in shock. "What?"

Ashton motioned to the space outside the small room. "She just threw herself off to the concrete below."

He stared at him. "I guess I'm supposed to feel sorry for her, but I don't feel anything, except maybe deprived of the vengeance I sorely want."

"I can understand that," Ashton shared. "Believe me that your desire for vengeance probably kept you going all this time."

He closed his eyes, nodded, adding, "And seeing Khan again. … You sure she's dead?"

"I haven't been down to the concrete to double-check it," Ashton replied, "but that will be next. I wanted to see what condition you were in and what you needed for assistance."

Sean shuffled upward, trying to sit upright on his own. "I would do better with a wheelchair. My legs have suffered quite a bit these last few days."

Ashton glanced around to see the evidence of his incarceration and nodded. "She really had a problem, didn't she?"

"Oh my God, you have no idea. That woman was just bad news all around." Sean stared at him and shook his head.

"I went to war and fought people who were absolutely horrific, but I never ever saw anything like her."

Ashton didn't have a whole lot to offer to make him feel any better, but he did try to explain. "What she told us was that you overheard something that could cause her some trouble."

"She mentioned that, but I don't even know who she is," he complained, staring at him. "And honestly, I don't know who you are either."

Ashton chuckled, and Crystal made sure he recognized her, then made quick work of the introductions.

"So, I'm at Oliver's place?"

"Yes," Ashton confirmed, "you are, and that woman had my grandfather in another building across the way—not that his accommodations were any easier or better than yours."

He stared at Ashton and asked, "Did he make it?"

"Well, he's alive, but he's in the hospital," Ashton replied. "The jury is still out on that at the moment."

"I'm voting he makes it," Crystal interjected. "That's my grandfather, so the alternative is not acceptable."

Sean looked at her, nodded slowly, and said, "I have no way to thank you, but I'm damn glad you found me. I wasn't sure how much longer I could keep this up." Sean looked from one to the other, tears in his eyes, and he whispered, "Thank you, thank you so much."

She leaned over, gave him a big hug, and said, "You are most welcome, and I am so sorry for this madwoman's crazy plan that she thought would work but was doomed from the onset."

"I don't even know what she was trying to do," he said, with a sigh. "It seemed like everything went wrong when I lost this guy." He leaned over, grabbing Khan and pulling him tight. He looked at the two people with him and asked, "Where did you find him?"

"We got him back from the couple who knocked you down and stole Khan from you," Ashton replied.

His eyes filled. "Nobody would believe me when I told them what happened. Like the deputies, they all but accused me of lying, just making it up." He shook his head. "I got to the point where I started to wonder if I had made it up."

"No, it happened all right. I found the couple with the War Dog, and, with any luck, you and Khan can have many happy years together."

Tears came to Sean's eyes again, and he sniffled, trying to brush them away. "I don't think I've ever cried this much in my long life. I don't know how I'll ever repay you."

"No thanks are required," Crystal stated. "It's partly our family who did this to you, so we should be apologizing to you."

He looked over at her and shook his head. "But *you* didn't do it."

"No, that's not my style," she confirmed, with a twinkle in her eye. "If I have to tie up a guy to get my way, I think I'll just keep looking. Now you, of course," she teased, "you're kind of a cutie, and if you were just a little bit younger, I might have gone for you." With that, she leaned over and gave him a kiss on the forehead.

"Lady, you do realize you just kissed an old fart who's been lying in his own piss for days?"

"Of course I do, and I'm so dang glad to see you that I'll do it again!"

He looked at her for a moment, and then his face wrinkled up, and he burst out laughing, easing any tension in the air. When he could settle down again, he smiled. "Thank you for that. It's been a long few days. She wouldn't talk to me. She wouldn't tell me what she was doing. Mostly endless silence with no explanation," he told them, building on the same bewilderment he had felt earlier. "I just didn't even know what to do anymore."

"Well, the good thing is, you are free now," Ashton stated. "I'm just wondering how she got you up there."

He sighed. "She had two idiots helping her, but she was nagging them the whole way up here, telling them they weren't doing it right. It took both of them because they were so inept, but that whiny one was *scared of heights*. I don't weigh much more than one hundred pounds, particularly after losing the leg, and those two buffoons still had trouble moving me."

Ashton nodded. "It's amazing how much difference that makes. I'm missing one myself," he shared. "I was a Navy SEAL and just got out of surgery and rehab. I'm on medical discharge and am still adjusting to life in this new situation."

"Sorry about that," Sean said, "because ain't no easy way to adjust."

"No, there sure isn't, but we do what we need to do, and we'll find a way to make it because that's what we do," he declared, with a smile.

Sean nodded. "That we will, but it's sure rough when the rest of the world seems to think you're some sort of a joke and a loser for getting injured."

"Of course they don't understand, and we don't expect them to because it's too much of a strain on their poor psyches," he quipped, with a smirk.

Sean stared at him and nodded. "You really do understand, don't you?"

"I sure do. I've been up against way too much judgment

myself. There's nothing quite like it, but here we are, and we're sure glad to find you alive. The next challenge is getting you down from this loft." He looked at the old man, looked at the ladder, and nodded. "Yeah, we got this. The question is, do you need medical attention before I move you?"

"No, sir. I would much rather get out of this hellhole first, no matter how we do it," he replied. "I can *scooch* down on my butt if need be, and that would probably a whole lot safer."

Ashton laughed. "No way, we can do better than that." In a move that surprised both Sean and Crystal, Ashton leaned over and lifted Sean up on his good foot, pulling him from that prone position over his shoulder, into a fireman's carry. Ashton stood tall with Sean draped over one shoulder and his back.

"You sure about this?" Sean asked.

"I'm sure," Ashton replied.

Crystal offered, "I'll go down first and spot you, Sean."

Both men got a good chuckle out of that.

"Hey, you guys, I can wrangle a horse, so don't test me."

The guys laughed again, as Ashton backed up to the ladder. "Gotta shift you now, Sean, into a cradle carry, so just hook one of your arms around my neck. Tell me when you got a good hold there."

"Got it," Sean called out.

Then Ashton swung Sean around so they now faced each other, yet a little offset. "Hang on, Sean. We're going down." Ashton hung onto Sean tightly with one arm, while his other arm steadied both of them on the ladder. Ashton continued to talk to Sean, as if to distract him. "I don't know whether forensics needs to be here or not, but they'll just have to work around our tracks," he noted. "God knows they won't be impressed when I call them back out here again."

"You would think they would be happy," Sean muttered. "At least I've been found."

Crystal looked up at Sean and nodded. "I'm sorry to say a whole lot of people were not convinced you were missing."

He shook his head. "I don't understand," he muttered. "How does the world find it so easy to dismiss people like me?"

Crystal shook her head. "It was Jenny. She was very good at misdirecting people into believing what she wanted them to believe. So, when you went missing, she would slide suggestions into conversations, making you seem depressed, things like that," Crystal explained.

"That I would never do," Sean declared indignantly. "I lived through war. I lived through losing my leg. I lived through losing Khan, but I gotta tell you. That was the worst of it all. I was beside myself. Nobody would believe me that those people stole Khan from me. I kept telling people how that couple took Khan and pushed me over and ran off, but nobody would even give me a chance or would even listen to what I had to say. It was heartbreaking."

Crystal nodded. "People can be so cruel. The good news is we found you both."

At that, Khan barked loudly beside them, making everybody laugh. "Hell of a dog that can climb up ladders …" But at that moment Khan jumped to a large hay bale then another and suddenly he was on the floor. "He made that look easy."

Piper and Joe milled around on the floor as they slowly made their way down.

Now at the bottom, Ashton noted, "I'll need to check on

her."

"Looks pretty dead to me," Sean said in a grumpy tone, as they stared at Jenny's prone body.

Ashton sat Sean on a nearby hay bale. "I'll grab you again in a second." With that, he walked over and checked on Jenny, but it appeared she had died on impact, just as he had surmised when he had first looked from above. "Nothing anybody can do for her," he said, "so we'll just call law enforcement." Then he proceeded to phone Richard.

"I'm really busy. You do know that, right?"

"Well, as it turns out, I am too," Ashton retorted. "Doing your job."

After a moment of silence, Richard asked, "What are you talking about now?"

"We just found Sean. He was also a captive at Oliver's place."

"What?" Richard roared.

"Yeah, he was in the upstairs loft of another outbuilding, the smaller equipment barn. And, no, Oliver did not hold him there. You need to get out here now, and, while I'm sure Sean will argue about going to the hospital, I think he should be checked over. We also have a dead body, so move it, will you?" Ashton ended the call to now argue with Sean.

Hearing the word *hospital,* Sean stared at Ashton indignantly, but Crystal was determined. "No way," she argued. "You need be checked just to make sure that in your excitement to get out of that place, you're not hiding another injury."

He frowned at her and asked, "Do I look like I'm somebody who would hide an injury?"

She gave him a cheeky grin and nodded. "Absolutely."

He chuckled. "Fine, I'll let them check me over, but

that's it. No way I'm staying in that hospital," he declared. "I spent way too much time in a hospital to want any more of that."

Ashton absolutely understood.

As they sat here and waited for the deputies, Ashton checked with the hospital for an update on his grandfather. The report he got lacked any real details, but he at least got word that the patient was doing better and that they could visit him later today. As it turned out, they wouldn't be available until quite a lot later.

It took Richard twenty minutes to get out here, and he arrived still pissing mad, until he walked into the barn, took one look at Sean, and then followed their gaze to Jenny's body on the concrete floor. He stared in shock and asked, "What the hell is going on here?"

"Yeah, we would like to get a few answers on that too," Crystal snapped smartly, looking over at him. "We told you that this guy was missing, how his War Dog was stolen from him. And now we have found both Grandpa and Sean right here."

Sean looked over at Richard and asked him, "Were you guys even looking for me?"

Richard frowned. "We had it on good authority that you may have possibly—" Then he frowned as he looked at the dead body on the ground.

Sean nodded. "That *good authority* wouldn't be the dead woman before you now, *huh*? Or the Wilfords, by any chance? The ones who knocked me down and who stole my dog?"

Richard closed his eyes and muttered, "Shit."

"Yeah, you're not kidding," Ashton noted. "And Jenny held both Sean and Grandpa as her prisoners."

"Both?" he asked, his eyes shooting open.

"Yeah, both." Ashton then tried to explain the nightmare that had gone on. "I recorded her."

Richard stared at him. "Holy crap."

"Yeah, holy crap is right. It's been a *not fun* trip all the way around."

"This shit is seriously wrong," Richard declared, staring back and forth between Ashton and Crystal. He looked over at Sean, who raised both hands in frustration, his face all shades of angry. "And I can corroborate," he stated animatedly, "because the crazy dead woman told me that she had another prisoner who she was still trying to figure out what to do with. So I figured it wasn't just me going a little bit crazy in here. But I sure never expected her to do what she did here," he admitted, as he looked over at the bloodstained concrete.

Richard frowned. "And she just dove off?"

Ashton nodded. "She just dove off, but, then again, it's not as if she was looking at an easy time of it going forward," he pointed out. "You and I both know that would have been quite a long list of infractions, even if you went easy on her. Plus, she held a rifle on Crystal and me just an hour ago."

Richard shook his head. "Yeah, there is no *easy* on something like this," he agreed, followed by a snort. "I mean, those are really ugly charges she would be facing."

"Exactly."

Richard groaned. "Okay, I already texted a request for the coroner. You do realize this is the most we've had to do in a very long time?"

"I know. Believe me that I know. And I sure hope this is the end of it."

"Well, if you're staying here, chances are it won't be,"

Richard grumbled, glaring over at his friend. "Feel free to go off into the wild blue yonder and decimate somebody else's town for a while, will you?"

"No can do," Ashton said, with a smile. "It seems like here in Missouri is probably home for me now."

Richard just rolled his eyes at that.

"I mean it," Ashton stated, with a quick glance over at Crystal.

She walked over and placed her hand in his. "Yeah, he's not going anywhere for a long time," she added. "I'm done waiting."

Richard looked from one to the other, then nodded. "Good, maybe you can keep him out of trouble then."

She chuckled. "I don't know about that, but I'll definitely see what I can do," she said.

"Well, at the very least, can you keep your grandparents out of trouble?"

"That depends," Ashton noted. "Apparently Grandma is sitting in a hotel somewhere, contemplating all the wrongs she may have committed in her life. At least according to Jenny."

"A hotel?"

"Yeah, at Jenny's suggestion, my grandmother not being the smartest kid on the block," Crystal explained. "Apparently Jenny had Grandma thinking that everything was all her fault and that she would end up on all kinds of charges. And, ever helpful, Jenny suggested Grandma go lie low in a hotel room and figure out what she would do next because Jenny was done covering for her."

"And did she cover for her?"

"Well, in truth, Jenny apparently had access to the financial records and probably Grandpa's login information,"

Ashton shared. "So, she's the one who took out the big chunk of money we weren't sure about, and she also had access recently and apparently may have been the one who took out the money from Grandpa's account, or the two of them did it together. However, Jenny was planning on taking the money herself, then siccing the law on Grandma, so Jenny would be free and clear. She knew that nobody would ever believe anything Grandma said about Jenny."

Crystal added, "But Jenny didn't quite know what to do with Grandpa and Sean and likely would have just let them languish as captives."

Richard stared down at Jenny's body. "Wow, really makes a guy think twice about having help at the house, doesn't it?"

"Unfortunately a lot of things take on a whole new meaning," Ashton noted. "I need to get Sean to the hospital to be checked over, and then call my lawyer and the bank to see if we can get the money back into the company account."

"Yeah, tell the bank to call me," Richard offered. "You'll need that in order to make some of those reversals happen."

"Hopefully your word expedites things, so we can move the money before everybody finds out and decides that our company is a completely lost cause." Ashton shifted his stance, his hands on his hips as he contemplated the mess in front of him. "I'll let you know if I need any more help."

"Jesus Christ," Richard muttered. "The whole lot of you are nuts. What the hell have you been doing when all this was happening right under your noses?"

"Funny how us good guys project onto the bad guys, not seeing what's going on. The good news is that things will get sorted out now," Ashton declared, as he pulled Crystal to him.

Richard stared at him, a warning in his gaze, before he turned to leave the barn.

Ashton called out to Richard, "You might as well get used to seeing us around because I'm not leaving again."

"Maybe then you'll stop raising Cain every time you wake up," Richard muttered, and, with that, he stepped forward and smacked him on the shoulder. "Glad to have you home where you can straighten out all this shit."

"Yeah, me too," Ashton agreed. "Too bad you couldn't do it yourself."

Richard glared at him, then laughed. "If you want a job, you know where to come."

"Maybe," he replied. "I'll see how all that works out here, after I get to the bottom of this other mess and see who is owed what," he shared.

"Just let me know." And, with that, Richard turned and walked up to greet the coroner, who had just arrived.

Ashton looked down at Sean. "You ready?"

Looking grim, Sean replied, "I promised Crystal that I would get looked over, but, man, please don't leave me there. You have to understand, … hospitals and me—"

"Say no more. I get it," Ashton said, holding up his hand, as if taking an oath. "Don't worry. We'll take you there, get you checked over, and then I'll get you home again, along with this guy," he added with a chuckle, as he reached down and rubbed the top of Khan's head. "You've got a great watchdog here. Make sure you look after him."

"Oh, I intend to," Sean declared. "I love this dog to bits. How did you even know to go looking for him?"

"Actually," Ashton shared, "some guardian angels out there look after these War Dogs and their owners too." He rubbed Khan's ears. "I came here looking specifically for

Khan. Word had it that he'd gone missing. So, guess what? I came right away to lend you a hand."

Sean stared at him in shock. "Well, shit, I didn't even know help was coming."

"Most of the time there isn't enough help," Ashton stated, "but the people running this program, let's just say that they are pretty special. And, by the way, if you're looking for a prosthetic to get you back up on your feet—"

"Yeah, there's no money for that kind of shit. You know that."

"Well, I got mine, and that's what Kat does."

"Yeah, I heard from a friend of mine about some sweetheart a few states over who does some great work on prosthetics," he muttered, "but the VA turned down my request years ago. I don't know how the hell they can do that."

"Well, I suggest we talk to Kat directly then."

"Do you know where she's at?" Sean eyed him hopefully.

"Yeah, you're looking at her one-of-a-kind design right here," Ashton replied, as he pulled up his pant leg to reveal the etched-in-steel prosthetic.

"Man, that's a piece of work," Sean noted, staring at it with envy.

"You can get one too."

"Do you think that's even possible?" Then he stopped and shook his head. "She'll just say I'm too old, and it's not worth it."

"No, she won't. I haven't heard those words come out of her mouth ever," Ashton said, with a smile. "But I can tell you that she'll want you to do some prep work before."

"Like what kind of work?" he asked.

"Physical therapy, some specific exercises to build up

strength. You'll have to build everything up so that it's strong enough for her to put in the screws and bolts and all that good hardware in there."

"You got hardware in there?"

"Yeah, I sure do," he confirmed. "This thing screws on and off just perfectly." They kept talking as they managed to drive him over to the Emergency Room.

The nurses were nice enough to get Sean into a shower and then found some clothes in the lost and found for him, all before the doc even looked Sean over. After a checkup and the okay from the doctor, they headed over to Sean's place. As they pulled up, they warned him that it looked like it had been tossed pretty well.

The old man stared at his place and sighed. "Of course," he muttered. "I mean, if anybody can steal five bucks from you, that's what they'll do."

"Do you need a hand cleaning this place up?" Ashton asked.

"Of course he does," Crystal interjected. "We're not leaving him here like this. This is hardly even inhabitable at the moment," she noted, frowning as she looked around. She asked Sean, "Do you have anybody in town who helps you at all?"

"Not in a way I can count on," he replied. "That would be way too easy."

She smiled. "Well, maybe you need to come back to our place for tonight, and we can get a crew over here tomorrow to clean up," she suggested, looking back at Ashton. "This is no way for Sean to live. Not after what he's been through already."

Ashton smiled. "Got it. I've been there and done that myself."

She stared at him and said, "Please tell me that you didn't have to live in a situation like this either."

"Not exactly like this"—he shrugged—"but things got pretty ugly for a time. Then I ended up over with Kat and Badger, and that completely changed things for me. So, we will prevail in the end." He looked over at Sean and asked, "So, are you up for bunking with us for the night?"

The old man looked at him gratefully. "I would be honored if you gave me a home for the night," he replied. "It's a little rough around here right now."

"And we'll have to find your wheelchair."

He nodded at that. "That'll be a sore point for me," he added. "A pair of walking sticks are in the closet here somewhere. I can use them if I have to, but I'm kind of out of practice with them. Maybe we can grab a change of clothes too."

They rummaged around, found the crutches and some clothes. Sean nodded. "Okay, this will do for the moment, until we can rustle up my wheelchair."

Ashton added, "Let me send a message to Richard, asking him to have his guys look around Oliver's place, since you are incapacitated without it. Jenny probably stashed it somewhere in that barn." With that done, he called out to them both, "Let's go home."

CHAPTER 15

W HEN CRYSTAL COLLAPSED on the couch at the main house several hours later, she looked over at Ashton, sadness in her gaze. "I don't know who I feel sorry for the most," she began. "Grandpa is absolutely devastated. Grandma is not happy to be found and is looking very much the worse for wear. I'm not sure which part is worse for her, Richard holding her overnight in jail or Richard talking about bringing her before a judge, asking for a psych eval. We probably do need her tested, which might explain some of the stuff Grandma has pulled in recent years. At least Sean is asleep in a comfy bed and is warm and full and hydrated for the moment, … or should be asleep soon. The whole town appears to have just lost it over the news."

Ashton sat down beside her, adding, "Everybody is trying to figure out what happened and how they all missed it."

"And what they missed is the same thing that we missed."

Ashton shook his head. "Jenny's betrayal hurt me, maybe more than Grandma's because I never expected Jenny to turn on us like that."

Crystal nodded. "Like Sean said, the ones you don't see coming …"

"Plus," Ashton pointed out, "Jenny was in love with Max, and none of us saw that either. How did that happen?"

he asked Crystal. "It seemed she was always here. She looked after the house, looked after Grandpa and Grandma, cooked all our meals, but she was apparently having a personal life too." He shook his head. "I'm glad she had a few years of happiness, but it's so very sad that it turned ugly so quickly."

Just then Ashton's phone rang, and Oliver was on the other end.

"Hey, wanted to thank you for going to bat for me and getting me out of jail."

"You were pretty much in the clear, especially once we realized what really happened."

"It's shocking as hell to find out about Jenny," Oliver said. "I know my brother loved her, loved her dearly, but honestly, I never trusted her. It's one of the reasons my brother and I fought toward the end, but he was happy, and I didn't want people thinking it was jealousy on my part. I just … I didn't have the same rapport with her that he did. Anyway, I'm exhausted, but I wanted to thank you for looking after the animals."

"You're more than welcome," Ashton replied. "Our family added chaos to your world that nobody needs. Give us a chance to sort out where things are at," he said, "and I'll get back to you about the deposit money. We've found it, and I think all of it is there, … but I can't be sure just yet."

"Yeah, that's tomorrow's problem," Oliver noted, fatigue in his tone. "It's a hard realization when you see just how much people are willing to do things … for all the wrong reasons." And, with that, he disconnected.

Crystal looked over at Ashton and muttered, "That's got to be rough."

"It's all rough," he declared.

She nodded. "People break other people's hearts, and yet

there was no reason for it, particularly what Grandma did." Crystal asked him, "Did you mean it? Are you here now to stay? Are you done gallivanting around the world, doing whatever you've been doing?"

He smiled at her, opened his arms, and tucked her up close. "Absolutely. You already know that."

"Well, I'm hoping that I know it," she clarified. "I just want what we have to be true and honest and that our communication is open and that we don't worry about what other people say."

He smiled. "I don't really care what other people say to begin with, … especially when we know what we know," he added, with a huge smile.

She leaned over and kissed him on the cheek. "So, can we go to bed now? I'm exhausted."

He laughed and said, "Absolutely. … Does that mean we are going to bed together or are you staying the night at your place?"

She looked at him and smiled. "After waiting six years? … Together, in your bed of course. Do you really think Jenny didn't know about me and you?" she asked, as they climbed the stairs to his bedroom.

"I don't know. I think she may have not wanted to know about us because that probably made it harder to deal with her own loss. Sometimes happy people make it harder for those without someone. And finding out more about Jenny at the end, she probably would not want either of us to end up being happy," he suggested. "I don't know that she had the capacity at the end of her life to be happy for anybody. I know that sounds terrible and sad."

"It does, but it also is probably quite true," she said, as she followed him into his bedroom. "I presume the twins helped her?"

H nodded. "They've been picked up along with Grandma. I don't know what the charges will look like but it's not going to be a smack on the hand and get released at this point."

"What about Sean?" She looked at him hesitantly. "Can he live in one of the dower houses? I think our family has put him through enough."

He caught her up and warm hug and nodded. "I was thinking of offering that to him. Not sure whether he'll accept or not, but I had thought to give him that option." He groaned as he looked out the window and muttered, "Who would have ever thought it?"

"Apparently both of us. But that's for tomorrow." She wrapped her arms around his waist. "Tomorrow's a whole new day. Let's get some sleep."

He twisted around to face her. "I don't want to waste any more time." And, with that, he nudged her backward until she fell onto the bed, laughing. "Unless, of course, you've changed your mind."

She just stared at him, her arms outstretched.

He smiled. "Good to know that you want me, that you still choose me," he said. "I would have been pretty devastated if I'd come back and found you with somebody else."

"And yet you kept making excuses," she pointed out, "delaying your way back here."

"Yeah, because, when I did come home, I had to be sure that I was coming home to you and only you. It wouldn't have been the same if you had left, particularly if you'd left with one of those two idiots," he muttered, with a groan.

She smiled and shook her head. "That would never happen."

He chuckled softly, a sound that resonated with warmth and affection, as he bent down to meet her lips with his own. The kiss was tender yet filled with a longing that had been building for what felt like an eternity.

When he finally lifted his head, she gazed into his eyes, a playful smile dancing on her lips. "I'm pretty sure we've waited long enough." Her words were a gentle reminder of the time they had spent apart.

With a graceful movement, she wrapped her arms around him, pulling him down closer to her. The world outside faded away, leaving just the two of them in their own private sanctuary. Their first time together was rushed, heated, a whirlwind of emotions and sensations, yet it was also a moment of profound connection. As he closed his eyes, he felt the weight of the world lift from his shoulders, holding himself back just enough to savor the moment.

She whispered softly, her voice a soothing melody, "This is just for us now, nobody else." Her words were a promise, a vow that this moment was theirs alone, untouched by the chaos of the outside world.

As he began to move, the rhythm of their past resonated with their future. She rose and crested before him, her body responding to his with an intensity that took his breath away. She held him tightly, as he finally surged above her, a wave of emotions crashing over him. He collapsed back down, enveloped in her arms, feeling a sense of peace and fulfillment that he had never known before. In that moment, they were a single entity, bound by their histories but building their tomorrows … together.

Crystal whispered, "Now we can sleep, and finally you're home where you belong."

RILEY COMBS WALKED into the boardroom and plunked himself down onto the nearest chair. Both Kat and Badger looked up. Badger frowned, and Riley frowned right back.

Kat laughed. "Badger, you should know by now that nobody thinks that frown of yours is very threatening."

"It should be," he grumbled. "Don't know when I lost that."

Riley snorted. "Somewhere around the time that you had kids, who wrapped you around their little fingers." He gave Badger a broad smile.

Badger shot him a look, just as his daughter raced into the room and threw herself into his arms. "I love you, Daddy."

He sighed, picked her up, and cuddled her close. Then he glared at Riley and grumbled, "What do you want?"

His daughter looked up at him and patted his cheek. "Talk nice, Daddy. That wasn't nice at all. You know you like Riley."

He sighed. "Well, Riley, *sir*, … what is it we can do for you today?"

Thoroughly enjoying the fact that big, bad, scary Badger—whom nobody ever talked back to—had been totally tamed by toddlers, Riley smiled at his boss and stated, "I just wondered if a K9 was over in my corner of the world that I could check on. That would give me a reason to go home."

Badger's daughter said, "Put me down, Daddy. I need a nap." Badger kissed his daughter on the head. "Give your mama a hug and then go sleepy-bye." The happy child did just that and skipped off.

Kat now focused on Riley again, eyeing him with interest. "I can't say I've ever had anybody ask for that," she noted, giving him a sharp look. "And why don't you want to go home to just visit family and friends, without another reason to?"

"Well, you know, family stuff."

"Oh, I do know family stuff," she replied, "but so much family stuff turns out to be just BS family stuff."

"What do you mean by that?" he asked, leaning forward, his gaze intent.

"If people would just sit down and communicate, 99 percent of all these problems would evaporate."

He shrugged. "You're probably right," he replied cheerfully.

"So, why do you need a case? Why not just tell the family that you're there but not for them?"

"Partly because it might be time for me to head in that direction, but I also want an out, in case I need it."

"And why is that?" she persisted, tilting her head at him.

That was the thing about Kat, you never really had a chance to pull anything over on her. She seemed to always know when crap was going on in your world.

"Let's just say, my mother contacted me, and somebody I may have known a while ago is apparently about to get married."

Kat's eyebrows shot up. "Ooh, and you want to stake a

claim?"

Badger stared at her, then turned to Riley and punched him on the shoulder. "That's not the way life goes, man," he declared. "If you wanted to stake a claim, you should have done it beforehand."

"I did … sort of," he stated.

"Okay, Riley. I need to hear a little more about this," Kat stated, a curious expression on her face.

"Yeah, you probably do, but it's a little awkward."

"Nope, doesn't sound a little awkward *to me*," she quipped, putting down the tools she was working with. "Yet it sounds way more than a little awkward *for you*."

Riley shook his head, then sighed. "Okay. So, … I was dating two sisters."

"That was your first mistake," Badger told him.

"It wasn't serious," he explained.

"Uh-oh," Kat said. "Until it was, right?"

"Yeah. Exactly. … I fell for one sister, but the other one claimed to be pregnant, by me. So the sister I fell for didn't believe me when I told her that I wasn't sleeping with, you know, … her sister."

Kat raised a hand, shaking her head. "Hang on a minute. This is too confusing. Can we just have names, please?"

"Debbie and Gail," he replied. "Debbie's the one who said I got her pregnant. Gail's the one I was falling for."

Kat asked, "And who is getting married now?"

"Gail." He sat back and sighed. "And I can't quit thinking about her since I heard the news."

"And yet if she had wanted you—" Badger began.

"Thanks for that," Riley snapped, followed by a grimace. "She may have thought there was no way forward from where we were."

"And is there?" Kat asked.

"Yeah," he declared, his tone forceful, "because Debbie finally told the truth and said she had been dating someone else. She ended up marrying that guy, the father of her child."

"Okay, so that's a good thing."

"Yeah, Debbie and her husband have a little girl and are very happy. I really want a chance to see Gail again."

"What does that have to do with us?" Badger asked, staring at him. "Unless my dear wife here has opened a booth for therapy by the hour, I don't see anything relevant to our operations."

Kat reached over and smacked him one. "That's because you're not thinking." He glared at her, and she smiled, noting, "Look at the track record."

"What about it?" And then he groaned. "Oh no, you're thinking that, if you can finagle Kat into this equation somehow, then maybe you'll end up as one of those lucky ones who ends up living happily ever after. Is that it?"

Riley looked at him with an impudent grin and shrugged. "Hey, it's worth a shot, right?"

Badger closed his eyes, shaking his head.

Kat replied, "You still haven't told me what corner of the world is *yours*." She tapped a folder she had sitting off to the side. "Because I do have a case here. I'm just not sure its location works for you."

He smiled at her. "Oregon would be great."

Her eyes widened. She flipped open the folder and double-checked it. "How does Portland sound?"

He muttered, "Perfect."

She nodded, a knowing smirk on her face. "Sounds to me like you're my next K9 bet."

He stood up, snatched the file folder off the corner of the table, then gave Kat a great big hug, whispering, "I'll take it." And, with that, he hurried out the door.

This concludes Book 32 of The K9 Files: Ashton.
Read about Riley: The K9 Files, Book 33

The K9 Files: Riley (Book #33)

Welcome to the all new K9 Files series reconnecting readers with the unforgettable men from SEALs of Steel in a new series of action packed, page turning romantic suspense that fans have come to expect from USA TODAY Bestselling author Dale Mayer. Pssst… you'll meet other favorite characters from SEALs of Honor and Heroes for Hire too!

When a shattered love resurfaces, so do the lies that broke it.

Riley Combs returns home to Portland on a multi-pronged mission: find a missing War Dog, confront the family who destroyed Riley's life, and get one last look at the woman who broke his heart.

However, when Gail Montoya learns the truth about the betrayal that split them apart, her world implodes all over again—because the lies weren't just cruel, they were engineered to send Riley into a war zone.

As old wounds and family power games and secrets buried in the Shanghai tunnels collide, Riley and Gail must decide whether love can survive the truth. With danger closing in underground and redemption on the line, one lost dog may be the key to exposing a deadly scheme—and maybe giving two damaged hearts a second chance.

A gritty, emotional romance … full of suspense, family drama, and hard-won hope.

Find Book 33 here!
To find out more visit Dale Mayer's website.
https://geni.us/DMSRiley

Author's Note

Thank you for reading Ashton: The K9 Files, Book 32! If you enjoyed the book, please take a moment and leave a short review.

Dear reader,

I love to hear from readers, and you can contact me at my website: www.dalemayer.com or at my Facebook author page. To be informed of new releases and special offers, sign up for my newsletter or follow me on BookBub. And if you are interested in joining Dale Mayer's Reader Group, here is the Facebook sign up page.
http://geni.us/DaleMayerFBGroup

Cheers,
Dale Mayer

About the Author

Dale Mayer is a *USA Today* best-selling author, best known for her SEALs military romances, her Psychic Visions series, and her Lovely Lethal Garden cozy series. Her contemporary romances are raw and full of passion and emotion (Broken But … Mending, Hathaway House series). Her thrillers will keep you guessing (Kate Morgan, By Death series), and her romantic comedies will keep you giggling (*It's a Dog's Life*, a stand-alone novella; and the Broken Protocols series, starring Charming Marvin, the cat).

Dale honors the stories that come to her—and some of them are crazy, break all the rules and cross multiple genres!

To go with her fiction, she also writes nonfiction in many different fields, with books available on résumé writing, companion gardening, and the US mortgage system. All her books are available in print and ebook format.

Connect with Dale Mayer Online

Dale's Website – www.dalemayer.com

Twitter – @DaleMayer

Facebook Page – geni.us/DaleMayerFBFanPage

Facebook Group – geni.us/DaleMayerFBGroup

BookBub – geni.us/DaleMayerBookbub

Instagram – geni.us/DaleMayerInstagram

Goodreads – geni.us/DaleMayerGoodreads

Newsletter – geni.us/DaleNews